# TED TAYLER

# NIGHT TRAIN

VINCI
BOOKS

## By Ted Tayler

**The Freeman Files**

*Fatal Decision*

*Last Orders*

*Pressure Point*

*Deadly Formula*

*Final Deal*

*Barking Mad*

*Creature Discomforts*

*Silent Terror*

*Night Train*

*All Things Bright*

*Buried Secrets*

*A Genuine Mistake*

*Strange Beginnings*

*Dead Reckoning*

*A Normal November*

*Into the Sunlight*

*Tame the Storm*

*One True Friend*

*Whispered Truths*

*A Morning Murder*

*Quick to Anger*

*Red Herring Season*

*Gathering Clouds*

*Still Standing*

Vinci Books

vinci-books.com

Published by Vinci Books Ltd in 2025

1

## Prologue

IVAN KENDALL LIVED IN PONTYCLUN, a village twelve miles from Cardiff. He was self-employed and ran a modest window cleaning business he'd developed since getting made redundant from a building materials supplier in 2008. Ivan had joined the company straight from school at sixteen.

Ivan was forty-five years old and married to Sally, his childhood sweetheart. Their daughter Alexa attended Y Pant Comprehensive on the Cowbridge Road and was weeks away from sitting her Year 11 exams. Alexa's ambition was to leave school and go to college in Bridgend. A fifteen-minute train journey allowed her to study at the Hair and Beauty Academy before starting her own mobile hairdressing business. Her mother, Sally, had left school at fifteen and worked as a shop assistant in various stores ever since, except for her six-month maternity leave.

Ivan, Sally, and Alexa lived in a three-bedroomed semi-detached house they rented from the local council. A life less ordinary would be hard to imagine. It was a constant battle for Ivan Kendall to keep his head above water.

His neighbours knew him as a quiet man who wore a distinctive salt-and-pepper beard. However, the stress the family experienced following Ivan's redundancy and the constant economic pressure meant those neighbours would freely admit that Ivan and Sally had a stormy relationship. Since 2008, the couple had separated on three occasions.

First, Sally left to go a few miles away to stay with her mother in Llanharry, taking Alexa with her. She returned after six weeks. In 2010, she moved to a gastropub in Cardiff to work as a barmaid. Ivan looked after Alexa alone. While in Cardiff, Sally started a relationship with the bar owner, Thomas Griffiths. Tommy was fifty-five, hard-working, and cared deeply for Sally.

On this occasion, it was eight months before Sally gave her marriage another chance. She moved back into the house in Pontyclun just before Christmas. Everything was sweetness and light in the Kendall household throughout 2011 and 2012.

The third and final time Sally left Ivan was in the summer of 2013. Once again, she ran away to stay with her mother. Within a month, Tommy Griffiths left his Cardiff pub and rented a flat in the village. Everyone realized Tommy wanted to take Sally away from Pontyclun for good. An uneasy period followed when Tommy Griffiths left Pontyclun and took over a busy bar on the seafront in Weymouth. Sally returned to Ivan a week later.

Saturday, the eighth of March, started as an ordinary day for the Kendall family. Ivan left in his white van at eight in the morning to visit six properties on his window cleaning round. Sally knew to expect him home by half-past twelve.

He would hand over most of the cash he'd earned and keep a few pounds back for himself.

While Ivan was out of the house, Sally got the washing up together and persuaded Alexa to help tidy the house. Ivan went to the rugby club on Saturday afternoons to watch a match and have a few beers. Sally and Alexa would visit the local supermarkets seeking bargains that eked out the pennies towards another week's food shopping.

It was rare for Ivan and Sally to venture out in the evenings. Alexa drifted around the village with friends. Her parents didn't know half of what she got up to and didn't seem that bothered as long as Alexa got home by ten o'clock.

Tonight there was a change in their predictable routine. Ivan had been later returning from the rugby club than usual. Sally could tell it wasn't because he'd kept drinking. Her husband was sober and yet was on edge. He couldn't settle for watching television for more than a few minutes. Sally didn't want to start an argument, so she held her tongue.

At half-past eight, Ivan left the living room and went upstairs. He came down ten minutes later and went out. As the door slammed behind him, Sally couldn't have known it was the last time she would see him alive.

Alexa crept in a few minutes after ten and looked in on her mother. She still had her scarf wrapped around her neck. Sally knew what that meant. She'd suffered enough love-bites in her teens. Sally prayed that whoever Alexa had been with used protection.

"Where's Dad gone?" asked Alexa.

"He didn't say," said her mother. "He will have gone to the rugby club or a pub in town, I expect. There was something on his mind."

"No," said Alexa, "we were near the station when I spotted him. He never saw us, but he got on the Cardiff train at five to nine."

"That doesn't sound right," said Sally. "He'll have to get a taxi home. I've no idea how he could afford that. What's his game?"

Alexa went to her bedroom. Sally tried to watch television but couldn't concentrate. She followed Alexa upstairs by half-past ten and fell asleep without hearing a key in the door.

### Sunday, 9 March 2014

WESTBURY IS a station managed by Great Western Railway that services a market town on the north-western edge of Salisbury Plain. It lies near the border with Somerset. Westbury is famous for the White Horse cut into the chalk face of the hillside above the town in the early eighteenth century. Murder is a rare commodity in this quiet corner of the county.

The station is a major junction, serving the Reading to Taunton line with services to and from London Paddington and Penzance in Cornwall. There are also mainline services to and from Portsmouth, Cardiff, and Swindon. In addition, local services from Bristol Temple Meads to Weymouth, plus services to London Waterloo, are available. For a town with a population of only eighteen thousand, including the numerous surrounding villages, it's a station that punches well above its weight.

Sid Dyer was a conductor who lived on the outskirts of town in Westbury Leigh and started his shift at six o'clock.

He parked his 125cc motorcycle in the car park, securing it with a chain to a large steel hoop set into the ground. He had thirty-five minutes before his first train arrived. Sid would cover the journey to Castle Cary and Taunton and switch trains returning through Westbury on the morning train that ferried passengers to the capital. He'd worked on the railways since leaving school. Nothing much surprised Sid Dyer. He'd seen all sorts over the years.

His first port of call was the Gents. At sixty-three, Sid knew the benefits of visiting the toilet whenever the opportunity presented itself. The platform near the main station buildings was deserted early in the day. The solid-looking red brick construction stood on this spot for over a century. Sid sensed something different to the thousands of other occasions he'd walked this platform as soon as he pushed open the door to the public convenience.

Each of the stalls was available, and there was nobody else inside. Yet as he stood at the urinal, Sid couldn't relax and kept glancing over his shoulder. Why was he so nervous? Sid washed his hands and dried them. He paid closer attention to the stalls.

When he pushed the end door open further, he saw the blood.

"Well, Sidney," he sighed. "I reckon you must wait for the Penzance train to rattle into the station before you get any conductor duties done today. There's far too much blood for there not to be a body somewhere. Time to call the police, I reckon."

Two local uniformed officers arrived by car, and a forensic crew and a detective soon followed. As the officers searched the station for a victim, the toilets were closed for the Crime Scene Investigators to do their stuff.

Sid Dyer sat in the station's award-winning buffet with a

mug of coffee, telling a DC Trainer everything he knew. The young man was green as grass, and Sid knew that he didn't know about the railways or how they operated.

"There was nobody on the platform when you arrived, and you didn't pass anyone in Station Approach as you rode in?" asked DC Trainer.

"I didn't see anyone on foot between Westbury Leigh and here. Nobody passed me in a car or van before you ask. If a bloke was staggering around in the town covered in blood, someone might have called you, don't you think?"

"How far is Westbury Leigh from here? One mile?"

"That's right. I used to walk to work in the old days, but when I've been on my feet all day walking up and down the corridors, I need to ride home."

"How did this supposed victim get here?" asked DC Trainer.

"It's not for me to tell you your job," said Sid, "but there was a lot of blood in that end stall. Dried blood. So, you need the answer to two questions. First, where did someone move him last night after they attacked him? Second, on which train did he arrive?"

"When did the last train stop here last night?" asked DC Trainer.

"The 21.30 from Cardiff pulled in around 23.45. The night trains you might have seen in the black-and-white films still exist, but they're few and far between these days. That train is as close to midnight as we get at Westbury. The Riviera Sleeper leaves London Paddington at around a quarter to midnight, but apart from Reading, its next stop is Taunton."

DC Trainer left Sid Dyer to finish his coffee. He went to find the forensic crew. Perhaps they could convince him this wasn't a waste of a Sunday morning. Instead, he soon learned their mystery man had been attacked by at least two men in the Gents' toilet. There were signs of a struggle outside the redbrick station building in the car park opposite where Sid Dyer parked his motorcycle. Scuff marks and blood spots showed someone got bundled into a vehicle and then left at speed.

When he returned to the police station, DC Trainer wondered how many stops there were between Cardiff and Westbury stations. It would be like finding a needle in a haystack. He had plenty of other things demanding his attention.

It might be quicker to wait for someone to call in about a missing person or for the blood results to come back. Then, with luck, they would match someone in the system. As for this Sunday afternoon, DC Clive Trainer had a date with England and Wales at Twickenham. It was England's first chance at a Triple Crown in eleven years.

IN PONTYCLUN, Sally Kendall had waited all morning for Ivan to return. Alexa was still asleep. Sally wondered whether to phone the police. Had something happened to Ivan, or had he left her? She dialled 999 and reported him missing.

WHEN SID DYER finished his shift in the early evening, he rode along Station Approach on his motorcycle. Where was the closest place to the station to dump a body? You would need somewhere it didn't get found right away. Sid slowed to turn right towards Westbury Leigh. Just ahead of him and to his left was Slag Lane, which led to the fishing lakes. They were as convenient a place as any. It was a muddy, boggy area with poor footpaths, although local councillors debated giving the popular amenity a much-needed face-lift. When he reached home, he called the number on the card DC Trainer had left on the buffet room table earlier that morning.

## Monday, 10 March 2014

A DIVER DISCOVERED the body of a bearded man, aged between forty and fifty years of age, at half-past seven in the morning. Robbery didn't appear to be the reason for the attack. There was cash in the man's pockets, although he wasn't carrying credit cards, a mobile phone, or any means of identification. He had a return ticket to Cardiff Central and Pontyclun in his back trouser pocket.

The victim suffered severe head injuries before he got thrown into the lake. Whether blunt force trauma was the cause of death would depend on the post-mortem. DC Trainer stood at the side of the lake and reflected on what the forensic boys had told him. Two assailants sounded right. The guy on the plastic sheeting on the bank was a well-built, stocky individual. He wouldn't have given in without a fight, and it would take an enormous man to lift him in and out of the car before throwing him into the water. No, it made sense that they were looking for two assailants.

Who was the victim, and what was the motive? The tickets ruled out the station permutations he'd fretted over yesterday afternoon as he watched England demolish Wales. His boss was already on the phone with South Wales Police checking for reports of a loved one not returning home on Saturday night.

THE SOUTH WALES police found it difficult to figure out why anyone wanted to kill this quiet family man. Ten days after the murder investigation began, officers arrested Tommy Griffiths in Weymouth and charged him with the murder. The bar owner was later released and cleared of the allegations. Griffiths always denied claims he was involved. He told reporters that the police were desperate for a motive, and he was the only one available.

Sally Kendall also believed in Tommy's innocence and was quoted as saying that although Tommy and Ivan weren't friends, for obvious reasons, they weren't enemies either. Tommy knew she was returning to Ivan when she left him in Cardiff. He'd followed her to Pontyclun because he was in love with her, but he accepted that Sally would never leave her husband.

Sally's and Alexa's whereabouts by the end of 2014 were unknown. The lack of motive for the killing and the mystery behind his journey to Westbury that Saturday night made Sally fear for her life. Her neighbours saw little reason for that fear, but they, too, couldn't explain why Ivan Kendall did something so out of character.

As for Wiltshire Police, they dismissed the murder as being caused by mistaken identity. Someone knew Ivan Kendall was on that night train, and his destination was Westbury. Did he argue with fellow travellers, or were two men waiting for him to arrive? What could have been so essential to cause Ivan to travel eighty miles late at night with no explanation to his wife?

Two weeks after the murder, a security man on an

industrial estate near Warminster reported an abandoned vehicle. He'd inspected the Toyota Yaris and spotted bloodstains around the nearside rear passenger window.

Three weeks later, the detective teams in Wiltshire and South Wales hoped a reconstruction of Ivan Kendall's last movements, starting from the approach to Pontyclun station, would jog someone's memory. They were mainly concerned about the two men in the Toyota Yaris in Westbury. But no one came forward. The Yaris had been stolen from a multi-storey car park in Bath on the seventh of March. There was no forensic evidence inside to identify the driver or his colleague.

Ivan Kendall's former workmates at the building merchants and customers on his window-cleaning round described him as a quiet chap who kept himself to himself. Officers travelled on trains on either side of the Bristol Channel, looking for passengers on the train that night. They showed pictures of Ivan, hoping someone might have seen something unusual.

The result was a familiar one. The murder appeared motiveless, the suspects never got identified, and the case disappeared into cold storage. DC Clive Trainer passed his sergeant's exams at the end of 2015 and transferred to Sussex Police based at their Headquarters in Lewes, East Sussex.

Sid Dyer retired at sixty-five in June 2016. On a stormy day in March of the following year, he got knocked from his 125cc motorcycle by a vehicle as he rode from Westbury Leigh into the town centre. He died in the ambulance en route to the Royal United Hospital in Bath.

# Chapter One

***

### *Sunday, 8 July 2018*

BLESSING UMEH WAS awake at dawn. After breakfast, she walked around the farm. It seemed so quiet. It would be a shame if her father thought it unsuitable.

Blessing's mobile phone rang.

"Hello, Blessing? It's Dave here, Dave Smith."

It was the hunky PC with the cornflower blue eyes. Oh yes, Blessing remembered.

"Is it my car?" said Blessing. "Did the garage fail to fix it and ask you to break the news?"

"No, it will be ready on Thursday. What if I help my brother-in-law by delivering it to you? Perhaps we could go out for the evening, and then I can get a taxi back to Chippenham?"

"That sounds great," said Blessing. "I'll see you on Thursday evening."

What an excellent start to the day, thought Blessing. I hope it lasts.

Blessing strolled around, thinking back over the events of the past twenty-four hours.

Yesterday saw a few changes around here. First, Gus Freeman and Suzie arrived early in the afternoon. Blessing had been reading in her room, and soon she heard Suzie and her parents talking in the kitchen. Everyone sounded excited.

It became impossible to continue with her book. Blessing spotted two cars in the yard beneath the landing first-floor window as she walked downstairs. That was odd. Why had Gus and Suzie not travelled to the farm together? She poked her head around the kitchen door to say hello.

John Ferris was shaking Gus by the hand. Jackie was hugging Suzie.

"Come in, Blessing," said John. "These two might need a helping hand later if you're free. Suzie's moving her final few belongings to Urchfont. There will be more storage room upstairs for you. I'm sure Suzie won't mind you utilising the wardrobe space in her old bedroom."

"It will be most welcome," said Blessing. "When my father arrives tomorrow afternoon, he will deliver those items that I couldn't fit into my car. I feel as if I've interrupted a family celebration. I'm sorry."

"Don't be silly, Blessing," said Jackie Ferris. "We might open a bottle of champagne later, but Gus and Suzie are driving backwards and forwards to Urchfont this afternoon. We can't raise a glass with them just yet. Nothing dramatic has changed. It's not as if Suzie's ever here for long these days, anyway."

"You make it sound as if you're glad to see the back of me," laughed Suzie.

"Any celebrations can wait until tomorrow," said John,

with a grin at Gus. "We invited you two to Sunday lunch when you were here the other day, didn't we?"

"You did, and we'd love to come over, John," said Gus. "We'll work up an appetite on the allotment in the morning. I hoped to get there this afternoon, but Suzie had other ideas."

"You know how it goes, Gus. We think our day has been mapped out, and the other half changes everything. So it's easiest to go with the flow."

Blessing forgot her book for the rest of the afternoon. John Ferris had a supply of old suitcases and cardboard boxes he unearthed from somewhere in the farmhouse. As items became ready to get stored in the Ford Focus or the VW Golf, Blessing helped John and Jackie carry them downstairs.

They soon loaded the cars. As Gus and Suzie disappeared along the track to the main road, Jackie turned her attention to refreshments.

"How about fresh scones and a mug of coffee?" she asked.

John and Blessing sat at the large kitchen table and tucked in.

I must join a gym, thought Blessing. This scrummy food is a nightmare. If only it didn't taste so good.

"You need to keep your energy levels up," said John, offering Blessing the last scone on the plate. "One more trip will see Suzie's move finished. Then, Jackie will want to clean her old room and shift a few sticks of furniture around."

"What John means," said Jackie, "is he'll be busy with the animals and other chores around the farm for the next four hours, so yet again, he won't be available."

"It never stops, does it?" asked Blessing.

"It's the life I was born into," said John, "I wouldn't swop it for a nine-to-five job for all the money in the world."

"I'll help you, Jackie," said Blessing. "I need all the exercise I can get to stop my weight ballooning with your lovely food."

"Thank you. It will get done in half the time, and you can decide what to store there," said Jackie.

John Ferris was right. When Gus and Suzie returned from Urchfont an hour later, only half a dozen boxes were left to carry to the cars. John and Jackie waved the couple off at the kitchen door.

As Blessing made her way upstairs with the Dyson, she heard John Ferris roar away in the Land Rover. The sooner she cleaned Suzie's room, the sooner they finished. Blessing wondered if Jackie would think her rude if she skipped the evening meal.

Of course, after two hours of hoovering, cleaning, and manoeuvring furniture, both Jackie and Blessing were ready for something to eat.

"Right," said Jackie, "you can use the wardrobe or any drawer space you fancy. Nobody else will use the room for the foreseeable future. So how do you fancy something light to eat and a glass of wine? I think we've earned it."

"That sounds perfect," said Blessing, "what about Mr Ferris?"

"John won't get back until after dark," said Jackie, "I'll prepare something when I'm getting our meal, and he can heat it when he's ready.

Blessing slept well last night, but she was awake early thanks to the sounds of the countryside and her concerns for the afternoon ahead.

When she finally returned to the farmhouse after her long walk, the smells from the kitchen enticed her indoors.

Blessing groaned. How could John and Jackie face a fried breakfast every day? Jackie understood that Blessing needed something different and had explained when she arrived last Sunday that if it was fruit, nuts and yoghurt that got her moving in the morning, that was fine. If she ever weakened, there was no shortage of eggs, bacon, and sausages. Why did life keep putting temptation in your way?

After their late breakfast, John disappeared to the furthest field on the farm to repair a fence, and Jackie prepared lunch. Blessing went to her room and tried to read.

Before she knew it, Blessing realised it was two o'clock. Her parents should be here soon. She heard a car entering the farmyard, but it was travelling far too fast for her father. It sounded more like Suzie's Golf, not his people carrier.

Blessing checked her dress was neat and tidy where she had been sitting. Her father expected her to look her best, especially on a Sunday. Suzie spotted her coming down the stairs.

"Wow, you've dressed to impress, Blessing. It's only Sunday lunch, not a formal occasion."

"You don't know my father," said Blessing.

Gus strolled in from the farmyard carrying two bottles of red wine.

"I'm not designated driver," he grinned, "and we've not had a lunch invitation before as a couple."

"I shall have a soft drink today," said Blessing, "my father disapproves. He used to worry that if I had a glass of wine in the evening, I still shouldn't drive to work the next morning."

"Have you heard about your sick motor yet?" Gus asked.

"I had a call earlier today," Blessing replied, "the garage fixed it and will return it on Thursday after work."

"Good, that's one problem solved," said Gus, "Luke and Neil will be off the hook for providing a taxi service."

"As long as I can remember how to get to the office on my own, everything will be fine," said Blessing.

"What time did you tell John to get back for dinner, Jackie?" asked Gus.

"Half an hour before I needed him," said Jackie. She already had a glass of wine in her hand. "Everything's ready and in the Aga. I'll dish up our food as soon as Blessing's parents arrive and are ready to eat."

"Do you need a hand, Mrs Ferris?" asked Blessing.

"No, my dear, I've coped alone for forty years of marriage and served meals to far more people than we'll have here today. It's not a chore. It's something I enjoy. Your best bet will be to unload your things from your father's car and get them stowed away. I'm sure Gus and Suzie will lend a hand after yesterday. You won't want to be doing anything strenuous after one of my Sunday lunches."

Blessing heard the chugging of the Land Rover as it swept into the yard next to the kitchen door. John Ferris stopped in the kitchen doorway.

"Sorry if I'm late," he said, "it took me longer than I thought."

"Don't worry. You've got time to have a shower and change into something presentable. Oh, and at least try to drag a brush through that mop of hair."

"Yes, Mum," said John, taking the stairs two at a time.

No sooner had he left than Blessing heard another vehicle pulling up outside.

Kelechi and Maryam Umeh had arrived.

Blessing went outside to greet them.

"Did you have a pleasant journey, father?" she asked.

"We attended St Peter's for morning service and left home in plenty of time," said her mother. "I persuaded your father to purchase a similar satnav to the one you have. Getting him to do as the woman told him was more difficult. It has taken us an hour and a quarter instead of forty-five minutes."

"You're here safely, and that's what matters," said Blessing.

"I can't see your car, Blessing," said Kelechi Umeh, "I hope it's under lock and key. There have been lots of thefts of property in the countryside in recent months."

"Nobody's going to steal my car, father. Don't worry. It's perfectly safe in the garage."

Blessing crossed her fingers behind her back, hoping her parents didn't want to inspect her car today and her accommodation. She'd avoided mentioning the breakdown to her mother when they'd spoken in the week.

Gus came to her rescue. He appeared in the farmhouse doorway.

"Hello there," he said, "you must be Blessing's parents. Pleased to meet you. I'm Gus Freeman, Blessing's boss."

"It is good that our daughter has an older man to supervise her progress," said Kelechi Umeh. "I am not in favour of promoting youngsters into managerial positions. They need to serve a longer apprenticeship."

Gus disagreed with the last piece of Kelechi Umeh's wisdom. Gus believed that if they were good enough, people should get the chance, no matter how old they were.

"It's good to meet you," said Maryam Umeh, "but I'm surprised to see you here. Blessing told me you live in another village, on the other side of Devizes. Do you know the Ferris's?"

Gus resisted saying he was supervising the progress of their youngest child.

"I've known John and Jackie for several months," Gus replied. "their daughter, Suzie, is a Detective Inspector stationed at London Road. She's a close colleague."

Nicely done, thought Blessing.

John, Jackie, and Suzie came out of the farmhouse together. Jackie had shed her apron for a few minutes to show a light summer dress. John now wore a white, short-sleeved shirt and navy-blue slacks. His hair was almost under control, but not quite. Suzie made the introductions and then moved closer to Gus.

"We can eat whenever you're ready," said Jackie. "If Blessing needs extra hands to carry her things inside, then these two are ready, willing, and able. Maryam, why don't we take a quick tour of our home? John, you could show Kelechi what we do here. Find a clean cloth to put over the truck's passenger seat, and don't take too long."

Blessing's head was in a whirl. Suzie seized the initiative and asked Kelechi for the keys to his people carrier. John bundled Kelechi into the Land Rover and drove out of the yard towards the stables. Maryam was already in the kitchen, and Gus stood by the vehicle's rear door, waiting for instructions.

Suzie opened the rear door.

"Blimey," she said, "how many clothes have you got, Blessing? I thought I was bad,"

Gus didn't offer an opinion.

"It's mostly shoes," said Blessing. "I don't mind getting rid of the dresses and coats I no longer wear. Now I've stopped growing, my shoe size will never vary, so an older style could always come back in fashion. It seems such a waste to throw them away when there's plenty of wear left in them."

Fifteen minutes later, Gus, Suzie, and Blessing had stored every box, suitcase, and carrier bag in one of the two bedrooms. They met Maryam and Jackie upstairs on the Grand Tour.

"What a lovely room, Blessing," her mother said, "I can tell your father I have no concerns for your welfare. I do hope he's alright with Mr Ferris. Kelechi is out of his comfort zone on a farm. He's happiest in a lecture hall with other computer geeks."

"Mother," cried Blessing, "he might hear you."

Jackie laughed.

"We understand one another, Maryam. John would be lost without his horses and his tractors. He relies on our two sons to advise him on whether it's worth investing in robotic equipment, and then they have to install and maintain it for him. I don't think they'll ever truly leave home. John's a technophobe, but it would be a dull old world if we were all the same, wouldn't it?"

When John and Kelechi returned, they found the others in the kitchen with a glass in their hand. Blessing, Maryam, and Suzie were enjoying a cold lemonade. Gus and Jackie had a large Malbec, or what remained of it.

"I hope you found your appetite," Jackie said, getting up from her chair and donning her apron. "Roast beef and trimmings are coming up."

The following two hours passed in a flash for Blessing. She couldn't believe how talkative her parents were. They seemed happy. Perhaps she needn't have worried, and her father would say she could stay.

Gus knew that, when required, Jackie Ferris could provide fast food. He'd seen her in action, but this afternoon it wasn't as much lunch as an afternoon event. It was five o'clock before anyone moved from the kitchen table.

Jackie took Maryam and Blessing into the kitchen garden and then the orchard. There was plenty to see, and Blessing's mother needed inspiration for her new garden at their home in Englishcombe village.

Kelechi couldn't resist walking upstairs to check Blessing's room. John and Suzie went to the stables to see the horses. When Kelechi returned to the kitchen, he found Gus Freeman pouring one final half-glass from the Malbec he'd brought from home.

"Do the Ferris's pass muster?" Gus asked.

"I can't believe how big this farm is and how bumpy the tracks are," he said, "as for the accommodation, it's excellent. I'm content. One day, perhaps you could allow me to visit your offices, Mr Freeman."

"People tend to have committed a crime, or at least we suspect them of having done so for us to invite them upstairs to our office," said Gus. "I can assure you that I've never worked in such smart surroundings. My superiors pulled out the stops to convince me to come out of retirement. Blessing has fitted in well, as I expected. Your daughter is a team player and has a bright future. Mr Umeh. You can be proud of her."

"Pride comes before a fall," said Kelechi. "Many dangers lie in wait for a young woman, and my daughter is in a profession with greater risks than in many areas she might have chosen. A father always worries about his children."

"I'll do my best to see that Blessing comes to no harm," said Gus. "We're working on cold cases which my colleagues failed to solve. Most of our work is in the office or the field interviewing witnesses. We work in pairs, as far as possible, so Blessing will always have one of the other three detectives with her or me."

"Blessing is a dutiful daughter," said Kelechi Umeh. "Maryam and I have done what we can to raise her properly. I'm pleased she has made a good first impression, Mr Freeman. I can return to Englishcombe village and prepare for the new term at Bath University with a glad heart."

"I can hear the others returning," said Gus. "I suppose you'll want to head home soon?"

"We wish to get home before it gets dark," said Kelechi.

Gus glanced at his watch. That shouldn't be a problem. It wasn't six o'clock yet. Maryam came into the kitchen carrying a bunch of flowers.

"These will brighten our living room, Kelechi," she said, "Jackie has a bountiful garden."

"It will take time to get our new garden as well-organised as the one we left behind," said Kelechi. "We've hardly had time to open everything we brought from Claverdon. I know my gardening tools came with us and are in the house somewhere. I may need to buy a ride-on mower, Mr Freeman. My lawn is extensive."

"It takes time," said Gus, "and there's no end to the work involved. Whether you commit to growing fruit and vegetables or to have a place to grow flowers and shrubs surrounding a neat stretch of grass."

Everyone was back in the kitchen now, and Blessing could tell that her parents wanted to be on their way.

"Thank you for a wonderful afternoon, Mr Ferris," said Kelechi, shaking John's hand. "You and your wife have been most generous hosts. We will make our way back to our new home now. Blessing, if you would come with us to the car?"

"Think nothing of it," said John, "we're happy to have

met you. Don't be strangers. You'll always be welcome while Blessing sleeps under our roof."

"Yes, Maryam," said Jackie. "I know you'll phone Blessing regularly. You've got my number if she's busy on a case and you need a chat."

Blessing walked outside with her parents to see them off.

"Safe journey home," she said as her father started the engine.

"As long as he listens to the lady on the satnav, we'll be fine," said her mother, shaking her head. "If not, we must ask someone for directions. Goodbye, Blessing. I'll call in the week."

"Listen to Mr Freeman, daughter," said Kelechi Umeh. "He's a good man, and he will keep you on the straight and narrow. I suppose Miss Ferris will give him a lift home later? I would run him home if I knew the way."

"Oh, that's too much to ask," laughed Maryam Umeh.

You're not kidding, thought Blessing as she waved until they were out of sight.

# Chapter Two

**Monday, 9 July 2018**

SUZIE NUDGED Gus a few minutes before seven.

"Time we made a move, sleepyhead," she said.

"What a day yesterday," said Gus, "we avoided letting the cat out of the bag and offending Blessing's parents."

"Blessing kept the news of her Micra being in the garage from them, too," said Suzie, "I saw her crossing her fingers behind her back more than once during the afternoon."

"Maryam got on well with Jackie, I thought."

"Mum gets on well with most people," said Suzie. "Dad mentioned when we visited the stables that the horse you rode still wonders when you're getting back in the saddle."

"I'll bet," said Gus. "Is that a none-too-subtle hint you'd like me to ride with you on Saturday mornings?"

"It would do you good," said Suzie. "Better than sitting outside your shed on the allotment mulling over matters related to a case. You can do that as we ride. Where you need my input, I'll be right beside you."

"I'll give it thought," said Gus. "Who's going into the shower first?"

"You go. I'll make breakfast. After that roast dinner and several glasses of red wine yesterday, you won't need anything too heavy this lovely July morning."

Gus headed for the shower. That was something to look forward to; muesli and yoghurt, not so much. After he had showered and dressed, he walked to the kitchen. Ah, things were looking up. Suzie had plugged in the waffle maker. Happy days.

Suzie passed him with a grin as she made for the bathroom. This living together business was a great idea. It was eight o'clock before he knew it, and Suzie was ready to leave for another day's work at Gablecross.

"How long before you're back at London Road?" he asked.

"If Gareth Francis pulls his finger out, we'll wrap it up before the end of the week. I'll see you at around six this evening."

"Drive safely," said Gus, "especially on the way to the gate."

With that, Suzie left, and Gus wandered into the lounge. The room still felt the same as when he shared this bungalow with Tess. Every other place in the house now contained items Suzie had brought from home. He couldn't be happier with things the way they were. But how could he stop feeling guilty for not keeping one place where memories of Tess hadn't got shoved to one side? Ah well, it was time to drive to the office.

When Gus reached the car park beneath the Old Police Station office, it surprised him to discover he was the first to arrive. He parked his Ford Focus and travelled up in the lift. His phone rang no sooner than he'd hung his jacket on the back of his chair.

"Good morning, Gus," said Geoff Mercer. "I have news on the Wakeley case that I'm sure you want to hear. The Metropolitan Police arrested Dominic Hurley and Caitlyn Bendick at an apartment in Chelsea Village yesterday evening."

"That was quick work," said Gus. "Did they come quietly?"

"Hurley's first request was for the family solicitor," said Geoff. "I don't know whether he was shocked to find the police at his door or relieved. According to the Superintendent I spoke with, Hurley never once mentioned his parents."

"Did he say anything more?" asked Gus.

"They constantly thought about getting caught," said Geoff, "but the rush was worth the risk."

"That's a quote," said Gus, "not Wardrip this time, but I've read it somewhere."

"Caitlyn Bendick didn't utter a word until the officers separated the couple and led them to the lift," said Geoff. "Then she turned to them, and with a broad smile, she told them, you can never separate us from our memories."

"They were as evil as one another," said Gus. "If only we could have stopped them earlier."

"Well, they're under lock and key now, Gus. We believe Salisbury will have priority in carrying the case forward. Ursula Wakeley's murder was on their patch and was the pair's first kill. The forces on either side of the Midlands will want their pound of flesh, but they must take their turn in the queue. I'm concerned about the gap year. It could be ages before we learn whether they were busy during that spell overseas."

"Alex uncovered the details of the Maisie Fletcher and Katherine McKenna murders by concentrating on the deaths of women living alone in the area near Warwick University. After Hurley and Bendick left, did they move to London immediately? If so, there may be other deaths to link to those two yet."

"I'll be in touch as soon as I hear anything," said Geoff. "Don't worry. I'll make sure those involved in the Far East and London know there may be more to come."

"We like to keep people busy, don't we, Geoff?" said Gus.

"Is DS Hardy still with us at the Hub?"

"Yes, he worked on the Burnside affair last week, breaking off to research the Hurley and Bendick murders. His progress is slow, but he's getting there."

"Would another pair of hands help?" asked Geoff.

Gus put his hand over the mouthpiece and groaned. Please don't say WPC Cranston is at a loose end.

"Who did you have in mind?" asked Gus, offering a silent prayer.

"DS Chalmers has returned to duty with us after working undercover for the past three months. He needs regular hours and less time chasing illegal immigrants landing on the beaches in Hampshire and Dorset."

"Rick Chalmers? My daytime companion during the Eron Dushka affair. Rick was the fast-food king, as I recall. He seemed a solid sort. How long could we have him?"

"A month tops?"

"I think we'll have found Grant's killer by then," said Gus, "or have given it up as a bad job. If you can find something useful for Rick to move to after a fortnight, I'm sure Alex will appreciate the help."

"Okay, I'll find Rick in a minute and send him to the Hub. Thanks, Gus."

As Gus ended the call, the lift doors opened, and the gang arrived. Lydia was in full flow, and the others were hanging on her every word. Something must have happened at the weekend.

"Hi, boss," said Lydia, "I'm just updating the others on the latest news of my father. I'll fill you in later."

Luke, Nick, and Blessing made their way to their desks, and once everyone had sat down, Gus told them what he'd heard from DS Mercer.

"That's great, guv," said Neil. "I can't wait for their case to get to court. Those two are as good a case for life means life sentences as I've ever come across."

"I reckon they'll put Hurley in Broadmoor," said Luke.

"Peter Sutcliffe's there, isn't he?" said Neil.

"They used to send women there too until ten years ago," said Luke, "but these days, someone like Caitlyn Bendick will go to Ealing in London."

"Wherever they go, I hope it's secure," said Blessing.

Gus reminded the team there could be other murders to add to the list.

"A sobering thought," said Lydia.

"Right," said Gus, "I suggest we carry out our usual tidy-up after completing our involvement in a case. Clear the decks for another cold case to get passed on to us by London Road. Also, double-check that everything on the Wakeley case in your part of the Freeman Files is up to date and ready for me to transfer to the ACC, or Salisbury, whichever shouts first."

An hour later, Luke and Blessing went to the restroom.

It was time for coffee. Gus thought it was as good a time as any to break the news.

When Blessing handed him his cup of black, no sugar, he whispered:

"Did you say anything to the others about Suzie?"

"No, guv," she replied.

"While you're taking five," said Gus, "I'll tell you before you hear it on the grapevine. Suzie Ferris finally left home on Saturday. For some inexplicable reason, she wanted to spend her free time with yours truly in Urchfont."

"You kept that quiet, Blessing," said Luke.

"About time, guv," said Neil. "I'm sure you'll be good together."

"I certainly hope so, Neil," said Gus. "That's my news out of the way. Has anyone else got something to add?"

"The kitchen's finished, guv," said Luke. "The ground floor redecoration will be complete with a few final touches in the hallway."

"My little Micra is ready to get back on the road," said Blessing. "The garage is sending someone over to Worton on Thursday evening."

"We walked around Salisbury shops for two hours on Saturday afternoon and bought nothing," said Neil.

"It sounds like each of you had a pleasant weekend then," said Gus.

"I'll come and sit with you, guv," said Lydia Logan Barre. "The others already know my news."

As Luke, Neil, and Blessing attacked the walls and whiteboards, Lydia brought her coffee to Gus's desk.

"You sounded animated when you arrived earlier," said Gus, "you and Alex must have made positive progress, am I right?"

"We knew it would be tough to trace my father from those few days in Da Nang in May 2007 until the present day. So, we spent Friday evening listing ideas on what jobs he might take when he could no longer go to sea. I remembered what you said about how high he'd climbed in the Merchant Navy. So, I confined my suggestions to engineering and logistics roles. But when I compared my list with Alex, I found that he'd attacked it differently. He reasoned that if my father couldn't face returning to life on board ship, he'd work in a port he'd visited. One that he particularly liked. Alex thought he'd pick a job that kept him in touch with people he used to work with."

"A sailor's mission?" asked Gus.

"That was one of several ideas Alex proposed," said Lydia. "but where would we start our search?"

"Did you return to London for a list of ports frequented by the shipping company that employed Chidozie?" asked Gus.

"We did, and there were several," said Lydia. "He only landed in Scotland on three occasions, whereas he sailed into Shanghai and Singapore dozens of times. Alex thought Chidozie would be more likely to move to Europe or the States. The most popular ports were Dubai, Durban, Rotterdam, Hamburg, Tangiers, and New York."

"What did you do next?" asked Gus.

"We slept," laughed Lydia, "by the time we'd driven to London and back, got the basic numbers we needed and aggregated the number of visits by port; it was midnight. We returned to it fresh first thing yesterday morning."

"Define first thing," said Gus.

"Around eleven," admitted Lydia.

"Suzie and I had done an hour's work on the allotment by then," said Gus. "We had to leave for Worton by half-past one for Sunday lunch with the Ferris's and Blessing's parents."

"Wow, how did that go?" asked Lydia, "Blessing hasn't said much yet."

"It turned out far better than she feared. John and Jackie Ferris are a terrific couple, and Maryam Umeh and Jackie clicked straightaway. Blessing's father, Kelechi, is more formal. He doesn't give much away, but it impressed him how well John and Jackie looked after his precious daughter. I hope they got home alright."

"Is his sense of direction as bad as Blessing's?" asked Lydia.

"Worse, if yesterday was anything to go by. Okay, so pick the search up from your late morning start."

"Yes, guv," said Lydia. "Alex started in New York. He found a social media page for a bar in the Bronx that mentioned a Chi-Chi working as a cocktail server. I couldn't believe it was my father. Alex argued that my father was only thirty-five at the time, and as a new arrival in the States, he would need to start small."

"Your Dad probably thought it better to be somewhere he could keep in touch with the sea rather than chase a better-paid job a thousand miles inland."

"That's what Alex said. He found a telephone number for the bar, and we called them later in the day. The bar owner confirmed that Chidozie Barre worked for him but left at the end of 2009."

"Did the bar owner know where Chidozie moved to next?" asked Gus.

"He thought he was heading for Europe."

"So, you could be looking at Hamburg or Rotterdam."

"Because of the time difference between New York and us, we had filled in the time before ringing the Bronx bar with searches in Dubai and Durban. I wondered whether my father might have returned to Africa. There had to be a reason he didn't go to Lagos after the shipwreck, but I hoped he might return to his place of birth in time."

"Did you find any trace of him?" asked Gus.

Lydia shook her head.

"After Alex spoke with the guy in the Bronx, we had a new start date. We looked for bars in Hamburg and Rotterdam majoring in cocktails. I searched social media for phone numbers, and Alex then chased owners hoping to learn Chidozie Barre was doing a Tom Cruise in his bar."

"Did you have any luck?" asked Gus.

"Do you have any idea how many cocktail bars there are in Hamburg?"

"They're not places I actively seek," said Gus, "the only time I approve of an umbrella is when it's raining."

"On the thirty-first phone call, Alex struck lucky. Chidozie worked there from February 2010 until he left for Rotterdam in April 2016. He opened a bar on Leuvehaven. That's a street running alongside the water on the west side of the port. It's near the Maritime Museum and makes it perfect for him to mix with seafarers and tourists eager to learn what it's like to get cast adrift in the South China Sea."

"What's the name of the bar?" asked Gus.

"Guess,"

"Chi-Chi's Bar?" replied Gus.

"No. My Dad called it the Lady Eleanor," said Lydia. "Isn't that sweet?"

"Did you call him last night?"

"It was too late. Alex suggested we visit Rotterdam next weekend."

"High risk," said Gus. "You don't know his reaction to

learning he has a daughter. I would call before dropping into the Lady Eleanor for jenever."

"You've lost me," said Lydia.

"It's a fiery gin drink that the Dutch enjoy straight from the bottle."

"We might need a couple of those before I broach the subject. I've waited so long to find my father, but now I'm so close I want to throw caution to the wind."

"Take a trip to Rotterdam, give your Dad a call from wherever you stay and take it from there. At no point in your Dad's history since that bar in the Bronx have you mentioned a family. Even though he's moved from the States to Germany and now the Netherlands, it doesn't prevent him from having gained a wife and children along the way.

"That's what Alex said when we traced him to that first cocktail bar. I could only visualise him as a lonely bachelor. Alex warned me of the old saying of a girl in every port. When Eleanor spoke of Chidozie, that wasn't the impression he made on her."

"NOT THAT I know much about it," said Gus, "but serial heartbreakers become very practised in hiding their past dalliances."

"Hark at you, guv," said Lydia. "I hope Suzie isn't a dalliance. Anyway, the name of the bar convinced me he'd not forgotten his first love. I might be an old romantic, but even the most despicable Lothario would avoid using a name from his distant past for his new business. It raises too many red flags."

"You may be right. I hope you are. Tread carefully,

Lydia, and I'm sure the team wishes you all the luck in the world."

After their coffee break, Lydia resumed tidying her files, ready for the next case. Life was never dull with the Crime Review Team.

When his phone rang, Gus was finishing his recommendations to the detective squad at Salisbury. It was Monday morning. Who else could it be?

"Gus Freeman," he replied.

"Truelove here," said the ACC, "I wanted to add my congratulations to you and the team for your excellent work on the Wakeley case. Quite a story, that one. I hadn't imagined it turning out the way it did when I handed you the file. I was confident you would solve the mystery, Freeman, but my money was on the brother."

"You would have lost, Sir," said Gus. "Arthur was never a suspect, despite religion playing a significant part in the case."

"As you may have guessed, passing on congratulations was not the sole purpose behind my call. Can you get here at noon? I have another cold case to hand you."

"The team have cleared the decks and is ready and waiting, Sir," said Gus.

The ACC ended the call, and Gus looked at the team members in front of him.

"Was I right?" he asked.

"Almost there," said Luke.

Neil and Lydia nodded their agreement. Blessing looked puzzled.

"I seem to have lost my copy of the Freeman Files," she said, "temporarily."

"No panic," said Gus, "I don't leave for London Road for another forty-five minutes. Plenty of time to get the entire package ready for me to take to the ACC. He can do the honours and chat to the top brass at Salisbury, then that's another one done and dusted."

"I'll take a look, Blessing," said Lydia. "It can't have gone far."

Between them, Lydia and Blessing replaced the errant file, and at eleven-thirty, Gus left the Old Police Station Office with the necessary case files and headed for Devizes.

The ACC was staring at him from his office window as he parked the Focus in the one remaining visitor's space. He resisted the temptation to wave and trotted up the steps to the main entrance. What were five minutes between colleagues? Gus blamed the binmen. They were on a go-slow today.

Gus bustled up the stairs and darted past the admin section with the cheery wave he'd kept in reserve. Vera Butler and Kassie Trotter were poised to pounce, but Gus pointed at the ACC's door. His friends nodded as they saw Kenneth Truelove in the doorway, waiting. They could wait. Gus knew he'd have to spare them five minutes on his way out.

As he made his way to the ACC's office, he remembered Alex Hardy. After he chatted with the ladies, he should drop by the Hub and check Alex's progress. If Geoff had found Rick Chalmers before someone else grabbed him, they should have had a good half-morning working on the Grant Burnside killer.

"Come on, Freeman," said the ACC, "stop dawdling. DS Mercer will join us in a moment. I have to leave for Salisbury by one o'clock for a funeral. Jimmy Calvert, the retired Police Surgeon. No doubt you remember him?"

"I do, Sir," said Gus. "Jimmy attended quite a few deaths while I worked in Salisbury. Old school. His name cropped up during the Ursula Wakeley case review. He was off sick with the flu, and Peter Morgan stood in for him."

"Yet you still solved it in double-quick time," smiled the ACC.

"My superiors considered me old school, too," Gus said. "With myself and Jimmy on a case, there were few loopholes for a defence lawyer to explore."

"Quite. Ah, that's Mercer, I can hear in the corridor. So we can make a start."

Geoff Mercer tapped on the door and didn't wait for an invitation to join them.

"Did you get everything sorted, Mercer?" asked the ACC.

"No problem, boss. My dress uniform is getting a quick going over by Christine. I can drive home, get changed, and pick you up outside at one o'clock."

"Excellent. Let's crack on. I'll run through the basics. If you have something to add, Mercer, then jump in."

"Got it," said Geoff, grinning at Gus.

"Who do we have this time?" asked Gus.

"Ivan Kendall," said Kenneth Truelove. "Does the name ring a bell?"

"Did he live next door to that bloke who never won Wimbledon?" asked Gus.

"Are you in one of those moods of yours, Freeman?" asked Kenneth Truelove. "This murder took place four years ago. The victim came from South Wales, but he left home on Saturday the eighth of March to catch a train to Westbury station."

"Not the most exciting place to visit on a Saturday night, Sir, I grant you, but what was this chap's background? Was he known to us?"

"No criminal record. Clean driving licence. Kendall ran

a small window-cleaning business centred on the tiny village where he lived with his wife and daughter."

"How old was he?"

"Forty-five, a year older than his wife, Sally. Their daughter was sixteen. Kendall lost a well-paid job through redundancy six years earlier. Neither he nor his wife was well-qualified, so they lived hand-to-mouth. They would have relied on public transport if he hadn't needed a van for his business."

"Life's been tough in those old mining communities for a generation and more," said Gus.

"Yes, and the stress told after that sudden change of circumstance," said the ACC. "Sally Kendall walked out for a short period within a year, then moved to Cardiff, leaving Alexa, the daughter, behind. Sally got involved with a bar owner, Tommy Griffiths, fifty-five and single. He wanted more than someone willing to share his bed after work, but Sally must have still loved Ivan despite their economic headaches. So Sally went back for a second time."

"There were no domestic problems where the police or social services got involved?" asked Gus.

"None whatsoever," said the ACC. "When things got too much, and another final demand landed on the door-mat, Sally disappeared. Ivan just kept working, looking after Alexa, and trying to get them out of the mire."

"When did his wife leave him for good?" asked Gus.

"She didn't. Sally spent a few weeks with her mother in the summer of 2013, but there was a reason for that. A lovelorn Griffiths had quit his job in Cardiff and moved into the village. There's no evidence he stalked Sally Kendall or tried to come between husband and wife. While Sally was at her mother's, Ivan got on with things as before. Tommy Griffiths realised he was banging his head against a brick wall and took a pub in Weymouth. Sally came home as soon as the coast was clear, and until the following March, everything was fine."

"At least on the surface," said Geoff Mercer.

"So, what changed in March?" asked Gus.

"If the detective teams in South Wales and up the road in Westbury knew that, they might have solved the case back in 2014," said the ACC.

"Well, they missed something," said Gus. "Because, so far, it's been an everyday story of country folk living on the bread-line. There's no mention of criminal activity, domestic abuse, alcohol-fuelled arguments, drug addiction, incest, or bestiality. What triggered this urge to travel on a train to Westbury?"

"Nobody knows," said the ACC. "After spending the afternoon having a couple of pints at the rugby pub in Pontyclun, Ivan came home, sat in the living room for an hour without saying a word, then got changed and walked out. The daughter came home at ten and told her mother she'd seen her Dad getting on a train to Cardiff. It was totally out of character."

"What did Sally do?" asked Gus.

"She went to bed, and when there was still no sign of him by early afternoon, she called the police."

"Did they start an immediate search for a body?" asked Gus.

"Why?" asked the ACC. "They couldn't even list him as a missing person after only twelve hours. Ivan might have gone to Cardiff, got drunk and slept it off somewhere. He could creep home later and tell his wife he just needed to escape the madness for a spell. It was his turn to take a break after all."

"Ivan was a quiet man by the sound of things. He kept himself to himself. Am I right?"

"Spot on," said Geoff Mercer.

"When things got tough, the wife walked away for a respite break. When she was ready, she returned. Ivan never altered his routine when Sally wasn't there on the other three occasions. He continued to graft as hard as possible to provide for his family. There are many men like Kendall that crack in the end. There are two ways things go from there."

"Suicide, or murder-suicide," said Geoff.

"Exactly. Perhaps, Ivan believed that Sally Kendall had decided to move to Weymouth," said Gus. "Tommy Griffiths had declared his love for her, and after wrestling with the problem for nine months, Sally had decided the South Coast was a better prospect. Ivan jumped on the train, planning to get off at an unscheduled stop or make for somewhere near Cardiff Central to lie on the high-speed line. What's to say he didn't plan on making it to Weymouth to sort out this Tommy Griffiths character?"

"Police found Ivan Kendall's body in a fishing lake in Westbury on Monday morning," said the ACC. "Someone murdered him."

"Nobody in South Wales knew that on Sunday lunchtime," said Gus. "In those first few hours after her phone call, they should have looked closely at the family dynamic. Was it possible Ivan Kendall was suicidal? Did Sally know where in Cardiff he might have gone? How far away is that village from the city? Ten or twelve miles?"

Kenneth Truelove nodded.

"A quick phone call and they could get their Cardiff colleagues to pay a visit to the likely addresses. By teatime, they should have known whether Ivan had reached the capital. Then they needed to check for a body on the line to Cardiff and CCTV at the city station to see if he travelled further afield."

"There's nothing in the file that I can see to suggest they went with the suicide angle," said the ACC. "I think they reckoned he'd turn up after a day or two."

"Did they check what ticket Ivan bought on Saturday evening?" asked Gus.

"A return ticket to Cardiff Central," said Kenneth Truelove. "I won't tell you what else they found on the body just yet. Run with your ideas on Ivan's motive for his sudden late-night trip. When you dig into the case with your team, no doubt something you think of in this first pass will prove useful."

"Nothing ever gets wasted, Sir," said Gus. "I now know that Ivan planned to return home. You don't buy a return ticket if you don't plan on using it. When we start work on the file, we'll double-check that South Wales Police confirmed the ticket purchase with the village railway station on Sunday afternoon. You said they discovered Ivan's body first thing on Monday morning. Who found him? I suppose it was a little old lady walking her dog. It usually is."

"Not this time, Freeman. A police diver went to the lakes with uniformed officers and a forensic team," said the ACC. "DC Clive Trainer got a call to attend Westbury station just after six o'clock on Sunday morning. A train conductor had arrived for work, and when he visited the Gents' toilet, he found a large quantity of dried blood in one of the stalls. A savage attack had taken place late the previous night. They found no trace of an injured man or dead body in an extensive search of the station premises. The forensic team discovered blood in the car park on the station forecourt and signs that a car had left in a hurry. The detective interviewed the conductor and learned that the only night train was the Cardiff service, which stopped at Westbury at a quarter to midnight."

"South Wales Police should have checked CCTV at Cardiff Central to see where Kendall went after he'd made the brief trip into the city. They were looking at a different scenario if he'd headed out of the station. As it was, he purchased another ticket."

"And that was a return ticket, too," said the ACC. "That was what police found on the body in the lake. He intended to get to Westbury and return, perhaps the next day. Ivan Kendall carried a modest sum of cash in his pockets but no mobile phone or credit cards."

"Surely, he had a mobile phone for his business?" asked Gus.

"No, the Kendall's had a landline. Alexa, the daughter, had a basic pay-as-you-go phone, not a smartphone."

"What did you mean by a modest amount of cash?"

"Sixty-five pounds, plus loose change. It surprised Sally it was that much, but then she wasn't sure how many customers Ivan called on for payment that Saturday morning. People were often at work during the week when he went to clean their windows. He was more likely to catch someone at home on a Saturday. The police didn't think it was unusual. Window cleaners often deal in cash. As for the credit cards, with money as tight as it was in the Kendall household, Sally told them it was out of the question. Ivan didn't want to risk getting into even more trouble."

"That could be another angle to pursue, Gus," said Geoff Mercer. "Ivan Kendall could have taken a payday loan from an unscrupulous outfit."

"I thought they were all the same," said Gus. "If Ivan did, then Sally didn't appear to know."

"There are national companies involved in that business," said the ACC. "But it's not uncommon for someone local to mount a smaller-scale operation on a town's housing estate. The interest rates still make your eyes water, but why Westbury? If Kendall were late with his payments, they would visit him at home or in a dark alley when returning from the rugby club."

"Loan sharks aren't daft enough to kill the guy either," said Geoff. "With Kendall, the main breadwinner, dead, there'd be even less chance of them getting the money back. I'll make tracks now, boss. I'll pick you up outside at one. Bye, Gus. This case looks to be a belter, doesn't it?"

"I'll reserve judgement until I hear more," said Gus.

Geoff Mercer left the room.

"What led this chap Trainer to search the fishing lake?" asked Gus once the door closed.

"It was Sid Dyer, the conductor, who suggested they look there. He wasn't impressed with DC Trainer. Dyer had arrived at six o'clock, found the large pool of blood on the bathroom floor, plus splatter around the cubicle and immediately phoned the police to report a murder."

"That's fair enough," said Gus. "Even though there was no corpse, it's hard to believe anyone could survive an attack like that."

"After they searched high and low for a corpse and found nothing, Trainer wondered whether it was a waste of his time. The forensics evidence they uncovered made him think again, but by then, it was lunchtime. DC Trainer was keen to watch an international rugby match on television. So, he let the case slide for four hours, thinking if there was a body close to the station and someone tripped over it, they would call 999."

"I imagine they've promoted him by now?" asked Gus.

"He's a DS in East Sussex," said the ACC. "Trainer wouldn't have lasted five minutes if I'd heard what he did. Sid Dyer travelled home on his motorcycle later on Sunday evening and thought of likely places to dump a body. The fishing lakes were dead opposite the entrance to Station Approach. He called it in as a suggestion. The diver was on the bank at first light."

"Did Ivan Kendall carry no ID?" asked Gus.

"None, but it didn't take long to work out from the train tickets that the victim came from Pontyclun. Westbury police contacted the locals, and South Wales Police called off the hunt for the missing window cleaner. They notified Sally Kendall within the hour."

"How did the victim die?" asked Gus.

"Blunt force trauma to the head," said Kenneth Truelove. "Nothing fancy, just a sustained attack to the head, torso, and legs with a baseball bat and a crowbar, or something similar. The head injuries proved fatal. He was dead before they threw him in the lake."

"Two armed men against one," said Gus. "I don't think they meant Ivan Kendall to use those return tickets."

"No, but there still wasn't a hint of what made Ivan take that cross-country journey or a clue to the identity of his killers. Kendall was a quiet, family man, despite the occasional separations."

"Which direction did the investigation take next?" asked Gus.

"After scratching around looking for connections between Kendall and anyone, this side of the Bristol

Channel DC Trainer's superior went to Weymouth to arrest Tommy Griffiths. They charged him with murder."

"That smacks of desperation," said Gus. "It's obvious that it didn't stick."

"Tommy Griffiths had enough alibis from his busy bar to convince the detective team he was nowhere near Westbury that night. Sally told the South Wales detectives Tommy had accepted that she would never leave Ivan. Killing Ivan wouldn't have altered her mind. She was never moving to Weymouth to be with him."

"How's Sally now?" asked Gus.

"Nobody knows," said the ACC. "Sally thought if someone had frightened Ivan enough to make him do something so out of character, she and her daughter could be in danger. She had no idea who might want to kill Ivan or why, but the pair disappeared several months after the funeral. There have been no sightings of them since the end of 2014."

"Blimey," said Gus. "Does that mean she was right, and they're six feet under? Or have they moved far enough away from a small village like Pontyclun to a big city where nobody gives a passer-by a second look?"

"You will need to look for them, I imagine?"

"I don't think we'll get far without them."

"Good hunting," said the ACC.

Gus took a moment to consider. How do you find someone who goes into deep hiding because they're afraid for their lives?

"Blessing will be my best bet," said Gus. "She can scour social media. Despite Alexa becoming a popular name in the cloud, by the time Sally and her daughter went to ground, it won't be hard to trace the daughter. Parents find it impossible to keep their kids away from it."

"And social media," said the ACC. "Although there was never any issue with the parents, the local police knew of the daughter. Alexa didn't commit any crimes, but a comment by one detective referred to her as being of easy virtue. Alexa was sixteen when her father died. The locals had seen her with other teenagers for the previous three years. Her behaviour is unlikely to have changed in the four years since. I agree DC Umeh will find her online somewhere."

"You had better get ready to leave for Jimmy's funeral, Sir," said Gus. "Was there anything else?"

"I'll let you read the files for yourself, Freeman. A week after they released Tommy Griffiths, the car used by the men to transport Kendall from the station to the lake turned up on a nearby industrial estate. Blood on the nearside rear passenger window was a match for Kendall. The car got stolen from Bath on Friday. Despite reconstructions on both sides of the Bristol Channel, they never found the attackers. Any leads they pursued dried up fast, and six weeks later, the case went onto cold storage."

"I might get something from that conductor," said Gus. "He had more common sense than Clive Trainer. At least Sid Dyer found the most likely place to look for the body. Kendall would still have been in the lake if Trainer had his way."

"More bad news, I'm afraid," said Kenneth Truelove, smoothing his dress uniform jacket. "Sid Dyer retired in June 2016 and died in a motorcycle accident nine months later."

Gus blew out his cheeks.

Geoff Mercer was right.

This one was a belter.

# Chapter Three

GUS GATHERED the files from Kenneth Truelove's desk and followed the ACC out of the door. Geoff Mercer was waiting at the bottom of the stairs. He gave Gus a wave.

"Rick Chalmers is working with Alex Hardy," he called out. "They're making excellent progress. If you ask at Reception, they'll issue you with a pass."

"Terrific," said Gus, "I'll pay them a visit in a minute."

"I hope you're not rushing off without a word?" asked Vera Butler.

Gus turned and saw Vera and Kassie Trotter hovering a few feet away.

"Don't worry," said Gus, "I know better than to visit London Road and not reach out to you two."

"You were much later today," said Kassie. "Most Monday mornings, you time your arrival to get offered a coffee and a bun."

"I took a coffee break mid-morning in the office," said Gus. "I spent it with Lydia Logan Barre. She's finally located her birth father and plans a trip to the Netherlands to meet him for the first time next weekend."

"That sounds exciting news," said Vera. "I suppose she and Alex will go together?"

"Without a doubt," said Gus. "Those two are inseparable these days."

"Like someone else that we know," said Kassie.

"Ah, the village telegraph is still in fine working order," laughed Gus.

"It was the frequent trips between Worton and Urchfont that did it," said Vera. "I was in town on Saturday afternoon, and a friend said she saw you and Suzie, in convoy, with both vehicles carrying loads of items on the back seats."

"Your friend couldn't see the stuff in the boot," said Gus. "Not that either of us can get much in there. Anyway, we've done it now. What did you two get up to this weekend? Anything exciting?"

"Unlike Lydia, I already knew where my birth mother and father were," said Kassie. "Not that we've had much to do with one another since I left home. Last weekend wasn't much different from any other, Mr Freeman. I came into Devizes on Saturday to do my weekly shop and baked on Sunday. It's getting boring."

"I can see you didn't just do your weekly shop, Kassie," said Gus. "You visited the hair salon to adjust the colour of your flash, or whatever you call it, from royal blue to emerald green. Your nails now display ten original designs, compared with two lots of five I noted on my last visit."

"Don't miss much, do you?" said Kassie.

"I'm a detective, Kassie," said Gus with a grin. "I can't see any additions to the tattoos, though."

"I live in hope," said Kassie, "one day, my prince will come. My love birds are getting fed up waiting."

Gus glanced at Vera and raised an eyebrow.

"What did I get up to?" she said. "Oh, nothing that exciting. The friend I mentioned was someone you saw in the Bear that night months ago. We went out for a meal and a few drinks on Saturday night. We hadn't done that for a while."

"Carol was one of the original FEW, Mr Freeman," explained Kassie. "Then she met someone, but it didn't work out."

The Frustrated Ex-Wives Club, yes, Gus remembered.

"When does Rhys Evans move into that property of Monty's, Vera?" asked Gus.

"Rhys starts work as our new Police Surgeon three weeks today. I believe he's collecting the keys from Monty ten days before that."

"I'll be free that weekend," said Kassie. "If he needs a hand."

"Rhys won't be short of offers of help by the sound of things," said Gus. "I'd better make tracks to the Hub. Good afternoon, ladies. It's been good to catch up."

"Don't be a stranger," said Vera.

"Do you want to pop back in an hour?" asked Kassie. "Mr Mercer's office will be vacant. I can offer you a coffee and a generous slice of my Victoria sponge."

"You're a temptress, Kassie Trotter, and no mistake," said Gus. "Have you invested in a book containing Welsh delicacies yet?"

Kassie blushed a deep red.

"You've caught her out, Gus," laughed Vera.

"I promise I'll get back later, Kassie," said Gus. "Suzie's finishing her stint in Swindon this week. I might not get an evening meal until late tonight, and I'll need something to stop my bones poking through."

With that, Gus trotted downstairs to chat with the Sergeant in Reception. As soon as he had the pass, Gus exited the main building and made his way across the yard to the Hub. The swipe card allowed him to safely negotiate the security doors on this occasion. During his first case, Geoff Mercer brought him here for a quick tour. Gus studied the pictures on the corridor walls again.

Because of the rapid succession of Chief Constables and the change of circumstances for a previous Member of Parliament, the images had reverted to pastoral scenes from the Wiltshire countryside. They were far less likely to end up in prison or worse.

Gus found Alex Hardy and Rick Chalmers's workstations and pulled up a chair.

"Good to see you again, Rick," said Gus, shaking the detective's hand.

"It's quieter than the last time we worked together," said Rick.

"I imagine it's better than the undercover role you had to play on Chesil Beach and other beauty spots too?"

"I lost count of the number of types of vessel these immigrants will use to cross the Channel, guv," said Rick. "They pay good money to get on a decent sea-going craft, but some will risk the journey in an inflatable raft designed for children. It's crazy, and the numbers keep growing."

"People I speak to can't understand the attraction." said Gus, "Anywhere would be better than the war-torn regions they're fleeing, but if you cross half a dozen countries to reach France, why bust a gut to go a further thirty miles? The weather's worse here, and the streets aren't paved with gold."

"Do you know what I noticed, guv?" asked Rick. "English was more likely to be their second language, not French, German, or Italian. Of course, they've forgotten every word as soon as you catch them. It never ends, guv."

"Well, now you're back at London Road, Rick, we're happy to use a man with your experience. Now, who will update me on the progress Geoff Mercer told me you two had made?"

"I suggested to Alex that we change tack from what he tried last week," said Rick. "If the red-headed sniper were part of a well-organised unit, he would be tough to find by a direct route. They'll be too good at covering their tracks. So instead, we could follow up on people who benefited from their unidentified help. They might help us find a way in."

"Fair enough," said Gus.

"We've found Tanya Norris, guv," said Alex Hardy. "The young girl Jack Sanders described."

"Was that through social media?" asked Gus.

"Yes, by a convoluted route," said Alex. "If you recall, Tanya was fifteen when she ran away from home in Oxford. She got dumped outside Swindon's major hospital two years later after an illegal abortion attempt. The young female doctor who treated Tanya persuaded her to tell her how she came to be in such a state. Tanya told her that running away was the simple part: finding a place to live and a job was something else. Unfortunately, Tanya was vulnerable, and after several weeks living on the streets, she was soon in the clutches of the Swindon grooming gang."

"The first thing the doctor did when she learned of the horrific life Tanya and the other girls had suffered was make a phone call to a national newspaper," said Rick. "Now, that sounds innocent enough. Members of the public phone in to various sectors of the media every day of the week. What does the next step in Tanya's life tell us?"

"Someone intercepted that call," said Alex. "Because a man and woman arrived within hours with enough accreditation to leave the hospital with Tanya. The youngster had gone when the doctor reported for her next shift. The story she got was that Tanya's parents had arrived from Newbury. Her birth parents hadn't moved to a new house in the past two years. So, who took her?"

"When the doctor rang the reporter to tell them what had happened," continued Rick, "he told her the newspaper had already received a call from a senior hospital manager telling him their source was unreliable. The doctor checked, but nobody from the hospital made any such call."

"So, someone was covering their tracks," said Alex.

"Nothing to see here. Move along, please," said Gus.

"We searched online for a Tanya Norris, who is now twenty-five or twenty-six years old," said Rick. "There were several potential matches, but we didn't have a photo of Tanya to be sure we had the right person. Alex didn't want to call her parents for an old photo in case it opened old wounds. Someone whipped Tanya away from the hospital before anyone could get Tanya's consent to contact her family. They are probably in the dark about what's happened to her since she left home a decade ago."

"I found an inactive account Tanya had with Facebook when she was fourteen," said Alex. "The profile picture was of her with the family's pet dog. The last posting was a few weeks before she ran away from home. I know Rick said we found her by a convoluted route, but to be fair, we were lucky. I searched for a girl with the first name Tanya, who resembled the girl on that profile. If she had altered her first name too, we could have searched for months without luck."

"Is Tanya married, with children?" asked Gus. He remembered sitting outside Jack Sanders's place, wondering what had happened to Tanya and the other girls caught up in that despicable business. He had hoped for the best but expected the worst.

"Tanya's single," said Rick, "we haven't heard her full story yet. We're interviewing her in Wantage tomorrow morning."

"We're hoping she can tell us about the people who took her," said Alex. "Who they work for, and where they're based."

"What about the lead you uncovered last week, Alex?" asked Gus. "Might we get to Grant Burnside's killer by speaking with people living in that apartment block in Marylebone?"

"We're hoping Tanya kept in touch with other girls, guv," said Rick Chalmers. "The class of person who occupied those apartments will expect to speak to someone with a higher rank than a Detective Sergeant and only with a solicitor present. Most of the occupants were at work in the City or something similar. If there *was* anyone home, they were domestic staff, and turnover can be high in that line of work. They'll be back in Portugal or the Philippines by now."

"Don't give up on that angle yet," warned Gus. "I want Burnside's killer. We'll explore every avenue."

"Got it, guv," said Alex and Rick.

"Call me when you return from Wantage tomorrow," said Gus. "I ought to get back to the Old Police Station office soon. The team will champ at the bit for their next case. Although, they might change their tune once they see what little we have to work with."

"That's never stopped us in the past, guv," said Alex.

"You're right, Alex," said Gus. "Something will turn up. We have to ask the right questions."

Gus left Alex and Rick to continue searching for potential links to the people who employed Grant Burnside's assassin. He crossed the yard from the Hub building to return to his car. Once he'd locked the Kendall murder files inside the Focus, he dashed upstairs to the admin area. The team could wait another thirty minutes. Kassie's cakes were too good to miss.

It was a quarter to three when he stood in the lift travelling to the Crime Review Team office. As soon as Gus exited the lift, he could see that his team had run out of valuable tasks.

"Are you carrying two files, guv?" asked Neil Davis.

"We've got a case that started in South Wales as a missing person but ended up as a murder in Westbury," said Gus. "That's why this landed on our desk. South Wales Police handled the initial inquiry, and Wiltshire took it forward once the victim's body surfaced. The killers had thrown Ivan Kendall's body into a fishing lake half a mile from the railway station where the murder occurred."

Gus took the team through the basics surrounding the case. He allocated tasks and watched as the pertinent crime scene photographs, local maps, and witness statements got pinned to the walls and whiteboards. By five o'clock, everything was ready for their review to start.

"Two minutes," said Gus, "and then we'll go home and start afresh on this in the morning. First impressions, anyone?"

"DC Trainer believed there were two men involved in

the killing," said Luke, "based on forensic evidence gathered in the toilets and the car park. Is that correct?"

"I see no reason to query the forensic evidence, Luke," said Gus, "but somebody could interpret your question two ways. Define what you mean by correct."

"Well, the victim did something his wife said was out of character. They had been married for twenty years, and Sally left him on three occasions. Something wasn't right in the marriage, and it might not have been entirely their economic circumstances. Sally took a lover when she was in Cardiff. Was Ivan Kendall gay?"

"There's no suggestion of that in the material gathered by the two separate police forces," said Gus.

"Luke's concerned about the murder site, guv," said Neil. "We don't understand why Kendall visited a Westbury station toilet late that Saturday night. Maybe he agreed to meet someone."

"Neither reconstruction produced a witness who remembered seeing Kendall on the train, alone or with anyone else. Police interviewed passengers between Pontyclun and Cardiff and several from Cardiff to Bristol Parkway and beyond. It's not conclusive, but it's easier to imagine Kendall arriving alone on the Westbury platform at a quarter to midnight."

"I agree, guv," said Lydia. "If Ivan were gay and used to finding casual partners throughout the marriage, he'd find them closer to home. Eighty miles on the train is a long way to travel on the off-chance that you get lucky."

"So, are we happy Ivan was alone when he got off the train?" asked Gus.

"How many other passengers got off that train at that time of night?" asked Blessing Umeh. "I'd be in bed."

"An excellent question, Blessing," said Gus. "I learned

much about Westbury station when the ACC stepped through the case notes with me earlier. For example, even though it's an important junction with services across the south of the country, only a few trains stop there that late at night. Nor would trains depart the station before the following morning. So, apart from the staff, Ivan Kendall was unlikely to have encountered many people. Either on the platform or in any other part of the station."

"Why pay a visit to the Gents toilet, though?" asked Neil, "a train travelling that distance from Cardiff Central would have had toilet facilities on board. Perhaps, Kendall approached someone in the Gents and picked on the wrong guy."

"How do we explain the second man that the forensics indicated?" asked Lydia. "Or did they make a mistake? Kendall was a stocky individual, not easily pushed around. It's possible his killer worked alone but was a giant of a man."

"We have to locate Sally Kendall," said Gus. "We need to confirm whether Ivan might have met another man. That's our first hurdle because nobody has seen Sally and Alexa since December 2014."

"There are too many imponderables," said Blessing, shaking her head. "We must come back to this with a clear head in the morning."

"I couldn't have put it better, Blessing," said Gus.

Blessing and Lydia left the office and travelled in the lift together.

"Who's running Blessing back to the farm this evening?" asked Gus.

"I am, guv," said Neil. "I just wanted to clear the air with Luke first. It wasn't judgemental, mate. I know gay men don't all look for rough trade in public conveniences. I was exploring the possibility that Kendall had an ulterior motive for making the journey."

"That's OK, Neil. I understand where you're coming from," said Luke. "I didn't take offence. If Kendall knew someone was meeting him, he might expect one man to greet him on the platform and take him to the waiting car and its driver. There had to be a house they were returning to nearby. Kendall couldn't carry out a business transaction and jump on the next train back to Cardiff. He realised he was staying in Westbury overnight when he left home."

"Why didn't he take a bag with him then?" asked Neil.

"He didn't want to raise his wife's suspicions, I suppose," said Luke.

"It's a puzzle we can't solve this evening, lads," said Gus. "Come on, let's go in the lift together. Blessing will be eager to get home for her dinner."

Gus watched Luke and Neil's cars leave the car park. How many more facets could this case have? A homophobic attack? He hadn't even considered it. Neither had the detectives on the case in 2014. It was time to find another subject to fill his mind. Tomorrow was another day.

As Gus drove through the gateway to the bungalow, there was no sign of Suzie. He had the place to himself. Gus sat in the lounge and stared at the four walls. It was almost four years since he and Tess had moved here and decorated the place throughout.

To him, it felt comfortable; it was home. He liked the odd bump and scratch it had gained over the last four years and wouldn't be in a rush to change it. Many of those bumps and scratches helped keep Tess's memory alive.

How did Suzie feel about the bungalow? Would she hint that the décor looked tired? What would she think if Gus dug in his heels and said it was fine as it was? He'd had quite enough upheaval in his life in the past few months, thank you very much. Gus closed his eyes and relaxed.

Gus heard Suzie's car pull up outside. He shook himself awake. How long had he been napping? He checked his watch. It was a quarter past seven. Suzie breezed into the hallway, chucked her car keys into the tray on the side table and dropped her bag on the floor.

"What a day," she exclaimed.

Gus emerged from the lounge and hugged her.

"I think we've both had a tough day," he said, "what can I get us for dinner?"

"We'll prepare it together," said Suzie. "You can unload your troubles on me, and I'll do the same in return. But, thank goodness, tomorrow will be the last day I must stand working with that idiot, Gareth Francis."

"Okay", said Gus, "although it sounds like you're going first."

An hour later, they'd de-stressed and eaten. Sitting in the lounge with a coffee, Suzie leaned on Gus's shoulder.

"I was thinking," she said.

Here we go, thought Gus.

"If we count Saturday as Day Zero, I've only lived with you in this bungalow for two days, yet it already feels like home."

"You don't have the urge to remove walls, scrape off wallpaper, or buy gallons of paint then?" asked Gus.

"Heavens, no," said Suzie. "Ever since you invited me back for lunch that Sunday afternoon, I've loved this place. It cocoons you and wraps you in a warm embrace."

"You could have offered to buy it," said Gus.

"It wouldn't be the same without you in it," laughed Suzie.

"That's a relief," said Gus.

"What shall we do for the rest of the evening?" asked Suzie.

"We could walk to the allotment to see how my vegetables are doing one hour before sunset. Or drop by the Lamb for a drink with Bert Penman. Why not open a bottle of wine and listen to one of the albums you brought over on Saturday?"

"Option three sounds preferable," said Suzie. "We'll take the first two options tomorrow evening. It will start the celebrations for finishing my work at Gablecross, despite DI Francis. You open a bottle of Malbec and bring us two glasses. I'll select something from my limited vinyl collection, and I hope you enjoy it."

### *Tuesday, 10 July 2018*

ALEX HARDY LEFT his home to drive to Devizes at the regular time. He gave Gus a wave as they passed one another at the bottom of Caen Hill. With Suzie Ferris needing to leave for Gablecross, his boss was up and about in plenty of time to reach the Old Police Station office at nine.

Alex had arranged to collect Rick Chalmers from London Road. The drive to Wantage would take them around an hour, and Tanya White (formerly Norris) expected them at ten o'clock. Alex did not know what Stockham Park was like. Rick was more familiar with the area.

When Alex carried out high-speed pursuits, there weren't opportunities to see much more than the motorway or the major roads. The drivers he chased weren't keen on giving him a chance of sightseeing.

As Alex parked his car outside the Hub building, Rick emerged and jumped into the passenger seat.

"Before we go," he asked. "Did you have a substantial breakfast?"

"I never leave home without one," said Alex. "Why?"

"My eyes were bigger than my stomach last night. I've got half a pizza in my car if you want to share it."

"No, thanks," said Alex. "So, what have you heard about Wantage and this estate we're visiting today?"

"Wantage is a quiet, market town with a population of eleven thousand, give or take. For one, a few famous people were born here, including Alfred the Great. As for Stockham Park, it's got its issues."

"I guess you can understand why Tanya lived there," said Alex. "She was born in Oxford, lived in Swindon for a while, and convalesced somewhere close. It's an area she knows. It sounds like she can exist there, raising no eyebrows; that's probably all she wants. To live her life with no one learning about her past."

"And here we are, on our way to open up those wounds again," said Rick.

As they turned on Portway on the outskirts of the town, Rick checked the time.

"Take a right onto Ham Road just up here, and we'll be outside Tanya's front door at one minute past ten. Let's hope she's got the kettle on."

Rick was spot-on with the timing. He was right about the estate, too, with the odd car on bricks in the front garden and damaged walls, windows, and doors crying out for repair. When they walked from the car to the entrance of the smart-looking two-up, two-down terraced property Alex wondered what they would find inside.

Rick pushed the bell. They weren't sure whether it worked as they didn't hear a ring.

Alex rapped the glass panel with his knuckles. The door opened at once.

"Alright. Keep your hair on. I suppose you're from the police that rang me yesterday?"

Tanya was petite, perhaps five foot two inches tall, with her blonde hair dragged tightly off her face and secured in a ponytail. Alex kept reminding himself she was only twenty-six. Tanya was barefoot and wore a loose-fitting sleeveless top and tight blue jeans.

Alex checked her arms for tracks but saw nothing fresh. He knew Rick would keep his eyes peeled for the usual drug paraphernalia inside. If cannabis had been Tanya's thing, the stench would have hit them already.

"I'm DS Chalmers, and my colleague is DS Hardy," said Rick. They showed Tanya their warrant cards. She stood back to let them in.

"Tea or coffee?" she asked.

"Coffee, white, one sugar for me," said Alex.

"Me too," said Rick.

"I don't know what I can do to help you," said Tanya as she walked to the kitchen. Rick followed her. He noticed that the room was tidy. There was food in the fridge when she collected the milk, and the cupboard was full when Tanya took out the coffee jar.

Alex stood in the hallway and looked upstairs, and listened. He didn't sense anyone else was home. He glanced through the open door into the living room. Although some would think it was sparsely furnished, it had everything a young woman living alone needed.

Tanya might have her demons, but she was doing her best to hold on to this place. Her landlord wouldn't have any cause to complain.

"We know how painful things were for you in Swindon," said Rick as they moved into the living room and sat. "We want to start with the time when things improved for you. Can you remember when you left the hospital and someone took care of you? What can you tell us?"

"I'd spoken with Michelle, the doctor," said Tanya, "and she promised to do more than help me get better. I think she phoned someone, but I was out of it for a while, not just because of what they did to get rid of the baby. They gave us girls all the drugs we needed, and everyone relied on them to get through the day. I was strung out for weeks but determined to beat it."

"Do you know who collected you from the hospital, Tanya?" asked Alex.

"I didn't recognise them," said Tanya, "they told the staff I was their daughter. That was daft. They were too young to have a seventeen-year-old kid. The lady was only ten years older than me if that. They drove me to a house. Not that far in the car, but I didn't know which direction we went when we left Swindon. A nurse looked after me there. She didn't wear the same uniform, but she knew what she was doing."

"How long do you think you were there?" asked Rick.

"Two weeks, maybe three," said Tanya. "Those two people came back to talk to me while I was getting better."

"The couple who posed as your parents?" asked Rick. "Did they ask about the men who made you work for them?"

Tanya nodded.

"Okay," said Alex, "did you learn where you were or who they were?"

"The nurse told me she knew them as Mr and Mrs Brown. They lived in Shrivenham. I stayed in what she called a safe house in Devizes until I was well enough to travel. Someone collected me at night after three weeks. I think the nurse gave me something because when I woke up, I was somewhere different. The doctors there helped get me off the drugs and told me none of what happened was my fault."

"Were you able to mix with other patients while you were there?" asked Rick.

"Did you find out where this new treatment centre was?" asked Alex.

"I had no idea how far we went when they drugged me," said Tanya, "but other girls were there. Girls I'd seen in the clubs and at the parties in the big houses in the countryside."

Alex and Rick realised that these other girls could help them in their search.

"Do you know the names of these other girls?" asked Rick.

"Vicki, Tasha, Billie, and Freya were the ones I talked to most. We got together because we were at the same stage in our recovery. That's what the doctors said."

"Did you leave at the same time?" asked Alex. "How did that work? Did they find a place for you, like this one?"

"We aren't supposed to tell anyone," said Tanya.

"What made you choose your new surname?" asked Rick.

"We didn't get to choose," said Tanya. "The doctor gave you the next name on the list: Black, Brown, Green, White. I didn't care. We just wanted to forget everything that had happened. I got told I could stay here as long as I wanted, provided I kept up to date with the rent. I had to stay in full-time employment and keep clean and not go back to what I did before, you know."

"Did someone find you a job?" asked Alex.

"I work from home," said Tanya. "I work for a charity that helps ex-servicemen deal with PTSD. I feel that I'm doing something worthwhile."

"Are you in a relationship?" asked Rick.

"I'm not ready yet," said Tanya, "I still need counselling to process what those men did to me. The doctor at the hospital in Swindon told me I'd have no children. Those men had done too much damage when they punished me for getting pregnant."

"I'm sorry, Tanya," said Rick. "We didn't wish to cause you distress. Have you got contact details for Vicki and the others?"

"Yeah. We're in a What's App group. We support one another."

"I'd appreciate those contact details," said Alex, "You can promise them we'll be discreet. We want to learn as much as possible about Mr and Mrs Brown and the others, that's all."

"What's the name of the charity you work for, Tanya?" asked Rick.

"I told you before, we aren't to speak about it," said Tanya. "My life has been heaven since they rescued me from the hell I suffered back then. If I want to go to college and pursue another career, they'll help me. Once I prove I can be independent, I can move on from here and get my own place. This house isn't a prison. If I meet someone, the same applies. They won't stand in my way. You have no idea how many people they're helping across the country. When we talk amongst ourselves, me and the girls think they're better off doing good things without publicising it."

"Where is the charity based, do you know?" asked Alex.

"Not a clue," said Tanya, "and that's the truth, honest. Every financial transaction and every email contact has always been from a numbered account or address. There's no way to link it to the specific name of an organisation. Before you ask, no, you can't see any of my bank details without a warrant."

"If I said we'd be back with a warrant tomorrow morning, what would happen?" asked Rick.

"You would find this place empty," said Tanya. "If I ever feel threatened, they said to call them. Look, I've said more than I should have already. What's the problem, anyway? I've not broken the law."

"Fair enough," said Alex, "Give us the phone numbers to get in touch with your friends. We won't push them to tell us more than they want. You said the people who masqueraded as your parents were too young. The woman was the same age as you are now, is that right?"

Tanya nodded.

"The man was older, but not by much."

"Can you describe them?" asked Rick.

"She was pretty. The man looked good, too, tall and athletic. They spoke like the actors in that 'Our Girl' series on the telly."

"The series about the British Army in Afghanistan?" asked Rick.

"Yeah, that one," replied Tanya.

"That's very helpful, Tanya," said Alex. "We'll let you get back to work as soon as we've got those contact details."

"I was hoping you'd forget," grinned Tanya. She

checked her phone and noted names and numbers on a scrap of paper before handing it to Alex.

"Thanks, Tanya," said Alex. "Remember what we said. We don't want to cause trouble. We're happy to see you're in a safe place and enjoying your work."

Tanya White walked them to the front door and watched as Rick and Alex returned to the car. As soon as Alex drove away from the kerb, she closed the door and went back inside.

"She'll be on the phone to these friends of hers, warning them we're on our way," said Rick.

"Call one of them now and fix a meeting," said Alex. "Even one confirmation of that description of Mr and Mrs Brown will help. Who knows, they might provide more details on this charity. Tanya said we wouldn't believe how many people they help. How can something be that wide-spread and not be general knowledge?"

"They've got financial clout, too," said Rick. "If they can support medical facilities to wean patients off drugs, re-house them, and fix them up with jobs."

"When I started this search, I was hunting a sniper who killed Grant Burnside. A military background seemed an obvious connection for a man capable of making that shot from a distance. Now we've uncovered other ex-military personnel involved in undercover work rescuing girls from a grooming gang. Could these people connect to the charity Tanya mentioned? A charity that helps ex-servicemen dealing with Post Traumatic Stress."

"Who are you ringing?" asked Alex.

"Freya," said Rick, "but it's gone to voicemail. Shall I leave a message?"

"Try Vicki next," said Alex.

Rick dialled the numbers Tanya provided, one after the other. He shook his head.

"I don't think Tanya gave us the wrong numbers," said Rick, "But she must have texted them and warned them not to answer. So they've gone to voicemail. I'll send them a text explaining who I am and why I'm calling. We'll just have to wait, Alex."

Alex thought for a second.

"Call Tanya," he said, "she'll recognise the number you rang to book this morning's interview."

Rick made the call.

"Guess what?"

Alex turned back at the next roundabout and sped towards Stockham Park.

"Who the heck are we dealing with here?" said Rick.

A local estate agent's 'To Let' sign confirmed what Tanya had told them. If she felt threatened, she only had to call. The furniture might still be inside, but Tanya White (formerly Norris) had gone.

## Chapter Four

ALEX AND RICK headed for the Hub building when they arrived at London Road. Gus Freeman needed to hear this news.

While Alex made the call, Rick started the hunt for Mr and Mrs Brown from Shrivenham. Tanya was sure the nurse had told her they lived there in 2012. If they had returned from active service in Afghanistan before that, they could appear in the 2011 Census.

"It's Alex, guv," said Alex. "We've got a problem. Rick and I interviewed Tanya in Wantage this morning. She wasn't eager to give much away, but we got a lead on who took her from the hospital."

"That sounds positive," said Gus, "so, what's the problem?"

Gus listened, tight-lipped, as Alex explained.

"Curiouser and curiouser," said Gus. "I wonder whether the girls have moved, or is it just Tanya? Can the Hub whiz kids help with that? Could they locate those phones? Do you have enough details to search for them on social media?

They'll be among Tanya's friend list, won't they? So keep calling those numbers and start looking online. Keep me in the loop."

"Will do, guv. Oh, I didn't tell you the girls' new identities. Tanya Norris is now Tanya White. Or she was when we spoke to her at ten o'clock. She didn't tell us what Vicki, Tasha, Billie, and Freya got called after they'd completed their recovery. Take your pick from Black, Brown, Green, and White. It will slow us down in finding the right profiles on social media. If Tanya's anything to go by, they will have covered their tracks before we find them."

Alex rejoined Rick, and they divided the tasks between them. Rick spent the rest of the day tracing the couple masquerading as Tanya's parents. Alex saw him sit back in his chair with a massive sigh at a few minutes to five.

"Any joy, Rick?" he asked.

"Got them both, mate," said Rick. "Hayden Vincent was twenty-eight years old in 2012. He served in Iraq and Afghanistan as a medic. Under fire in Helmand, he met Kelly Dexter, a Lance Corporal in the Logistics Corps. Kelly, twenty-six at the time, took shrapnel in the legs after a mortar attack. They returned in 2010 and recovered from their ordeal at a facility in Hampshire before leaving the army. They were a couple. Where one went, the other followed. They moved to Shrivenham in November and appeared in the Census the next year. Both of them entered their occupation as a joint cleaning company owner."

"Terrific," said Alex, "let's see them tomorrow. We won't announce our arrival. I'll collect you from home at seven o'clock. We can get to them before eight."

"If only it were that easy, Alex," said Rick. "While you chased the GPS locations, I asked another expert on this floor for a helping hand. He found Kelly Dexter and

Hayden Vincent in November 2012. Avon and Somerset held onto several CCTV images captured during a Royal visit to Bristol. The Queen attended the Old Vic Theatre and the M Shed. After a terrorist scare, the Queen's car exited stage left at a rate of knots. There was a large police presence in the city, but nobody could identify several other people on the scene during the excitement."

"Dexter and Vincent were definitely there that day?" asked Alex. Rick showed him the images.

"Look, there they are on Prince's Street, mingling with the crowd. Do they look like sightseers to you?"

"Not a bit," said Alex, "if I had to hazard a guess, I'd say they were security forces. Look at the bulge in that jacket Vincent's wearing. He's carrying a gun in a shoulder holster. I bet the woman has a weapon in that large handbag too. Who could they be with?"

"No idea, but it puts a whole new meaning on working for a cleaning company," said Rick.

"You told me to hold on. Have Vincent and Dexter left Shrivenham? Where did they move to?"

"They cleared out towards the end of 2013," said Rick. "Destination unknown. There is one more thing that will interest you, Alex. Gus will rub his hands too. Look at this image from Prince's Street that same afternoon."

Alex stared at the screen. A man was talking to a police-woman. He had his back to the camera, and the young officer looked up at him. The mystery man had to be over six feet tall, and despite the baseball cap and scarf, he had red hair.

"It can't be a coincidence," said Alex. "Kelly Dexter and Hayden Vincent being on the same street during a large-scale security exercise. Could we identify that policewoman? What rank is that? I reckon she's a DS from Avon and

Somerset wearing a dress uniform for the Royal occasion. Check for any video covering other venues the Queen visited. That officer might have appeared at several of them if she coordinated security. She's using the Airwave unit on her left shoulder as she walks away from our mystery man. We'd better get in touch with Portishead."

"Maybe someone from Portishead can tell us who these people work for," said Rick.

"Whoever the red-haired guy was, that officer looked star-struck. They have to be special forces. It changes things, doesn't it? I'll call Gus again."

"Hang on. A neighbour in Shrivenham told me nobody knew where Vincent and Dexter went. One day his people carrier and her Porsche 911 vanished. They did a moonlight flit. Another couple rented the property within days. The new occupants ran a removals business."

Alex laughed.

"Of course they did. I bet they were part of the same organisation. No matter. Where do we look for Vincent and Dexter now, then?"

"I've started search routines with my new friend on the other side of the office. So if Hayden Vincent or Kelly Dexter has appeared on CCTV anywhere in the past five and a half years, we could be lucky and be able to retrieve it."

Alex was going to call Gus when he realised how late it was.

"Gus will be on his way home now," he said. "We'll come back to this first thing in the morning."

"You didn't mention how the mobile phone search went," said Rick.

"I called those four numbers from my mobile and the Hub landline without luck. Every call went straight to voicemail. As for the GPS traces, the report I got back was confusing. All four phones pinged from the same tower. So the girls live in the same house or on the same street. I've asked another techie on this floor to check whether the kit malfunctioned. That's something else we can pick up again tomorrow."

Alex and Rick left the Hub office and returned to the car park.

"See you here at the usual time then, Rick," said Alex standing by his car.

"Let's hope we can solve a couple of these riddles, mate," said Rick. "Have a good night. There's a Chinese meal in that takeaway near the town centre with my name on it."

"Do you ever cook for yourself?" laughed Alex as his colleague started to walk into town.

Rick stopped by the Wiltshire HQ entrance and called back:

"Don't be daft. How many dishes can you cook? Five or six at most, I bet. My mother was the same. So I can eat something from a different cuisine every night of the week and never get bored."

With that, Rick strode along London Road.

Alex passed him as he drove home. It takes all sorts.

AS ALEX HARDY drove towards Chippenham to spend the evening with Lydia Logan Barre, Gus Freeman pulled up outside the bungalow in Urchfont. He'd called Suzie before leaving the Old Police Station office. Suzie expected to reach home by six, so Gus had told her he'd booked a table at the Lamb for eight. She'd find him at the allotment if she wanted a chat.

Gus opened the front door and walked inside. A quick shower and change out of his work clothes, and he could tend to his long list of outstanding jobs within twenty minutes.

Gus reflected on the day so far as he showered.

Blessing Umeh had started the search for Sally and Alexa Kendall.

Luke Sherman had contacted Ieuan Arlett, the steward at Pontyclun Rugby Football club. The interview would take place tomorrow at two o'clock.

Tommy Griffiths wasn't hard to find, either. He'd agreed to meet with Neil and Lydia at eleven tomorrow morning.

Gus had been on the phone, too, chasing the name of Clive Trainer's superior, the officer who ran the Westbury end of the initial investigation. Gus found him in Shaftesbury and had arranged to chat with DCI Eddie Sinclair at ten in the morning. Luke and Gus would leave after that call and visit the Cardiff Central HQ in King Edward VII Avenue before heading for Pontyclun. A DI Dai Williams would fill in the gaps concerning work by South Wales Police in those critical eighteen hours after Ivan Kendall's disappearance.

Gus towelled himself dry and found his gardening clothes. They were in the same place he'd left them, which pleased him. But, as he strolled along the lane towards the church, he thought about the one phone call he'd received today.

The news from the Hub was disconcerting. Since that meeting with Jack Sanders, Gus had agonised over Tanya Norris's welfare. Still, Alex persuaded him that Tanya had survived her ordeal and had a half-decent chance of making a good life for herself. Then everything went pear-shaped. Gus hadn't heard the questions the lads had asked, nor did he know whether they pushed too hard. That was something he needed to find out tomorrow.

Whatever triggered Tanya's reaction didn't help matters. The two experienced officers would spot if Tanya deliberately misled them. There was another unseen hand in this business. Gus had felt it from that first morning under Jack Sanders's apple trees.

Gus could tell as soon as he passed the church and turned into the gateway to the allotment that he had company. Bert Penman toiled away on his patch. This evening he had a willing helper. His grandson, Brett, was wielding a fork and working up a sweat. Bert continued hoeing steadily and looked up as Gus reached his garden shed.

"Evening, Mr Freeman," he said.

"Good evening, Bert," replied Gus. "How's your apprentice coming along?"

"He must learn to pace himself," said Bert, "The plants don't take kindly to getting assaulted. They respond best to a gentle touch, like a woman, if my memory serves me well."

"No sign of the Reverend tonight?" asked Gus.

He noticed Brett straightening his back, leaning on his fork, and taking a breather.

"No doubt she'll be along directly," said Bert, "It's been a warm day, and I saw her cycling around her parish this afternoon. I reckon she'll have spent an hour in the shade with Irene while we've been working on the land. Irene's experimenting with a new lime cordial. I don't believe the Reverend knows yet that it has gin and honey in the recipe."

"She will once she's had a glass or two," said Gus.

"How's your week going so far, Gus?" asked Brett.

"We have a new case that might prove tricky and an old

one that refuses to give up its secrets. Nothing out of the ordinary, in other words. Are you well-prepared for your interview?"

"My CV speaks for itself, Gus," said Brett. "Just because I've treated as many moose as I have poodles, I hope they don't hold it against me. I heard a rumour in the Lamb on Saturday evening. Was that fake news?"

"Not a bit," said Gus. "We never attempted to keep it secret. Suzie will be home from Swindon soon. She told me last night that the job's over and done with now. She returns to duties at London Road tomorrow. I've booked a table for eight o'clock in the Lamb to celebrate."

"You two are living over the brush now, Mr Freeman," Bert said, leaning on his hoe.

"We haven't held hands and jumped over a broom made of twigs, Bert," said Gus.

"I've no idea what you two are on about," said Brett.

"It's a custom that dates back centuries, Brett, when couples couldn't get married in a church. So they showed their commitment to one another by jumping over a broom. An ancient form of marriage."

"Do you think marriage will follow in time?" asked Brett.

"I haven't given the matter any thought," said Gus. "It's only a couple of days since Suzie cut the apron strings with her family home."

"There's another old saying for you, Brett," laughed Bert. "Times have changed, Mr Freeman. There was no question of Cora and me living together before we married, but that was in the early Fifties. This church next door to us would have been packed every Sunday back then. Those trees behind you bend with the wind, and old beggars like me have also learned to bend with the times. I can see how happy you two make one another, so you'll get no lectures from me. I can't say how the Reverend views such matters, though."

"Thank you, Bert. Are you two staying for a while?" asked Gus.

"We've finished for the day," said Brett. "We'll drop by the pub for a pint on our way home."

"I'll let you get on then," said Gus. "I have my list to tackle. I need to dash back by half-past seven to get myself ready."

Bert and Brett packed up and left ten minutes later, and Gus switched his attention to his allotment. When he locked his shed and made his way to the bungalow at half-past seven, there was still no sign of Clemency Bentham. Perhaps she was already in the Lamb, making eyes at Brett Penman.

"The wanderer returns," said Suzie as Gus strolled into the hallway.

"You're a sight for sore eyes," said Gus.

"Off you go," said Suzie, "get out of those gardening clothes. I've left a shirt hanging on the wardrobe door."

"Will I like it?" asked Gus.

"You'd better," said Suzie.

Fifteen minutes later, they walked along the lane arm-in-arm and arrived at the Lamb at five to eight. The landlord informed Gus that Bert and Brett Penman had left twenty minutes earlier. Gus spotted Clemency Bentham and Irene North sitting in the beer garden. While Suzie ordered the drinks and studied the menu, Gus went across to them.

"We missed you at the allotment this evening," he said.

"The Reverend's feeling light-headed," said Irene.

"My diet's still going well," said Clemency, "another two

pounds lost this week. But I'm wondering if I'm overdoing it."

Irene North winked at Gus.

"Bert told me you've come up with a new recipe, Irene. Is that right?"

"I have, Mr Freeman. Honey and lime cordial. We tried the first batch this afternoon."

"I see you're both on elderflower cordials this evening," said Gus. "Perhaps you should ask Irene for the full details of that other drink, Reverend. It might carry a stronger kick than you thought, especially as I saw your trusty steed outside. I'd hate to see you arrested for being drunk in charge of a bicycle."

"Irene North," said Clemency, "you swore to me that drink was non-alcoholic. No wonder I'm all over the place. It was so delicious we polished off the entire bottle this afternoon."

"I'll use less gin in my next batch, Reverend, I promise," said Irene.

"I'll leave you two to enjoy those cordials," said Gus. "Take care on your way home, Clemency. Suzie and I are having a meal inside, so bye for now."

"That's what *you* need, Reverend," said Irene. "Get yourself fixed up like Mr Freeman and Miss Ferris."

"Oh, that wouldn't do at all, Irene," said Clemency, "no matter how appealing it might be. Why is life so difficult?"

Gus left the two ladies to put the world to rights and rejoined Suzie inside.

"What are we having?" he asked.

"It's the duck for me," said Suzie. "I don't want to spoil our first meal as co-habitants. You can choose whatever you want."

Gus scanned the menu. Co-habitants indeed. Could he risk ordering the surf and turf?

"What do you have lined up for tomorrow?" asked Gus.

"I'm meeting Geoff Mercer as soon as I arrive in the office," said Suzie. "Geoff wants a debrief of my time at Gablecross, and then he says he's got a new case for me. He's given me no details yet. How about you?"

"We've arranged a series of meetings with people involved in our latest case. Luke and I are driving to Cardiff at eleven. We should get back before five. Neil's got a day trip to Weymouth with Lydia. Small steps, but I can't see us making significant inroads until we trace the wife and daughter of the victim. I might know more by the weekend. Perhaps we could discuss our various problems on the allotment one evening or Saturday afternoon?"

"I'll still go riding on Saturday morning," said Suzie, "and I know I must work on you for a while before you agree to join me. So that means the weekly shop will be your job on Saturday mornings if you want to keep the afternoon free."

"That's a plan I can work with," said Gus. "There was one worrying item that cropped up earlier. Alex Hardy has been working at the Hub to solve the mystery behind Grant Burnside's murder. Rick Chalmers joined him this week, and they've made progress. As usual with that case, it's three steps forwards, and two steps back, and they interviewed a grooming gang victim this morning."

"I remember hearing of that gang operating in Swindon six years ago," said Suzie. "I was still a Detective Constable and had nothing to do with the case. So how is the poor girl?"

"Tanya is twenty-six now and living in Wantage. When Alex and Rick spoke with her, they learned what happened when she left Swindon hospital. The NHS had treated her physical wounds, and Tanya needed time to recuperate. Someone whisked her away to a clinic, or a private house, in Devizes, where a nurse looked after her. When she was well enough to travel again, someone transferred Tanya to a unit where doctors tackled her drug dependency and the psychological damage her ordeal had caused."

"Who arranged this?" asked Suzie, "and where? It's not a place I recognise."

"Beats me," said Gus as their food arrived.

Gus picked up the tale after eating and enjoying a last glass of wine.

"I hoped Rick and Alex could learn more from Tanya and several of the girls rescued at the same time. Unfortunately, whoever arranged Tanya's recovery did the same for at least four other girls. According to Alex, Tanya was offered accommodation and a job once she was well enough to get discharged from this facility. She's worked for a veteran's charity for the past six years. I assume the others received a similar offer."

"Who was behind it then, another charity? One helping victims of crime. I can't think of anyone with that much financial backing, not locally, at least."

"I can't either," said Gus. "If you thought that was odd, when they left Tanya's house, Rick called one of the mobile numbers she'd provided for girls who'd also got exploited in Swindon. He got no reply, so Alex suggested they stop and try every number. They got the same result. So Alex turned the car around and drove back into Wantage, and guess what they found?"

"Had Tanya deliberately given them duff information?" asked Suzie.

"Alex couldn't check because Tanya had disappeared,

and there was an estate agent's 'To Let' sign in the front garden."

"You're kidding," said Suzie, "in that short a time? Who on earth could manage that, and why? What's going on, Gus?"

"I'll talk to the lads in the morning. I asked them to find Tanya on social media, look at her friend list, and name these four girls. Fingers crossed, it was only Tanya that did a runner. And we can find out more about the organisation behind this deception. I don't question the merit of the job they did getting Tanya and the others back on track, but the way they're covering their tracks suggests they have something to hide. That concerns me. I won't rest until I've got to the bottom of it."

"It's very James Bond, isn't it?" said Suzie. "It's exciting and yet troubling. Of course, life's never dull with you, is it?"

"Don't build your hopes up too much," said Gus. "It's only been three days. The routine nature of it will kick in before you know it."

"Finish that drink and let's go home," said Suzie.

"Now that's a routine I don't mind sticking to," said Gus.

### Wednesday, 11 July 2018

"IF I'M STAYING at London Road for the foreseeable future, then you could drop me off at work in the mornings," said Suzie.

"If we both could guarantee to keep regular hours, I

could collect you at half-past five every evening, too," said Gus.

"Maybe we'll be able to do that once or twice a week," said Suzie. "It would save money."

"Did you have something in mind to use the extra cash?" asked Gus, dreading the answer.

"Riding lessons for you," she replied.

"We both need to drive today," said Gus, "We'd better move."

Suzie slid out of bed and headed for the shower. Gus started on breakfast. It was another routine he could get to enjoy.

Gus sat patiently in the Focus at half-past eight while Suzie manoeuvred her VW Golf in the driveway and drove through the gateway. Gus followed as closely as he could, but the extra grunt her car possessed meant the only time he caught up was at road junctions and traffic lights.

Suzie gave Gus a wave as she turned right into the London Road car park. He continued through Devizes and made for the Old Police Station office seven miles away. He was last to arrive this morning, and when he exited the lift, he saw four eager faces.

"We waited until you got here before shooting off to Weymouth, guv," said Neil.

"Any last instructions?" asked Lydia.

"Do we believe Tommy Griffiths killed Ivan Kendall?"

"No, guv," said Neil.

"Do we think Tommy paid someone to murder Ivan?"

"I wouldn't rule it out until I've met the bloke, guv," said Neil.

"He was in love with Sally Kendall, guv", said Lydia. "Love can make you do daft things."

"You can work that angle for a while, Neil," said Gus.

"One thing that might help us is learning whether Tommy knew something about Ivan that even his wife didn't know. There had to be a reason for taking that train trip. Don't overdo the homophobic attack angle. Ease it into the conversation. See what reaction you get."

"I've got the idea, guv," said Neil.

"Off you go then," said Gus, "and good luck."

Gus's phone rang within a minute of Neil and Lydia leaving the office.

"Hello," said Gus.

It was Alex Hardy ringing from the Hub.

"We discovered something late yesterday afternoon, guv," said Alex.

He described Hayden Vincent and Kelly Dexter as Mr and Mrs Brown. Alex also told Gus about the CCTV images captured by Avon and Somerset Police in November 2012. When he mentioned the tall red-haired man caught on camera speaking to a police officer, Gus sat up straight in his chair.

"I need to look at those images, Alex," he said. "This could be the lead we've been desperate to find. That officer can identify him."

"I understand that, guv," said Alex. "But he's someone the police were comfortable working alongside that day. So why would he lie on a warehouse roof blowing Grant Burnside's brains out eighteen months later?"

"Let's tackle one thing at a time, Alex. First, find the officer, and get her to name the man we saw. Then, we'll drag him in for questioning if he's our mystery man. Get Rick started on that, then come back to me. I'm tied up from ten o'clock onwards."

Gus ended the call. What was it that Alex had said that rang a bell? Gus went over the conversation he'd had with

Jack Sanders. The Porsche 911, that was it. If Dexter drove the Porsche, it was her at the traffic lights in Old Town that night. Dexter and Vincent were in this from the beginning. They didn't just turn up to collect Tanya Norris. They also helped to eliminate the members of the grooming gang.

Gus grabbed his phone on the first ring.

"Alex, is that sorted? Right, carry on."

"Rick's on the phone to Portishead now, guv. Another Hub staff member is hunting more recent CCTV images of Vincent and Dexter. The other angle we tried yesterday afternoon was locating the girls' mobile phones using their GPS. I thought the kit malfunctioned the first time because it suggested the five phones were pinging off the same tower. The kit was AOK. We've just searched again for the five numbers, and they're still in the same area."

"Where's that?" asked Gus.

"The GPS pinpointed a place a few miles outside Bath," said Alex. "In the countryside between Englishcombe and Wilmington."

"I know exactly how long it will take us to drive there," said Gus. "Blessing's parents live in Englishcombe village. We can be there in less than forty-five minutes. All we have to do then is find the building containing these phones. Then whoever is holding them will need to give us answers. Well done, Alex. It's coming together nicely."

"When do we leave, guv?" asked Alex.

"I need to speak to DCI Eddie Sinclair about the team's latest case in half an hour. We'll be in better shape if we've got something more on Vincent and Dexter, plus whatever Rick gathers. I'll drive to London Road from home in the morning. If you and Rick meet me there, perhaps I can persuade Geoff Mercer to go with us. We might need someone with clout. It will do him good to get out of the office."

"Okay, guv," said Alex. "In the meantime, we'll keep digging, and if those phones move, I'll warn you."

"Fair enough," said Gus.

"Don't tell me my father has moved my mother into a danger zone," said Blessing.

"I hope not, Blessing," said Gus. "How are you getting on with the social media searches?"

"Nothing yet, guv," said Blessing. "I don't think Sally Kendall has a digital presence of any kind. Alexa will be the one to use a raft of sites. On my first pass, I stuck to Alexa. Perhaps when you speak to people in Pontyclun, they might know whether her schoolmates called her Lexie or something similar. I'll keep going as I am and adjust my parameters when I learn more. Fingers crossed they didn't change their names altogether."

Gus wondered whether he should tell Blessing to look for people with Black, Brown, Green and White surnames. Stop being negative, he thought. Today has had a decent start.

"Blessing, you'll be in the office alone after eleven o'clock. Are you okay with that?"

"I've worked alone at my old place, guv. We're not expecting visitors, are we?"

"No, and unless they have a swipe card," said Luke, "they can't use the lift, anyway."

"If we're expecting a visitor, we switch on the camera over the lift door," said Gus. "The switch is on the panel on the wall. So if you know who's there, send the lift for them. But, as Luke says, we're not expecting visitors."

"Neil and Lydia will be back before mid-afternoon," added Luke. "Gus and I should be back by five."

"I wasn't worried until you started explaining how it worked," sighed Blessing.

"Come on, Sinclair," said Gus, looking at his watch. "I want to get moving."

"We've got a lot of plates spinning in the air, haven't we, guv?" said Luke.

"We do, Luke. Of course, it doesn't help that we're trying to solve two cases at once, but if we were dealing with live cases, we'd have even more to cope with."

"Andy Carlton often had five jobs running at once, guv," said Blessing.

"My first Inspector told me that any detective that landed himself with that many ought to find another career. Although, they were different times and in my book Andy Carlton is a good copper."

Blessing made her way to the restroom. Luke looked at Gus.

"I need a cuppa, Luke. But, yes, better safe than sorry. Give Blessing a helping hand with the Gaggia. Neil said it frightens her when it gets noisy."

"To be fair, guv, every pump-driven espresso machine has a unique sound. Ours is a cross between a cement mixer and a strimmer."

"I blame Geoff Mercer," said Gus. "He told me it was the bee's knees when I came here to inspect the office."

"It makes a decent cuppa, though, guv," said Luke.

"So did my mother, but she never made such a song and dance about it."

# Chapter Five

BANG ON TEN O'CLOCK, DCI Eddie Sinclair called.

"Thanks for ringing, Sir," said Gus. "I know my colleague DS Sherman explained who I was and why we needed to get details from you. Can you remember the Ivan Kendall murder back in March 2014?

"I can, Gus," replied Eddie Sinclair. "I'd not been in the town long when that case landed on my desk. A strange affair."

"You had a DC Trainer working for you, is that right?" said Gus.

"Trainee, more like, and green as grass. Still, we all had to start somewhere. Clive got nothing wrong as such. However, it was a big mistake to leave everything unfinished overnight while he watched a rugby match and had a few too many jars with his mates in the aftermath."

"What did you make of the crime scene photos?" asked Gus.

"A savage attack. If only we'd had a wide CCTV coverage on the platforms. I wanted to see who left the train with Kendall. I thought he'd gone to that cubicle with a partner, and someone walked in on them. But that didn't work. When I worked there, we had our fair share of troublemakers, but it wasn't common for someone to wander onto the station platform or anywhere else in town with a baseball bat and an iron bar. The forensic people convinced me there were two attackers. So, it was two-on-one in the cubicle, not a homophobic attack. The two thugs had planned the attack and arrived with the necessary tools."

"That's my interpretation of events, too," said Gus. "Kendall didn't travel from Pontyclun expecting to get a vicious beating, so something happened in the first few minutes after he got off the train. Did you, Trainer, or anyone from the Cardiff end come up with a motive for the murder?"

"What are these arguments usually about?" asked DCI Sinclair. "Drugs and money was our next avenue of enquiry. We looked into that aspect without finding evidence tying Kendall to the drug scene. I believed that the men Kendall met were locals. We analysed each of our likely suspects, but they were in prison or had irrefutable alibis."

"So, these two weren't on your radar? Perhaps, because they'd never got caught before, or Kendall's trip had something to do with a business you never considered."

"We looked at the crime figures. Violence and sexual offences ranked highest, anti-social behaviour and arson attacks were next on the list, but nothing sprung out as a connection in this instance. It was a violent crime with no identifiable motive."

"Were there any newcomers in the area?" asked Gus.

"There's a permanent Wiltshire Council site out Dilton Marsh way," said Eddie Sinclair. "Several permanent caravans, with up to seven pitches. A few travellers caused trouble, minor stuff mostly, but they move on, don't they? Then turn up like a bad penny the next year. I can't recall names, but that's a possibility for new faces back then. Good luck finding them now."

"If it's an official site, then there should be a record," said Gus. "They should have paid council tax, utility bills and the like. Thanks. That might be worth a look."

"I'm sorry I can't be more helpful," said Sinclair.

"You've given us more than we had before, Eddie. We'll let you know if we close this one for you."

"I'd be grateful," said Sinclair, "the Kendall murder is one of three cases that kept me awake over the years. You know what I mean?"

"I do," said Gus. "It was the reason I came back. My boss warned me he'd never let me review one of my unsolved cases, but he promised that if I cleared just one case from the books, I'd have the undying gratitude of the detective involved."

"You can't beat job satisfaction, can you?"

"You certainly can't," said Gus.

DCI Eddie Sinclair ended the call. Gus made a note of Dilton Marsh on the whiteboard.

"That's interesting," he said as he checked the local map, "it's next door to Westbury Leigh, where that train conductor lived."

"Luke's gone to the restroom, guv," said Blessing. "You'll be leaving soon, won't you?"

Gus nodded. He decided he should make himself comfortable before undertaking the two-hour car journey. He passed Luke on his way back from the restroom.

"Did I miss anything, Blessing?" asked Luke.

"Gus realised Westbury Leigh and Dilton Marsh were next to one another. He thought it was interesting."

"Did he?" said Luke. "I wonder why. It's a mile further on the same road into the town."

When Gus returned, he and Luke gathered their things and headed for the lift.

"We'll see you before going home time, Blessing," said Gus. "Good hunting."

"And you, guv," said Blessing.

NEIL DAVIS WAS HUNTING for a parking spot on the Esplanade in Weymouth.

"Why couldn't this Tommy Griffiths live ten miles inland?" he moaned. "It's the build-up to the holiday season, and this place is packed."

"There's a car moving away on your right, Neil," said Lydia.

"Excellent spot," said Neil, "even if I scared the living daylights out of that little old lady when I crossed in front of her."

"Her hair was already white, Neil," said Lydia.

"What was she shouting? Could you make it out?

"My lip-reading skill isn't highly developed," said Lydia, "but she used three swear words in succession."

"Right, let's find this pub. It's along the seafront some-where. A decent spot to attract holidaymakers throughout the day."

"I wonder why Sally Kendall didn't throw her lot in with Tommy. Weymouth has to be a more pleasant place to live than Pontyclun."

"Here we are," said Neil. "Good. The board outside says they serve food from half-past eight in the morning."

"We're here to interview the landlord, not to give him a rating on Trustpilot," said Lydia.

They entered the pub and asked the young girl behind the bar for Tommy Griffiths.

She took a second look at Lydia, then disappeared into a back room. Thirty seconds later, the fifty-nine-year-old landlord limped through the door. Lydia wondered what had attracted Sally Kendall to the overweight, balding man who faced them.

"You'd better come through to the office," Tommy said, lifting the flap on the counter at the end of the bar.

Neil and Lydia eased their way past the sullen young barmaid and along a corridor. It was a stretch to call the cramped, overcrowded space an office, but it contained a desk and a chair. Tommy leaned against the desk, and Neil and Lydia stood as close to the door as possible. Lydia thought a windowless cupboard described the room best, and Tommy's hygiene left a lot to be desired.

"What do you want me to tell you?" asked Tommy.

"The truth," said Neil. "I need not remind you that Ivan Kendall's murder is an open case. His killer is still at large."

"It wasn't me then, and it isn't me now," said Tommy. "I've tried to put it all behind me."

"How did you meet Sally Kendall?" asked Lydia.

"She walked into my pub in Cardiff one afternoon. We were quiet, so I chatted while she had a drink. I asked if she'd come to the city for shopping or sightseeing. She said she'd left her husband, needed a place to stay, and was looking for a job. I had a few rooms upstairs for the staff. I didn't live on the premises myself. A week earlier, I discovered one of my bar staff had their hand in the till, so I was looking for a replacement. Sally took the room and started work the same evening."

"When did the relationship start?" asked Neil.

"Six to eight weeks after she moved in," said Tommy.

"She was a good worker, warm and friendly with the customers. We became a good team behind that bar, then one night after we closed up, you know, one thing led to another. After that, Sally slept at my flat several nights a week. Then after six months of me believing we were a couple, she ups and leaves, just like that. We'd had a busy weekend, with regular customers eating and drinking. One reason they kept coming to us was because of Sally. She always made everyone welcome. I was behind the bar, checking the stock when Sally came from her room to start work. Or so I thought. She had her bags in her hand and said she'd decided to give her marriage another go. I was gobsmacked. I told her I loved her, something I hadn't done before. Sally told me she didn't feel the same way. I was just scratching an itch, she said."

"That must have made you angry," said Neil.

"What if it did?" said Tommy. "It didn't stop her leaving, did it? Anyway, if I was angry at Sally, I didn't have cause to kill her husband. I'd never met the bloke."

"What prompted the move to Pontyclun?" asked Lydia.

"With Sally gone, my regulars dwindled, and the pub felt empty. My heart wasn't in the place anymore. I looked for something else—a new challenge as far away from South Wales as possible. Like a fool, I thought my best chance of making a success of it was for Sally to come with me. This pub came on the market, and when I'd handed in the keys to the gastropub, I gave our partnership one more try. I rented a room in the village and tried to speak to Sally about this place. I could see how profitable we could make it if we worked at it together. Sally left her husband again, and I thought I'd convinced her to give us a go. But she went back to her mother and refused to talk to me. I realised I'd been an old fool, left my flat and took on this pub alone. I've got several local staff who have stayed loyal. With the summer trade picking up, I've got casual staff like Terri out in the bar for the next eight weeks, and then it will be down-hill to Christmas. It's a living, but nothing as great as it might have been."

"Did you ever meet Ivan Kendall?" asked Neil.

"He knew who I was," said Tommy. "Sally told him she'd met someone when she was in Cardiff. Ivan took her back anyway. He never hit her. Sally swore that Ivan was never a violent man, even though she had left him repeat-edly. He never hit their daughter either, despite the worry she caused them. How she reached sixteen without getting pregnant was a miracle."

"Did you ever speak with Ivan or Alexa?" asked Lydia.

"I passed Ivan in the street twice while I stayed in the village. He just nodded to me but never spoke. As for the daughter, she was always with a different bloke if I saw her at night. Alexa gave me the death stare a few times. I don't think she would have come with Sally if things had worked out differently. The only other times I saw the daughter was walking the dogs. Well, getting dragged along by the dogs is a better way to describe it."

"Did Sally ever get in touch after you moved here?" asked Lydia.

"I didn't hear from anybody in that family after moving here, " Tommy said. "When the police found Ivan's body, they messed around for a week, then came straight here and dragged me out from behind the bar in handcuffs. They charged me with Ivan's murder without a scrap of evidence. All they had to go on was that Sally and I had a fling. Because of that, I wanted her husband dead. It never made sense. Sally would have told them it never meant a thing to her, but they didn't let it go until half a dozen of my staff and regulars said I was behind the bar while a karaoke singer murdered songs from the Sixties. I would have loved to be somewhere else that night, but thank the Lord I wasn't."

"Thanks for your co-operation, Mr Griffiths," said Neil. "Call me if you remember something you think might help our investigation. I don't think we'll revisit you. What did you do to your leg, by the way?"

"The limp, you mean?" said Tommy. "Both my knees are knackered. The doctor says I need to lose weight. My right knee's worse than the left this week."

"Did you know that Sally and Alexa disappeared nine months after the murder?" asked Lydia.

"I told you I hadn't heard from them," said Tommy. "Why don't you check upstairs and see whether they're hiding under the beds? Sally wasn't interested four years ago. I don't think she will change her mind, do you?"

Lydia and Neil left Tommy Griffiths in his glorified cupboard and returned to the bar. Terri was hovering by the doorway. Neil thought she'd been listening to the conversation.

"Is this a good place to eat, Terri?" he asked.

She seemed surprised that he knew her name.

"There are fish and chip restaurants further along the Esplanade that are ten times better," she said.

When they were outside on the pavement, Lydia turned to make her way to the car. Neil was searching for the restaurants.

"We should get back, Neil," she said.

"Maybe they do takeaway," said Neil, "We're at the seaside; it's traditional to have fish and chips. It's lunchtime. Gus doesn't begrudge us taking a break."

Lydia had to admit that Neil was right. After interviewing Christine Gates, Dennis Gates's birth mother, she had enjoyed a lovely Italian meal with Gus on their way home from the Isle of Wight.

"Alright then, you win," said Lydia, "but we're eating indoors. Have you seen the size of the seagulls on the sea wall over there?"

GUS AND LUKE were over the second Severn crossing when Neil was snaffling his first chip. Lydia rapped him over the knuckles with her fork.

It had been an uneventful drive for Gus and Luke, with brief delays at the M32 junction and the toll bridge. There was plenty of time to drop into Cardiff Central before meeting Ieuan Arlett at two o'clock.

"I wonder whether Dai Williams ever wishes he could get promoted, guv?" asked Luke.

"Possibly," laughed Gus. "Wales can be a funny place. I came here with Tess for a holiday one year when we were younger. We stayed at a B&B on the coast. Hot and cold running water in all beds, the brochure said. We realised what it meant when we slipped under the sheets later that night. The place was damp. As for the entertainment, well, they loved their bingo in the pubs and clubs. Sometimes they had a beat combo playing either side of the quest for a full house. On Sunday night, they had a comedian, Wit Munday. His name was nothing to do with the seventh Sunday after Easter and little to do with comedy either."

"What was the weather like?" asked Luke.

"Typical summer weather for Wales," said Gus. "It rained every other day."

"Oh, hard luck. That must be awful."

"Not really, it was a pleasant holiday. Despite the occasional oddball, the Welsh people are terrific company."

Luke parked in the visitor's car park, and he and Gus negotiated the eternally tricky Reception area. Ten minutes later, they wore visitor's badges and had an escort to DI Williams's office.

"Prynhawn Da," said Dai Williams.

"Good of you to see us, Sir," said Luke. "I'm DS Sherman, and Gus Freeman, my boss.

"You're with a Crime Review Team. Is that right?" asked DI Williams.

"That's correct. Wiltshire Police investigated the murder of Ivan Kendall in March 2014," said Gus. "I spoke with DCI Eddie Sinclair this morning. He gave me the story from his side of the Bristol Channel. We're here this afternoon to hear your version. We've got an appointment in the victim's home village in just over an hour."

"Right, we'd better get on with it then. Yes, I remember that case. I was Senior Investigating Officer, although we didn't accept that we were looking for a dead body at the outset. The officers in the sticks thought the wife had panicked. The couple's relationship wasn't rock steady. Mrs Kendall called Pontyclun police station at around two on Sunday afternoon. She reported her husband, Ivan, missing. We've known husbands celebrating in Cardiff two days after the national team won a Triple Crown, a Grand Slam, or beaten the All Blacks. It felt premature, but we did the necessary and followed the correct protocol in these instances."

"Did you verify the ticket purchases?" asked Gus.

"Hold on, let me find my report on my computer. I don't think we were aware of Kendall's destination. Here we are. Forgive me while I refresh my memory. That's it.

Sally Kendall told us her husband had left home and their daughter, Alexa, said she saw her father board the Cardiff train at 20.55 on Saturday night."

"What happened next?" asked Gus.

"Later that Sunday afternoon, two uniformed officers visited Mrs Kendall to take a statement, and then they went to the railway station. Passengers purchase tickets from a machine these days, of course, so there was no way to confirm who bought what if they paid in cash. The station employee on duty that afternoon wasn't working the previous night. He wasn't much help. So, they couldn't swear to the fact that Mr Kendall had even boarded the train. We only had the daughter's word for that, and Pontyclun had had many dealings with that little madam."

"Why would the daughter lie?" asked Luke, but DI Williams ignored him.

"Were you happy with how the first part of the case got handled, Sir?" asked Gus.

"I think it's fair to say both the rural officers and ourselves paid little more than lip service to a search for Ivan Kendall near the station or on the line between the village and the city centre. We were unconvinced he was missing and certainly had no reason to believe he was suicidal. However, everything rapidly changed gears on Monday morning when his body turned up eighty miles away in Westbury. At that point, my officers confirmed that Kendall travelled from Cardiff Central to Westbury after arriving from Pontyclun. Later, we learned that our checks matched the evidence Wiltshire Police found on the body."

"When you knew you were dealing with a murder, did you uncover a motive or identify potential suspects?" asked Gus.

"We must have interviewed everyone in Pontyclun who

ever had contact with Ivan Kendall and his family," said Dai Williams. "He was a hard worker, according to former workmates. Nobody had any complaints about his window cleaning. 'A quality job for a bargain price'. That was the motto on the side of his van. His neighbours said he was a quiet man...."

"Who kept himself to himself," said Gus.

"Quite," said Dai Williams.

"What about the rugby club?" asked Luke.

"Nothing different to anywhere else. Kendall watched matches occasionally and used the bar during and after the games."

"What did you think persuaded Ivan Kendall to travel to Westbury that night?" asked Luke.

"My first thought? Well, his wife was there one minute and gone the next. What would you do? I thought he had looked elsewhere. Crumpet, that's what I expected to find responsible for his acting out of character. A woman who Ivan Kendall found online on one of those dating apps who told him she was willing and invited him over for a night of passion."

"Westbury's a long way to travel though, Sir, isn't it?" asked Luke.

"Not if sex was a dead cert, DS Sherman. We've all spent half the night and most of our cash trying to get off with someone your mates assure you is a sure thing, and then we've gone home alone."

"If you say so, Sir," said Luke.

"Although that was what you *thought* was behind the journey, you didn't pursue that angle, did you, Sir?" asked Gus.

"We did not," said Dai Williams. "Because, based on every witness statement we received, Ivan Kendall never looked at another woman after he met Sally. He waited for her to return each time she left him, and there were never any recriminations."

"Was there anything else you looked at, Sir?" asked Luke.

"We realised there was little progress from the Wiltshire end, and we tried to devise a logical list of reasons for the journey. Then, as with so many other cases, I got a call from my Assistant Chief Constable, asking when I would close the case. We carried out a reconstruction, trying to jog someone's memory or prick someone's conscience. That proved to be a waste of time and effort. My boss didn't wait any longer for closure. Ten days later, I got assigned to another case."

"What did you make of Sally's disappearance?" asked Gus.

"I wasn't aware she had disappeared," said DI Williams.

"Neither Sally nor Alexa Kendall has been in the Pontyclun area since the end of 2014," said Gus.

"That's not a disappearance," said Dai Williams. "The police have never been contacted by anyone to say Mrs Kendall was missing. She left Pontyclun after her mother died. The rumour in the village was that she could be in danger because nobody could explain Ivan's death. I can't see any foundation for that belief. Sally and her daughter simply moved away. No law says a person can't live in a different part of the country without telling their neighbours. At least, not yet. They'll be living somewhere in Wales, I reckon. Sally was a home bird. I can't see her flying too far from the nest."

"If we get something from Pontyclun that we think helps, Sir, we'll pass it on," said Gus. "Many thanks for seeing us today. Good afternoon. That *was* what you said when we arrived, I presume?"

"It was, Mr Freeman," said DI Williams, "I spoke Welsh at home until I was five and attended school. So English was the first foreign language I learnt."

Gus and Luke retraced their steps from Dai William's office and were soon outside in the car park.

"What did we learn from that, Luke," asked Gus.

"South Wales thought the answer lay on the other side of the Severn Bridge, guv. They went through the motions with their investigation from the outset. I wonder whether DI Williams was right about Sally Kendall. Perhaps Blessing should concentrate on a smaller area of the country?"

"I'll make a mental note," said Gus, "but you had better remind me when we get back to the office. Those spinning plates are getting too many to count."

"We'd better get our skates on if we're going to make the rugby club by two o'clock, guv," said Luke.

As they pulled out of the Cardiff Central Police Head-quarters, the rain started.

"What did I say, Luke?" said Gus. "We crossed the Severn Bridge in glorious sunshine. The weather looked set for a perfect summer's day. Welcome to Wales."

"It's a passing shower, guv," said Luke.

"That's what Tess assured me when we were here for that holiday. The trouble was, there were as many showers as there were sheep. It wasn't long before you saw another one."

Twenty-five minutes later, they entered the village.

"I'm guessing this place has grown over the years," said Gus. "It has to be larger than Mere, where we spent much of last week."

"Pontyclun has a population twice the size of Mere,"

said Luke. "In the past ten years, people have come south from the valleys and west from Cardiff. Just look around you. It's a green and pleasant land, to coin a phrase."

"Where's this rugby club, then?" asked Gus.

"On Llantrisant Road, guv," said Luke, "we'll be there in five minutes."

As Luke swung the car through the rugby club entrance, he remembered it was the close season. No doubt they would cut the long grass before the end of next month, and the club's various teams would be in training for the coming league campaigns. But, for now, just one car was parked in front of the modern-looking clubhouse.

"You can understand why clubs such as this became the heart of the community in South Wales, can't you, guv?"

"A large green field, surrounded by housing," said Gus, "and if my eyes don't deceive me, several allotments. What's that over there, a kids' play area? As you say, I bet this place gets used throughout the year by various clubs and societies. Then, they'll cater weddings and funerals to boost their income. Anything to keep the overheads under control. Right, let's get inside and find the club steward."

When Gus and Luke entered the building, the notice-boards confirmed their thoughts. Something was going on every day of the week. Gus wondered whether Sally and Alexa Kendall ever came here, or was it just Ivan that visited?

Ieuan Arlett appeared at the end of the corridor. Gus could tell he was a former rugby player, even from this distance. Gus had never shown much interest in sports at school, nor in the years since. But he'd seen enough photographs to distinguish between participants in the different types of sports loved by so many.

There was something of the classic front-row forward in

Ieuan Arlett that meant, apart from powerlifting, Ieuan would have realised early on that he didn't fit in to any other on-field activity. Ieuan was five foot six inches tall with a well-padded muscular body.

When he was younger, he was wide-shouldered, narrow at the hip and excelled in the pack because of his strength and endurance rather than any pretension for speed. The club steward didn't have a neck as such, but Gus could tell, as the man lumbered towards them, that the collar size of the red shirt stretched over his ample torso would start with a twenty.

"You're the police officers from England, I suppose," said Ieuan. "Welcome to Pontyclun RFC. My office is behind you. Follow me."

Gus and Luke followed their host to a bright, well-appointed office overlooking the rugby pitches.

"It was Ivan Kendall you wanted to talk about, is that right?" asked Ieuan.

"That's correct," said Gus, "I'm Gus Freeman, a consultant with Wiltshire Police. It was DS Sherman here who contacted you asking for this meeting."

"Is it official then?" asked Ieuan. "Only you must be out of your jurisdiction here."

"This isn't an interview under caution, Mr Arlett," said Gus. "We've come from a meeting with DI Williams in Cardiff. We're cooperating with colleagues on both sides of the Severn, seeking answers that weren't forthcoming four years ago."

"Were you club steward then, Mr Arlett?" asked Luke.

"I've held the position since 2010," said Ieuan.

"When did you stop playing?" asked Gus.

"My last game was in 1999. Twenty-six seasons, man,

and boy, I never wanted to turn out for anyone else. This club is one big family."

"We can see evidence of that outside and inside this building," said Gus. "Ivan Kendall, was he a player or just a lover of the game?"

"Ivan played rugby at school. He had the build to make a decent second-row forward or lock. However, he didn't stick at it after he met Sally and got married."

"Did you know Ivan and Sally from your schooldays, then?" asked Luke.

"I'm fifty-nine," said Ieuan. "ten years older than Ivan would have been today. Sally was younger. I remember seeing them around the village when they were small kids. I was a teenager and already playing rugby. We didn't mix socially. Pontyclun was a smaller place back then. Everyone knew everyone else."

"What did you think when you heard Ivan was dead?" asked Gus.

"It came as a shock," replied Ieuan.

"When did the police come to speak with you?" asked Gus.

"I'm not sure, sometime in the week after we heard about the murder."

"Really?" said Gus, "I thought it would have been sooner."

Ieuan Arlett looked puzzled.

"According to the file we received from South Wales Police, Ivan Kendall came here on Saturday afternoon for a few beers and to watch a match."

"He did," said Ieuan. "Ivan was a regular here for years. It first started a few years after he got married. Their daughter, Lexie, was a handful, even as a toddler and Ivan escaped here on a weeknight too. When Ivan lost his job, he didn't come in the evenings anymore, but he continued to drop by on Saturday afternoons. I was on the Committee back in 2008, and I asked if we could do anything to help. It was me that gave him the idea of the window-cleaning business. Look at the amount of glass in this place, I said to Ivan. We need someone to clean these windows. Why don't you take it part-time while looking for another job? When people saw him up the ladder, they asked if he'd do their windows. Before we knew it, Ivan had his van and was up and running, working on homes, offices and the football club at the park."

"What time did he leave the club that Saturday?" asked Luke.

"I don't know that he was here," said Ieuan.

"His wife told the police that Ivan had cleaned the windows of half a dozen customers and collected outstanding fees in the morning," said Luke. "Then he came here while she went shopping at the supermarket. Sally said Ivan got home later than usual but was sober. She wasn't certain he'd even had a drink."

"Why did you look puzzled when we mentioned the police visit, Mr Arlett?" asked Gus.

"Well, it may as well come out now," said Ieuan, "it can't do any harm. Ivan used to come here every Saturday afternoon, as I say. We paid him weekly in cash, based on what he charged us for cleaning the windows twice a month. I don't know what he told Sally, but it meant he always had enough to pay for his drinks. The daft thing was that Ivan wasn't a big drinker. What he did with any spare cash, I don't know."

"How could that do any harm if it had come out earlier, Mr Arlett?" asked Gus. "Despite the number of times Sally left Ivan, there was never any report of a serious argument between them. Certainly, nothing physical."

"That was only half of it," said Ieuan, "Ivan stopped coming into the bar in the summer altogether. That was over a year before someone killed him. Ivan turned up for the first game of the season in August 2013. He never gave a reason he hadn't been in for a pint, and he'd started dropping into the office on Saturday mornings to collect his money. Ivan never let us down, though; he always arrived in his van to clean the windows every other Wednesday. I just assumed he wasn't socialising as much because money was tight."

"Did he keep attending throughout the season?" asked Luke.

"I couldn't put a date on it," said Ieuan Arlett shaking his head, "but the longer time went on, the less frequently I'd see Ivan in the bar. We get busy on match days, so I might have missed him when I got called away. Most weekends, we have an ambulance to ferry a dislocation or broken bone to the hospital. As for that Saturday in March four years ago, I can't swear that Ivan was even here. He called in for his cash in the morning. I'd recorded that and could show the police when they asked me their questions."

"So, the police knew about the cash-in-hand transactions," said Gus. "But what about Ivan coming here now and then rather than every week as his wife believed?"

"I omitted to tell them that, Mr Freeman. I didn't know what Ivan was doing, so I decided Sally had enough to handle. What if Ivan had a lady friend he'd met on his rounds, and she wanted him to do more than see to her windows? Sally had an affair with that Cardiff chap, didn't she? Nobody would blame Ivan if he'd found comfort with another woman. You would have to ask the police why they didn't arrive until Wednesday morning to confirm the details they had from Sally's statement. They asked whether he used to come here for a drink on Saturday afternoons. I said yes, but didn't elaborate."

"That's a pity, Mr Arlett," said Luke, "That might have been another line of enquiry for the police to follow, a jealous husband, perhaps."

"Ivan cleaned windows in the village," said Ieuan. "His round didn't include any houses in Westbury."

"There's no need to be facetious," said Gus. "Ivan Kendall died in a savage attack. Whatever he got involved in ended his habit of coming here for a few pints and got him murdered. The killers have a four-year head start because you withheld information, Mr Arlett. You were mistaken in believing it couldn't do any harm."

"Maybe," said Ieuan Arlett. "But you don't catch that many, no matter how much information you've got, do you?"

"One last thing before we leave, Mr Arlett," said Gus. "You referred to Kendall's daughter as Lexie. Is that what most people called her?"

"Everyone bar her parents," said Ieuan. "Sexy Lexie, that was her."

"Did you know her well, Mr Arlett?" asked Luke.

"She did like them older," said Ieuan, "but my cauliflower ears and broken nose helped keep her at bay. I think she had more luck at the football club. There's more space up there to exercise the dogs."

"I can't recall any mention of Ivan and Sally keeping pets," said Gus.

"Maybe they belonged to a boyfriend," said Ieuan. "Ivan wouldn't have brought them here."

"Do you know where Sally took Lexie when they left Pontyclun?"

"I remember reading in the local paper that Sally's mother died later that year. At first, I thought Sally moved to Llanharry to live in her mother's place, but it was on the market in the New Year. Life goes on. We were having a decent season, and it was the summer before I noticed Sally had left. No matter who you asked, she had told no one where they planned to go. Before I knew it, the next season got underway. As long as the new firm we hired to clean our windows kept turning up and doing a good job, there was never any reason to reminisce about Ivan Kendall."

Time to go, thought Gus. He'd give Dai Williams a call in the morning. His people could have handled things better in the first few hours after Kendall's disappearance. It was sloppy police work not to have asked more probing questions of someone supposed to have been in Kendall's company less than eight hours before his death.

It was water under the bridge—time to deal with the here and now.

## Chapter Six

"THAT'S ANOTHER MENTAL NOTE, GUV," said Luke as they left the rugby club car park. "Blessing needs to search for a Sexy Lexie online."

"That Kendall girl's twenty now, Luke," said Gus. "Heaven knows what site she's on these days. Blessing will have palpitations. That Arlett character was an idiot, too. Why didn't he mention Ivan Kendall wasn't using the rugby club as much as his wife believed? What was the big secret?"

"I agree with your hypothesis, guv," said Luke. "It had to connect to the murder. His behaviour altered in the summer of 2013, and the new attraction occupied him every weekend. Then, Kendall returned to the rugby club in the autumn and winter months."

"Arlett said there was a progressive increase in the frequency with which Kendall stayed away from the club during the rugby season. So much so, he couldn't say whether Kendall was there on the last Saturday he was alive. What activity does that suggest?"

"Whatever it was, Ivan Kendall didn't share it with his wife," said Luke.

"I dismissed Dai Williams's idea of there being a woman involved in Westbury as ridiculous. Arlett didn't discount the idea, though, did he? He didn't want to drop Kendall in it after his death, so he kept his mouth shut about something that could have blown this case wide open."

"There's nothing that points to another woman, guv. Not in my book. We're looking for a summer activity that needs support during what could be the off-season. Oh, it's so frustrating."

"Where's our sporting superstar when we need him?" said Gus.

"Neil will be back in the office by now, guv. I bet he'll come up with something as soon as we give him the parameters. Sports and pastimes aren't my thing."

"Home, Luke," said Gus, settling in his seat for a nap, "and don't spare the horses."

ALEX HARDY and Rick Chalmers had had a busy day in the Hub.

After his two phone conversations with Gus Freeman, Alex had sent the images from Prince's Street, Bristol, to the Old Police Station. Gus would view the six-year-old photos after he returned from Wales.

Alex continued to monitor the five mobile phones throughout the morning, but their location never changed. He wondered what that meant. What would they find if they searched for a building or group of buildings in that remote location tomorrow morning? The bodies of five young women or five mobile phones discarded in a waste bin? He couldn't believe whoever was pulling strings in this pantomime collected those girls from their homes and killed them because he and Rick had paid one of them a visit.

Just before lunch, Rick Chalmers reappeared. He slumped into a chair beside him.

"That doesn't feel promising," said Alex.

"I've identified the young policewoman in that CCTV image," said Rick.

"Great," said Alex, "who is she, and where is she stationed now?"

"The first bit was easy," said Rick. "I didn't find her face anywhere on current Avon and Somerset staff at Portishead, so I widened my search. Do you remember the floods on the Somerset Levels in 2012?"

"I remember the news reports, but we didn't suffer too badly in North Wiltshire. They reckoned those in Somerset were the worst in living memory."

"Our young Detective Sergeant, Zara Wheeler, earned herself a Queen's Gallantry Medal for rescuing a baby from a car trapped upside down in a swollen river. The mother died after her car got swept into the River Sheppey when a bridge collapsed."

Rick showed Alex a photograph from the local paper.

"The Chief Constable, DS Wheeler, and the grateful grandparents with the toddler," said Rick.

"Why do I sense bad news coming?" said Alex.

"DS Wheeler left Avon and Somerset Police within months and went into charity work."

"What sort of charity work?" asked Alex.

"Unspecified," said Rick. "I called Portishead as soon as I'd learned the woman's name. They told me she had moved to Portishead from Manvers Street, Bath, and was one of their most promising officers. They were sad to see her leave."

"So she won this medal at the back end of the summer, and then in November, she was in Bristol for the Queen's visit. Who did our mystery man work for? Was it the security services or the Royal Protection Squad?"

"Portishead had no idea whatsoever," said Rick. "He wasn't with the RPS, and the security services didn't show their face until the day after the explosion on Pero's Bridge. If any branch of the security services had intelligence concerning an attack from IS jihadis, they didn't make themselves known to Avon and Somerset Police on the day. So the red-headed man is still a mystery, I'm afraid."

"As are Vincent and Dexter, I presume?" asked Alex.

"I asked the ACC at Portishead if he could tell me about those two. He's new in the position but wasn't aware of any undercover people on the streets that day, and they aren't known to the police for criminal activity."

"That new ACC must be the guy who replaced Dominic Culverhouse," said Alex. "I missed out on some of that case."

"I heard about your troubles from Luke, mate. Don't worry. It's behind you now. Onwards and upwards."

"Thanks," said Alex. "Where does that leave us, though?"

"If we believe Vincent, Dexter, and Red work for the same team, then we're nowhere," said Rick. "They never appeared together, so maybe they're unrelated. Did Red ever appear in Swindon during the grooming gang affair?"

"We've only got those few images, plus what Tanya told us," said Alex. "We can't say for sure."

"Any movement on the phones?" asked Rick.

Alex checked once more.

"Nothing," he replied. "Any luck with the CCTV search for Vincent and Dexter?"

"Nothing so far," said Rick. "My tame techie worked wonders on the social media hunt, though. She identified Vicki, Tasha, Billie, and Freya among Tanya's friends on Facebook, Twitter, and Instagram."

"I take it we now have those false surnames?"

"Black, Black, Brown, and Green, in that order," said Rick. "Although, I'm not sure it helps that much."

"The fact you traced the names suggests their accounts haven't closed," said Alex.

"No, but there hasn't been a posting on either account since we left Tanya's house. My new friend has downloaded profile photos and details of friends the five girls had in common. They might be other girls from Swindon who recovered faster or slower than the Famous Five. Or they could be unconnected."

"Gus might want us to get one of these extra contacts to spill the beans about the charity," said Alex. "I tell you what, ask your techie to monitor those accounts for the next day or two. If they remain active, it suggests they're unrelated. If they hibernate, we should analyse everything they've posted to date to work out where they're living and then visit a couple. Then, we might catch a break and find them home when we knock on the door."

"Do you fancy a spot of lunch?" asked Rick. "We could walk to Gregg's and back within thirty minutes."

"Eating something unhealthy as we're walking back, do you mean?" said Alex.

"When we get back, we'll search for that Wheeler woman," said Rick. "If she worked in Bath for a couple of years before moving to Portishead, perhaps she lived there?

Maybe, she still does? There are plenty of charity shops in the city."

Alex laughed.

"Come on," he said. "I need the exercise. Sitting here for hours doesn't help my leg. As for the charity shops, I doubt that a bright young thing sorely missed by the brass at Portishead is sifting through donations from the public. So we'll be looking for an executive in a Head Office at least."

Rick and Alex started the search for addresses connected to Zara Wheeler by half-past twelve.

"Here we go," said Rick, "In the 2011 Census records, she was living with Mary Trueman, a widow. The older lady needed the company, and Ms Wheeler rented a room."

"How would we tell whether she moved closer to Portishead when she transferred?" asked Alex.

"She'd be on the Electoral Roll," said Rick, continuing to hunt for clues. "Ms Wheeler was registered to vote and living at the same address, but she was alone by June 2013. Mrs Trueman must have died. I wonder whether she got left the house in the will. No sign of her at that address one year later. Okay, so is it worth hunting for addresses in Portishead? No, because we know she left her job there in July of that year."

"Oh, what a tangled web," said Alex. "Let's assume Zara Wheeler stayed in Bath throughout. Is she not showing anywhere in the city? She must pay Council Tax, mustn't she? Hang on. Did she get married? Let's check for that."

Rick and Alex kept turning over pages of data hunting for Zara Wheeler. Finally, they asked Rick's technical whiz to look for the young woman's name on social media. Three hours later, it was getting near the end of play for the day. All three had drawn a blank on every front. Zara Wheeler's name didn't feature in Births. Marriages or Deaths. Her digital footprint was non-existent.

"Now what?" asked Rick.

"The only way she could live in the Bath area is if she changed her name," said Alex.

"I added Black, Green, Brown, and White to the social media search routine," said Divya, the techie. "I knew you'd remember to ask, eventually."

"You'll go far," said Rick.

"Shall I try Gus?" asked Alex. "To see if they're back yet?"

"We've still got thirty minutes. I'll keep looking. You give Gus a bell."

NEIL DAVIS and Lydia Logan Barre arrived at the Old Police Station office just before three. When they emerged from the lift, Blessing Umeh was nowhere in sight.

"Blessing?" called Neil.

Lydia heard a muffled sound.

"She's in the restroom,"

"You go," said Neil, "I'll start entering the details of our interview into the Freeman Files. A white coffee, one sugar would be great if Blessing can remember how to use the Gaggia."

"Stop teasing her, Neil. She's sensitive."

Lydia disappeared behind the restroom door and returned several minutes later with Neil's coffee. Blessing carried hers and Lydia's on a tray.

"Alright, Blessing?" asked Neil.

"I'm fine," said Blessing, "just equipment failure."

"Don't tell me the Gaggia blew up? How did you make this cuppa?"

"There's nothing wrong with the machine, Neil," said Lydia.

"We might as well tell him," said Blessing. "I got locked in the loo. I broke a nail trying to get out. Lydia fixed it so you won't suffer the same fate."

"How long were you in there?" asked Neil, trying to keep a straight face.

"An hour, more or less," said Blessing. "Well? How did you two get on?"

"We enjoyed a smashing fish and chip lunch on the seafront," said Neil.

"The interview went well, Blessing," said Lydia. "Trust Neil not to get his priorities right."

"Before you were otherwise 'engaged', did you hear from Gus?" asked Neil.

"Not a word," said Blessing. "He said to expect him back before we leave."

Neil and Lydia updated their digital files, and Blessing wondered how she'd live it down. If only Luke had been here, he would have rescued her and forgotten it already.

Gus and Luke came up in the lift at a quarter to four. Neil and Lydia waited to give Gus their news, such as it was.

"First things first," said Gus.

"Coffee, guv?" asked Neil.

Gus nodded. Blessing followed Neil into the restroom.

"We had a pleasant trip to Weymouth," said Lydia, "although we didn't learn much from Tommy Griffiths."

"We had several passing showers on the other side of the Severn Bridge," said Luke, "but we discovered a potential lead."

Neil and Blessing returned with Gus and Luke's coffee. Blessing hoped the noisy performance of the Gaggia had masked the few strong words she'd shared with Neil.

"Neil, if I asked you to name a sport or pastime carried out in the summer months which attracts several spectators on odd occasions in autumn and winter, what would you say?"

"Dogging, guv," said Neil.

"I was being serious, Neil," said Gus.

"So was I, guv. If it's an outdoor sport, it rarely carries on outdoors in the winter. An indoor sport like snooker can carry on throughout the year. I can't think of one off-hand, guv. Football works the other way around. The regular season is autumn and winter, and if there's a cup competition, it can run in the summer months."

"Keep thinking, Neil," said Gus, "I'll tell you why later. Right, what did Tommy Griffiths have to say?"

"He explained how he and Sally got together six to eight weeks after she started working for him in Cardiff, guv," said Lydia.

"When Sally returned home, it knocked Tommy sideways, guv," said Neil. "He thought they loved one another, but Sally told him she had never stopped loving Ivan."

"Every step Tommy took us through only embellished the story you gave us, guv," said Lydia. "He told us about the move to Pontyclun and how he tried to convince Sally the pub was a goldmine if only she went with him. Tommy took us through his arrest and what a joke the murder charge had been. We asked whether he'd spoken to Ivan, but he hadn't."

"We asked whether he spoke to the daughter," said Neil, "but although he saw her, she never spoke. Tommy said Alexa didn't leave him in any doubt about how she felt about him trying to take her mother away. He said Alexa was with a different bloke every night, and apart from that, the only time he saw her was when she was out with the dogs. Tommy said they nearly pulled her arms out of their sockets."

"Well, I never," said Gus. "That's interesting. Ieuan Arlett mentioned dogs when we spoke to him earlier. Don't you find it odd that there's nothing in either murder file that suggests Ivan and Sally Kendall had pets?"

"Ieuan Arlett qualified his statement by saying they may have belonged to one of Lexie's boyfriends, guv," said Luke.

"Fair comment," said Gus, "but I hate coincidences. If only we could find Sally Kendall. Ah, that reminds me. Blessing, narrow the parameters of your search for Sally. First, Mr Arlett, the club steward, thought Sally would stay close to her roots. Secondly, your guess about the name was correct. Alexa's friends had a nickname for her. Everyone knew her as Lexie."

"Sexy Lexie," added Luke. "You might need to close at least one eye when you find her online."

"Does it have to be Blessing that does the searching, guv?" asked Neil.

"You'll be far too busy solving my riddle, DS Davis," said Gus, "plus, we're off to the country in the morning."

Gus explained to Lydia and Neil what Alex and Rick uncovered.

"Englishcombe is where your parents live, isn't it, Blessing?" asked Lydia.

"For the time being," said Blessing.

"Neil, I'll give you and Lydia the headlines from today's conversations. You can read the unexpurgated version in the Freeman Files tomorrow. DCI Sinclair mentioned a traveller's site a few miles out of Westbury. Unfortunately, the forensics collected at the murder scene didn't match any of their likely lads. However, Eddie Sinclair still believed the killers were locals, so we need to investigate that site. Could that be the place linking Ivan Kendall to Westbury?"

"We might have to cast our net wider, Neil," said Luke, "because those men are sure to have moved."

"DI Williams at Cardiff Central confirmed what we suspected," said Gus. "Uniformed officers at Pontyclun would not start a finger-tip search of the railway tracks for a husband who had gone walkabout only twelve hours earlier. They knew Sally had left Ivan three times previously, so they likely wrote it off as tit-for-tat. That cost the investigation valuable time. Dai Williams thought Ivan Kendall had sought female company online, which explained his unscheduled trip to Westbury. That was never at the fore-front of the investigation this side of the Severn. Today was the first time a Welsh detective threw a liaison with an unknown female into the mix. Luke and I didn't believe it for a minute; we thought it was a fantasy. However, when we talked to Ieuan Arlett, he dropped a bombshell. The Pontyclun police never approached Ieuan on Sunday, when Ivan's disappearance was reported. On Wednesday, the Cardiff detectives joined the murder hunt and sent someone to speak to him. They asked him a simple question. Did Ivan Kendall come here for a drink on Saturday afternoon?"

"Sloppy police work, guv," said Neil. "Far too general. I would have asked what time Ivan arrived, how many beers he had, what time Ivan left, who he spoke to, and half a dozen more that I'd have prepared earlier."

"Sloppy, Neil, yes," said Gus. "But, even if I'd only asked one question, I would have learned something of value. By adding one word, Ieuan Arlett had to give a truthful reply. As it was, the detective gave him a chance to be evasive."

"Did Ivan Kendall come for a drink *that* Saturday afternoon?" said Luke.

"Wasn't Ivan Kendall there then, guv," asked Lydia.

"We don't know, Lydia," said Gus. "Ieuan Arlett admitted that Ivan stopped coming during the summer and reduced the number of visits he made during the rugby season. We don't believe he was seeing a woman, but we need to check. Luke and I reckon that Ivan found something more interesting than a quiet out-of-season pint in a clubhouse full of kids, gardening club members, and wedding guests. That's what we hoped you might help us with, Neil. Keep thinking, and bear this in mind. Remember how much money was in Ivan's pockets when the police recovered the body? Sixty-five pounds. Not much in the grand scheme of things, but Ivan and Sally scraped by, didn't they? The main cause for her walking out was the constant pressure of balancing the household budget. Ieuan Arlett told us that Ivan wasn't a big drinker. He had a contract to clean the rugby club's windows. Ieuan paid him cash in the office on Saturday morning or from the till in the afternoon. We week she thought Ivan collected each week. Still, it's plain from Ieuan's statement that he spent less of his earnings on beer after that summer when Ivan started his new activity. How large an amount did he gather, and what was it for?"

"Perhaps Ivan didn't gather a large sum, guv," said Neil. "Was he a gambler? There you are. I might have stumbled on it. He placed bets during the flat racing season to get his family out of a hole. There are more than enough variables in the summer to cope with, and when you add in dodgy weather and fences in the winter, it's even more of a mug's game. What if he had gambling debts?"

"That's a line of enquiry to follow, Neil," said Gus. "He'd never tell Sally what he was doing."

"Did you see the screens in the main bar, guv?" asked Luke.

"I missed that, Luke. I was checking those club and society notices on the noticeboard."

"They had a big screen in the corner of the room," said Luke. "The club has a multi-screen facility to offer its customers a variety of sports. So Ivan didn't need to leave the club to watch the races on which he'd had a bet."

"Ivan didn't have a mobile phone," said Blessing. "So, if he wanted to place a series of bets, he had to do it at the bookies."

"True," said Gus, "but he could have fitted in a visit between cleaning a client's windows and collecting money owed."

"Real gamblers don't bet that way," said Blessing, "or so I'm told. They want the latest odds, any minor change in the running. Andy Carlton had an account and tinkered with every little variable on his phone before finally committing himself. He was a nightmare when I was on an evening stakeout with him. I asked Andy one night how much he bet each time. He said he set himself a maximum spend per week of twenty quid. So Andy bet fifty pence here, a pound there. He didn't have any other hobbies. I ask you. What a fuss for twenty quid."

"Ivan Kendall could have bet larger sums, guv," said Luke, "and kept going higher to recoup the losses."

"Ivan never had sufficient funds to get himself in that deep, Luke," said Gus. "As Blessing pointed out, he didn't have a mobile phone or a credit card. Therefore, he could only spend the cash he had in his pocket. We're not there yet. Keep thinking, Neil. I know you'll get the right connection in time. Let's get stuck into these Freeman Files updates. I won't get everything finished before the end of the day, but I want as much done as possible while things are still fresh in my mind. I suggest you do the same, Luke."

"Got it, guv," said Luke.

At a quarter to five, the phone rang. Gus answered.

"Alex, good to hear from you. I've put you on speaker-phone for the others to listen. What have you learned today?"

"I'll keep it brief, guv. I know everyone wants to get home. We've seen no movement on the five phones we're monitoring. Rick identified the policewoman with our mystery man in Bristol in November 2012. She's DS Zara Wheeler, holder of the Queen's Gallantry Medal. Joined the Durham Police after leaving University. She moved south to Bath in 2010 and transferred to Portishead the following year. Wheeler was a rising star, guv, but left in July 2013, months after our image got captured on CCTV. We found an address in Bath where she lived until the end of 2013, but after that, she disappeared. Rick and I scoured social media but found nothing. The only clue we have is that Portishead believed she went into charity work when she quit her job with them."

"Another charity, or the same one, I wonder," muttered Gus.

"Portishead didn't have a clue who DS Wheeler was talking to that day, guv," said Alex. "He's not from any organisation connected to the police or security service."

"It begs the question, Alex," said Gus, "did DS Wheeler know this man? Why on earth would she engage with a total stranger during a Royal visit showing signs of turning ugly?"

"Exactly, guv," said Luke. "you only need to glance at that image to see she's not challenging him. She trusts him."

"Anything else, Alex?" asked Gus.

"We now know Vicki Black, Tasha Black, Billie Brown, and Freya Green were Tanya White's best friends. Rick has identified other girls of the same age who were friends with the five girls in that What's App group. The social media accounts for the five girls have gone quiet since we visited Tanya. That's as far as we've got, guv. I'll continue to monitor the phones and warn you if they move. If everything stays as it is, Rick and I will meet you at London Road at nine in the morning."

"That's the plan, Alex," said Gus. "I've not contacted Geoff Mercer yet. Neil's staying in the office tomorrow with Lydia and Blessing. Luke and I will meet you outside the Hub."

With that, Gus ended the call.

"What do we do to make that happen," asked Gus.

"I'll collect Blessing from the farm in the morning," said Neil, "Luke can drive direct from Warminster to London Road."

"It's only for tomorrow, guv," said Blessing, "I get my car back tomorrow evening."

"I've finished my updates, guv," said Neil. "What can I work on in the morning?"

"Follow up on the traveller's site out at Dilton Marsh. I need the names of the men staying there at the time of Ivan Kendall's murder. Then trace where they are today. That should keep you busy. Please think of the activity that became so important to our victim every spare minute you have. Blessing and Lydia can double up on the search for Sally and Lexie Kendall."

"Will do, guv," said Neil.

"Okay," said Gus, "I suggest you get off home. Have a good evening."

The office emptied, and Gus sat at his desk alone. He'd updated his files for the conversations with Eddie Sinclair and Dai Williams. Another thirty minutes would see the Ieuan Arlett interview finished. As for what Alex told him, that was something to chew over while he relaxed at home.

Gus knew that evenings at home would never be as carefree as they had been in the past. Should he call Suzie and tell her he would be late? Had she left London Road already? How would she react if he took work home with him? This living together business was more complicated than one might imagine.

Discretion was the better part of valour, Gus thought. He noted the points he had to include in the Arlett file update and closed his computer. Then, as he travelled to the car park in the lift, he considered the issues Alex had passed to him since first thing this morning. It was vital, even if it meant lying awake to mull over tomorrow's potential outcomes in the countryside near Bath.

Gus drove into the gateway to the bungalow at a quarter to six. He parked the Focus next to Suzie's Golf and went indoors.

"Dinner's almost ready," said Suzie. "Nothing too heavy. I imagine that you're tired after your trip to Wales. I recommend a quiet night in front of the TV."

"That sounds perfect," said Gus. "you read my mind."

Perhaps I'll be able to get off to sleep straight away, thought Gus. Then, I can plan for tomorrow while pretending to watch another riveting cookery series.

"What new task did Geoff Mercer set you?" asked Gus.

"He had to rush off for another meeting," said Suzie. "In the few minutes he could spare, he referred me to the latest message from the Police and Crime Commissioner. The latest figures show that Wiltshire continues to punch well above its weight for a small, rural force and delivers the best service possible within the funding awarded. Overall, Wiltshire is a safe county, and the latest figures highlight the hard work done to maintain that aspiration."

"Which are the hot potatoes these days in our game of Whack-A-Mole?" asked Gus.

Suzie gave him a gentle thump on his arm.

"Cheeky monkey," she said. "Burglary and vehicle crime have dropped considerably in the past twelve months. But, despite the positives, there was a twenty-five per cent increase in stalking and harassment. That increase concerned Geoff Mercer. He's tasked me to respond to the PCC and the wider community's concerns about these crimes. We need to get the message out that victims will be heard and must be confident to report a crime to us. We must assure them they will receive support from their first call - and throughout the criminal justice process - when they do."

"At last, something worthwhile for you to get your teeth into," said Gus.

"Talking of which," said Suzie, "our lamb chops will be ready. Let's eat."

# Chapter Seven

***Thursday, 12 July 2018***

GUS AWOKE EARLY and was out of bed by seven. Suzie stirred as he left the bedroom but did not rush to follow suit.

"I'll get breakfast this morning," he called out. "It will be on the table by the time you get out of the shower."

Gus heard the groan but ignored it. He wanted to get to London Road and start the hunt for the red-haired man. Gus reckoned they'd find him near the location of those five mobile phones. It was the only thing that made sense. The look shared between the mystery man and the former detective in Bristol was significant. Gus knew that look.

Once Gus heard the shower running, he dropped four slices of bread into the toaster. His Wiltshire sausages, bacon, and eggs were sizzling in the pan. All was right with the world. At least for now.

"That smells terrific," said Suzie. "Even though I know it's not good for me. Or you, come to that."

"Get stuck in. You can wash up these few things while I take my shower."

"It's very regimental here this morning," said Suzie. "What happened to the lovely chap that was here last night?"

"Today could be a game-changer," said Gus. "Every minute that passes and Alex doesn't call to say those phones are on the move is a step towards me solving the Burnside murder. I can feel it. Who knows? We might uncover something of national significance this morning."

"That might be a stretch," said Suzie. "I remember you telling me about the grooming gang and their mysterious disappearance. I can think of several innocent explanations for them not being seen in Swindon since that night. It is tough to swallow the idea that a secret organisation spirited them away, perhaps disposed of them, and rescued the girls the gang exploited. Now you want me to believe they treated the girls' physical and mental ills and found them accommodation and employment into the bargain. Have you any idea how much an enterprise like that would cost? It would be immense. How could anyone undertake that without the world and his wife knowing?"

"I don't profess to have the answers," said Gus. "My copper's nose tells me we're close to uncovering the truth. That's good enough for me. I'm only concerned with finding Grant's killer. After that, others can decide how to progress the case through the courts and handle the fallout."

Gus left the kitchen to shower and get dressed. Suzie tidied away the breakfast things and considered what Gus had said. She still couldn't see those past events his way.

Suzie hoped Gus wouldn't be disappointed with how things panned out later today.

"Are we ready?" asked Gus, standing in the kitchen doorway, suited and booted.

"You look smart," said Suzie, "and your hair's starting to grow back. I told you it would."

"You think I'm overreacting, don't you?" said Gus. "I thought about what you said while I was in the shower. I know a simple explanation is more likely, but why did someone need to whisk Tanya Norris away within thirty minutes of Alex and Rick leaving? It's the latest in a series of occasions when I've sensed an unseen hand orchestrating events."

"Well, if you're right, and you're dealing with a sizeable organisation, they might not appreciate someone poking their nose into their business. It could be dangerous, Gus. But I don't want to lose you. You will be careful, won't you?"

"Of course, darling," said Gus. "I've got three capable young men with me. I didn't think it necessary to ask Rick and Luke to acquire firearms for this morning's visit because I don't expect trouble. We'll follow my usual proce-dure. I'll ask a series of questions and only step up the pace if I don't hear the right answers. At the first sign of trouble, we'll withdraw. I'll leave Luke and Rick on the scene to stop anyone doing a runner and return with a warrant and armed support. How's that?"

"A little happier," said Suzie. "We'd better get moving. I'll see you tonight. Better still, call me at lunchtime or as soon as you return to the office."

Gus and Suzie left the bungalow, breathed in the fresh morning air, and got into their separate cars. Suzie was nervous about the day ahead. Gus was eager to reach the countryside on the outskirts of the Roman city of Bath.

Suzie swung the Golf into the car park at the front of

the main building on London Road. Gus eased through the yard to reach the Hub building. Rick Chalmers and Alex Hardy stood waiting on the steps outside.

"Luke Sherman is hunting for a parking space, guv," said Alex. "He won't be a minute."

"We'll take my car, guv," said Rick. "No disrespect."

"Fair enough. Any change on the phones, Alex?" asked Gus.

"All quiet on the western front, guv,"

"Divya, our techie friend, found another sighting of Vincent and Dexter, guv," said Rick as the three men transferred to Rick's car.

"Where and when was this?" asked Gus.

"I can only show you the image on my phone, guv," said Rick. "But it's them in a van with Dexter driving. Vincent's in the passenger seat. We think they were on their way to their house in Shrivenham based on their travel direction. This image comes from the afternoon of Sunday, the twenty-second of July 2013."

"Vincent looks uncomfortable," said Gus. "Or is that me?"

"No idea, guv," said Alex, "but that's what we've found for them. But, unfortunately, as with several others connected to this case, they dropped out of circulation soon after."

"Don't let anyone tell you there's a shortage of coppers on the beat," said Luke Sherman, arriving at a trot. "It's a devil finding a parking spot in this place."

"Well, you found one," said Gus. "Hop in, and let's get going."

"Didn't you want to tell DS Mercer where we're going, guv?" asked Alex Hardy.

"Suzie knows our destination," said Gus. "Geoff Mercer

was ultra-busy yesterday. So we won't be off the radar for long, anyway."

Rick eased his car into the rush-hour traffic. Gus wondered whether he'd been optimistic with the forty-five-minute travelling time. He sat back in the passenger seat and relaxed. They soon passed the Seend turning that took him to the Old Police Station each morning, and after they'd driven through Southwick and onwards to Rode, they made for Hinton Charterhouse. Gus reminisced over the hours he'd spent in a squad car with a colleague back in his Salisbury days. Hinton Charterhouse was in the same mould as Melton Mowbray. They could have been stars of 1940s black and white movies with the right agent. The latter struck the two police constables as a romantic lead. Hinton Charterhouse was more of an action hero, an ex-public schoolboy.

"We're entering Englishcombe village now, guv," said Rick.

Guv shook himself. He'd almost nodded off there.

"Nothing to report on the phones, guv," said Alex. "The signal is still constant. If we follow Whiteway Road towards Wilmington, those phones should stay on our right-hand side. The property they're in is less than three miles away."

"What's that one hundred yards ahead, on the right," said Rick a little later.

"A 'No Through Road' sign," said Gus. "We've travelled for two miles. Try there. The building we want must be in that direction."

"It's a remote spot, isn't it?" said Luke.

After negotiating a series of bends, they reached a straight stretch of road. From the passenger window Gus could see acres of rolling fields behind a solid-looking dry-stone wall. The land fell sharply away to the valley below.

"We can't see much from the lane," said Gus. "This area is typical of Bath and the surrounding countryside, all hills and vales. No wonder the Romans thought it reminded them of home."

"Here's the entrance to the property," said Rick.

He turned left through stone pillars, and the car rumbled across a cattle grid. Rick drove them along the winding driveway, and Gus heard the audible gasp as Rick was first to spot the imposing manor house appearing through the trees.

"I never expected that," said Rick. "I thought we were driving towards a farmhouse and a few outbuildings."

"This is the place," said Alex. "Those phones are dead ahead."

Rick stopped twenty yards from the house as a man walked along the centre of the driveway towards them. Gus Freeman got out of the car. Rick, Alex, and Luke joined him.

"I've changed my mind about the four of you three times already," the man said with a smile. He was well-dressed and fifty years old.

"At first, I thought you were the Charity Commissioners arriving for one of your snap inspections. Then, I thought you were lost and missed the junction sign telling you there was no exit. But, now that I've seen you out of the car, I recognise you as police. It takes one to know one. My name's Callum Wood. I worked at Manvers Street in Bath."

"So you knew DS Zara Wheeler, then?" asked Gus.

"I remember her. Yes, Zara came to us from Durham."

"What does she do here?" asked Gus.

"What makes you think Zara's here?" asked Callum.

"What do you know about Tanya Norris?" asked Gus.

"The name doesn't ring a bell," said Callum.

"Tanya's mobile phone is here," said Alex. "We've monitored it since it disappeared from her home in Wantage. Along with the phones of four of her friends. What can you tell me about that?"

Gus saw another man appear from the front door of the main building. He marched briskly towards them. As he reached the group, he looked at Gus.

"You must be Freeman, am I right?"

"And you are?" asked Gus.

"Head of security, this phone call is for you."

Gus took the phone that was thrust towards him.

"Freeman?" It was the ACC.

"That's me, Sir? What can I do for you?"

"Cease and desist, Freeman," said Kenneth Truelove. "Return to London Road at once. You've done it this time, Freeman, good and proper."

"I haven't completed my enquiries, Sir," said Gus.

"I want you in my office within the hour," said the ACC.

Gus returned the phone to the middle-aged man with a military bearing.

"It's best if you turn around and go back the way you came," said Callum Wood. "I'm sorry you've had a wasted trip."

The security head had already turned back to the manor house. Callum Wood watched Rick negotiate the three-point turn in the driveway and then came to the car's front passenger side and indicated to Gus to wind down his window.

"You're Gus Freeman, from Salisbury. I thought I recognised you. How are you enjoying working at the Old Police Station? It's changed since I worked there with my old boss, Phil Hounsell, but I have fond memories of the place. It's where I met my wife, Debbie."

Callum stood back and watched the car until it crossed the cattle grid and left the stone pillars far behind. Then, he walked back to his office and signalled the all-clear.

Gus and the others drove back to Devizes in silence. There was little to say. Luke was re-writing his CV in his head in anticipation of getting the sack. What had just happened? Who had the clout to make a phone call to get them dragged away from a legitimate investigation?

Rick and Alex blamed themselves. They must have pressed too hard on Tanya White when they spoke to her. They could never have expected this outcome.

Rick stopped the car outside the Hub. Gus had five minutes before facing the music.

"Have you noticed anything, guv?" said Rick.

"Sorry, I was going over everything that's happened since I started investigating Grant Burnside's murder. Who ordered the ACC to drag us away from that big estate, and why?"

"Several vehicles weren't here earlier—two unmarked vans over there on your left for a start. There seems to be more activity inside the Hub, too, with people moving around near the windows. They've usually got their heads down, staring at a screen. Something's going on."

"We'll get inside and check it out, guv," said Alex. "You need to get upstairs to see the ACC."

"I'll drive back to the Old Police Station," said Luke. "Should I keep this morning's episode to myself, guv, or can I tell the team?"

"It's not our finest hour, Luke," said Gus. "I don't see why either of us wishes to mention it. But I'll see you when I see you. Just stay on top of the Kendall case. If we could solve that, we might salvage a scrap of our reputation."

With that, the four men exited the car. Gus headed for

the main building. His heart sank when he recognised the vehicle parked in Geoff Mercer's spot.

The Reception area was busier than usual. Gus felt several pairs of eyes boring into his back as he signed in. The officer on duty didn't pass a comment. Instead, he just raised an eyebrow. Was that aimed at him, Gus thought? Or a general comment on the madness that had taken over today. Gus trotted upstairs to the admin area. He needed to find a friendly face.

"Are you calm enough yet, Gus," asked Vera Butler. She intercepted him as he made for the ACC's office. He wasn't standing by the door waiting today. The door was firmly closed.

"I'm confused and livid in equal measure, Vera," Gus replied. "Don't know what the heck's going on."

"Suzie told us how close you came to thumping him the last time he was here," said Vera. "Whatever you've stumbled upon, it's brought him back. Last time he was alone. This time he's got company, and it feels serious. I've never known the ACC so nervous."

"Is Geoff Mercer in there?" Gus asked.

"Geoff's off-site today," said Vera.

"I must go it alone," said Gus.

"Just take it steady," said Vera, "and count to ten."

Gus shrugged his shoulders. He crossed the office floor and tapped on the ACC's door.

"Come in," said Kenneth Truelove.

The ACC sat at his desk, which was never a good sign.

Brendan Curran sat opposite him. His suit was several months older but still looked immaculate. That's what you can expect if you pay two grand for a three-piece suit from Savile Row. Gus took a chair beside the OCTF supremo more than an arm's length away. In case he failed to reach ten.

"Can someone please explain why we've stopped a legitimate enquiry?" asked Gus. "And why are there so many strangers on site today?"

"Our people at Citadel Place have closely monitored events over the past week," said Brendan Curran. "Actions by junior officers under your command raised a red flag. As a result, we couldn't allow your investigation to continue. It would not be in the national interest."

"Hang on, Citadel Place? That's the National Crime Agency HQ, isn't it?"

The ACC nodded.

"Brendan transferred there with his team three months ago, Freeman. So I had no idea where you were this morning or your intentions."

"I've informed you of progress on each of our cases, Sir," said Gus. "You knew DS Chalmers had joined DS Hardy to use the Hub facilities to the fullest extent. Their diligent work this week uncovered a valuable lead. Jack Sanders told me about the mystery surrounding Tanya Norris's disappearance. My lads found Tanya in Wantage and went to interview her. Tanya's surname has changed to White, although she was never married. She told them what happened to her after she left the hospital in Swindon."

"There's no need to fill in the gaps, Freeman," said Brendan Curran. "Your boss need not hear it. It's not relevant. My team is removing every trace of the data you gathered relating to Tanya and others during your hunt for Burnside's killer. From now on, you and your team will never investigate the matter again. Do I make myself clear?"

"It stinks," said Gus.

"Kenneth, will you leave us now, please?" asked Curran. "I'll take Freeman into my confidence. It's for his ears only. I'll get him to sign the necessary."

The ACC stood and left the room. Brendan Curran took his seat,

"Just because there's a desk between us, it won't stop me, you know," said Gus.

"I know how you must feel after this morning, Freeman. That's why I will explain what I can about why I had to do what I did. There's too much at stake. Before you arrived, I had a word with Kenneth. He should never have selected the Burnside case for your Crime Review Team to tackle. He wasn't to know the number of red flags attached to those files, but I knew we were in trouble once I was aware that you had reopened the case. You're too bloody good, Freeman. I thought we'd got away with it when you solved several cases related to the Burnside family and moved on to another cold case."

"I couldn't let it lie," said Gus. "We had a description of Grant's killer, but it didn't match anyone on our database. Although it was probably unconnected, I found Jack Sanders's account of the grooming gang mystery intriguing. The more I puzzled over it, the more I convinced myself there was someone behind the scenes pulling strings. I never imagined for one moment that it was you."

"It wasn't me. Not back then, Freeman, I promise you," said Curran.

"Don't keep me in suspense," said Gus.

"This is between these four walls, Freeman," said Curran. "I'll need you to sign the Official Secrets Act."

"Just when I thought this morning couldn't get any weirder," said Gus.

"Like you, I've been at this game a long time, Freeman,"

said Curran. "If you plan to make your way to the top in this profession, you don't make many friends. However, I had one friend I'd known for over twenty years. I was well-established when he joined the Met at eighteen. His name was Mitch Ferguson. Mitch was one of the best undercover operatives this country has ever known. He worked in Newcastle for ten months, gathering intelligence on a gang of loan sharks in 2014. His efforts enabled us to demolish their operation, but Mitch couldn't have done it without help from an outside agency."

Gus was going to jump in, but Brendan Curran held up a hand.

"Let me continue, Freeman; we'll get through it much quicker. When Mitch returned to duty after the Tyneside case concluded, he told his bosses what had happened. You can imagine their initial reaction. Find these people and put them out of business. However, Mitch persuaded his bosses to consider working with them. Organised crime has a firm grip on daily life in the UK, Freeman. We need all the help we can get."

"I'm uncomfortable with where this help is coming from," Gus said.

"You must concentrate on the bigger picture, Freeman," said Curran. "My best friend died in early 2015 before he saw his idea come to fruition. Someone shot him at close range on the driveway of his house and dumped his body in Cannock Chase. Within a week, his killer, Steve Nash, was dead. You can draw your conclusions. We're fighting a war, Freeman. Sometimes, the ends justify the means. When Mitch Ferguson, and other coppers like him, go undercover, we know they're working in the margins. Just look at what happened to Ricky Gardiner. The lines between right and wrong get blurred, and those lines can too easily get crossed."

"Gardiner was a rogue," said Gus.

"I agree," said Curran, "but he was our rogue for two decades. His superiors applauded every instance when Ricky delivered intelligence that produced a positive result they could brag about to the media. But, if you pressed hard enough, you might learn that they were also aware of when he crossed the line, but they ignored it."

"They were looking at the bigger picture," said Gus.

"Quite," said Curran. "Within weeks of my best friend's murder, the picture changed. The outside agency lost its cutting edge. He was another victim of the UK's organised crime lords. The people he worked with had to adjust. But, over the past four years, Callum Wood and other ex-police personnel have helped move forward the spirit of co-operation that Mitch championed."

"How do I explain this to my team," said Gus. "Tanya White, as she now calls herself, told them she worked for a charity helping veterans suffering from Post-Traumatic Stress. So what happened to the other girls? Why were the phones inside that manor house?"

"You can tell your people the truth, Freeman. The charity recycles mobile phones and distributes them to veterans who have fallen on hard times. Even a refurbished early smartphone is better than anything these men and women can afford. The girls will continue to work for the charity, but we felt it necessary to move them. I can explain how they're involved if you wish?"

"I'm guessing I will not get any more details?" said Gus.

Brendan Curran smiled.

"The British Legion reckon six thousand veterans are living on the streets of this country today. Many other veterans are on the breadline. All they want to do is work, but for many, it's impossible. The challenges they face differ from others that are out of work. They need more support. During recent periods of austerity, thousands of veterans got pushed to the breadline after being judged fit for work. Severely wounded veterans from Iraq and Afghanistan, who were once entitled to incapacity benefits, were told they no longer qualified."

"What a mess," said Gus, "wasn't there supposed to be a safety net?"

"Ten years ago, the Community Covenant came into being, which should have given those veterans priority on affordable housing. Instead, local councils passed their housing problems onto a third party, and the housing associations who now control things have no binding obligation to help veterans. In 2012, the Armed Forces Covenant enshrined in law the government's duty of care to its serving service personnel. The government also agreed to sustain and reward them for the rest of their lives. Our veterans should have been better protected than ever before."

"Another example of joined-up thinking nobody followed through with actions to ensure its success," said Gus.

"The facility you visited today aims to help veterans through their PTSD and find accommodation. It might be a flat, a hostel, anything that keeps them off the streets, and they become eligible for benefits there."

"A noble ambition," said Gus, "but what about Grant Burnside?"

"Burnside was vermin," said Curran. "He died when a covert operative strayed into those blurred lines I mentioned earlier. It has to be this way, Freeman. The red-haired man you seek is beyond your reach. The girls your officers wanted to meet with again can't help you identify him, as they've never met. We've both had similar cases. No matter how hard we try, we can't find the key."

"In this case, you've got the key in your pocket," said Gus.

"And that's where it will stay," said Curran.

Brendan Curran stood and approached Gus. He held out his hand.

"I hope I can rely on you to back off on this one, Freeman. You've got a tremendous amount to offer this county's force with the work you and your team are doing. I should hate to see it curtailed. Tell your team as much as you need to and no more. I wish you luck with your latest case. Do we understand one another?"

"I think we do," said Gus, shaking Curran's hand.

Brendan Curran left the ACC's office.

Ten minutes later, the two vans and their personnel left the car park.

## Chapter Eight

THE ACC FOUND Gus Freeman standing by the window.

"What are you doing in my spot, Freeman?" he asked with a wry grin.

"I was watching the world go by," said Gus.

"I'm sorry if I was rather abrupt when I called you," said Kenneth Truelove. "Brendan descended on us with his troops and told us to stop everything. It was plain that you had stepped into a hornet's nest. Are things clearer now?"

"As clear as mud," said Gus. "But no matter how much I want things to be different, Curran has marked my card. Provided you've checked you're not handing me a ticking bomb, then I can continue tackling cold cases. Cases like Burnside are off-limits."

"I'm sorry, Freeman," said the ACC. "I didn't realise it would prove so contentious."

"It wasn't your fault," said Gus. "The NCA, or whoever pulls strings these days, should make their red flags more visible."

"What do you plan to do now?" asked the ACC.

"Get back to base," said Gus. "I need to rally the troops and tell them as much as Curran will allow. Then we'll get on with the Kendall case. When do you expect Geoff Mercer back? I want to know whether Rick Chalmers is leaving us now that the task he was helping Alex with has collapsed."

"Mercer will return on Monday morning," said Kenneth Truelove. "I'd appreciate an update on the Kendall case, whether or not you've cracked it. Perhaps we can meet at ten o'clock and discuss staffing levels then?"

"That sounds good, Sir," said Gus.

"One last thing before you leave, Freeman," said the ACC. "Brendan's people had to know about the Freeman Files. I had no choice. Your people will be entertaining his men as we speak. So when you get back to the office, please ensure they know where to find every scrap of data you've recorded on Burnside's killer and the related issues. Don't be clever."

"I wish you'd told me sooner, Sir," said Gus. "Lydia and Blessing will be alone. Neil Davis was in Westbury, inter-viewing people connected to the Kendall case."

"I called ahead, Freeman," said Kenneth, "and told Ms Logan Barre to let them in. The ladies don't know why they were getting raided, but they knew what to expect."

Gus left the ACC's office and made for the stairs. "Not so fast," said Suzie.

"I didn't expect to see you before tonight," said Gus. "Were you caught in the madness?"

"They had no reason to commandeer any of my stuff," said Suzie. "Nothing similar has ever happened here at London Road. You have a knack for finding trouble, don't you?"

"Sorry that I didn't call you," said Gus. "My feet didn't

touch the ground once we got the elbow from the manor house. I imagine Alex and Rick are talking with Divya to learn what the NCA removed. I need to speak to them before they reveal what they were working on to other staff members in the Hub,"

"Don't worry, Gus," said Suzie. "The stormtroopers warned everyone it was beyond their remit. The Hub staff were told to carry on with whatever they were doing and forget that the NCA was ever here. I warned you to be careful."

"We weren't in danger," said Gus, "as far as I could tell."

"Vera tells me your old sparring partner, Brendan Curran, was in the building."

"He's halfway to London by now," said Gus. "We'll never be bosom buddies, but he was more forthcoming than last time. Curran asked if we understood one another. His isn't a job I would enjoy, but I appreciate the tightrope he has to walk. We shook hands before he left."

"Blimey," said Suzie, "that's quite a shift in your relationship."

"With luck, we'll never meet again," said Gus.

"I wondered whether you'd leave it a few weeks and have another go," said Suzie.

"I can't be selfish," said Gus. "I have the livelihoods of others to protect. But, if I were a lone wolf, who knows, perhaps I'd risk another visit."

"Put it behind you, Gus," said Suzie. "Plenty of other cases to tackle."

"Do you know what Callum Wood said?"

"Who's he?" asked Suzie.

"Callum works at the manor house," said Gus. "Previous to that, he was a detective in Bath. Guess where he worked before he moved there? In the building that now houses our office. Callum worked there alongside Neil's father, Terry. Their boss was Phil Hounsell. How many more times will that name surface? Somehow, those people are connected. Wood, Hounsell, Wheeler, and the red-headed man. How many others we may never know."

"You're struggling to let it go, aren't you?" said Suzie. "I'm worried for you, Gus. Please, drop it. Keep busy on your other case for the rest of the day, and I'll see you tonight."

"You're right," said Gus, "but it flies in the face of everything I value. I hate leaving the pieces of a jigsaw scattered on the table, especially when I know how most of them fit together. I keep reminding myself of what Curran said, that pursuing Burnside's killer wasn't in the national interest. Curran's men are at our office grabbing everything we've got on file there. They're thorough. I'll give them that."

"Do the necessary," said Suzie. "I'll see you later. If you want to talk, I'm a good listener, but be warned, I won't let you throw everything away for a thug like Grant Burnside."

Gus trotted downstairs and left the building. He glanced across the yard to the Hub but decided against a visit. A call to Alex before he left the car park would suffice. It was hectic enough in that building already.

As Gus battled early afternoon traffic, he knew Alex and Rick would be on their way after his quick phone call. They would reach the Old Police Station office within seconds of one another. How long the NCA people were staying was uncertain. Gus tried to work out how to explain matters to his Crime Review Team. A speech that didn't give much away but enough for his colleagues to accept without asking probing questions. Why wasn't there a government minister around to ask for advice when you needed one?

THIRTY-FIVE MINUTES LATER, Gus stood below the office with Alex and Rick. Two burly detectives barred their path to the lift door. Gus checked their identification and accepted their barked instructions. He and his two colleagues must wait for work upstairs to finish before gaining entry.

Gus knew that thanks to the well-organised system Alex, Neil, and Lydia had helped him install, it would be a simple task for the detectives upstairs to carry out a seek-and-destroy mission. He prayed they left everything unrelated to the Grant Burnside case in its usual pristine condition.

Forty minutes later, the lift descended, and four men emerged carrying closed cardboard boxes. The six NCA detectives then crossed the car park to their van, loaded up the evidence, and left without a word.

Gus rode up with Alex and Rick. As they walked into the office, they found Neil and the others tidying the mess the searchers had left behind.

"Leave that for a while," Gus said. "You deserve an explanation."

The team gathered around his desk. Gus knew the probing questions would come, regardless of how he couched the words from Brendan Curran. The men and women in front of him had proved they were a crack team of investigators during the cases they'd worked on together. However, he needed to stress that they had zero options if they wished to stay in business. Toe the line, or they were history.

"What's going on, guv?" asked Neil Davis. "Why have

Alex and Rick joined us? I got back from Westbury as their dark blue van arrived in the car park. I wondered what was going on when I saw them clamber out mob-handed. Luke arrived while I tried to persuade the two heavies downstairs to allow me up. Finally, they relented, and we came up together. Luke said he couldn't elaborate on this morning's events. He said you got told to get back to London Road, and the ACC would explain everything."

Lydia Logan Barre and Blessing Umeh sat beside one another, waiting for Gus to speak.

"I proceeded along the driveway in an orderly fashion," said Rick, trying to make light of the matter. "Someone handed Gus Freeman a phone. The next thing I knew, we were back in the car and returning to Devizes."

"Rick and I went inside the Hub," said Alex. "Senior detectives rifled through filing cabinets, downloaded files onto memory sticks, and shredded printed documents. Divya, the girl who helped us collect data this week, told us it was our data they seized and nobody else's."

"What's that about then, guv," asked Neil.

"Do you ever watch US TV shows," said Gus, "where the local police take on a case, and when things look interesting, FBI agents descend on the squad room and whip the case from under their nose? As often as not, the case impinges on the FBI's major investigation. The locals might have enough evidence to arrest and charge a low-level criminal gang member, but the FBI insists it has its eyes on a bigger prize."

"Is that what's behind this morning, guv?" asked Luke.

"In simple terms, yes," said Gus. "We're the local cops, and the National Crime Agency are our equivalent of the FBI."

Gus hoped he could get away with his following statement as the last word.

"The matter fell outside our jurisdiction, and we would do more damage than good by continuing."

The room fell silent while the team considered what Gus had said.

"So, the NCA took everything we had on the Grant Burnside case," said Lydia. "They didn't tell us that. They said to sit still and keep quiet."

"I imagine they did the same here as they did at the Hub," said Gus. "They didn't just take copies of the Freeman Files; they deleted every scrap that could help us progress the case. Then, Brendan Curran ordered me to leave it alone."

"How did they explain the business about the mobile phones?" asked Blessing.

"There's a recycling centre at the location we visited this morning refurbishing phones for ex-service personnel," said Gus. "Alex and Rick's visit to Tanya White coincided with an upgrade for phones issued to charity staff."

"I suppose that's reasonable," said Luke. Neil looked unconvinced.

"The other four girls haven't moved to a new house," said Gus. "Alex and Rick assumed they had disappeared, the same as Tanya, but apart from having their phone numbers, we hadn't yet confirmed where the girls were living."

"Tanya did a runner, though, guv," said Alex.

"Tanya didn't see any reason to tell you she was moving into a house with another girl that day. She couldn't see it was any of your business. After her experiences in Swindon, she needs time to learn to trust someone. I think we can appreciate that."

"What happens now, guv?" asked Rick.

"We continue the hunt for Ivan Kendall's killers," said Gus. "Geoff Mercer isn't available to give you a new assignment yet, Rick. I'm meeting Geoff and the ACC at ten o'clock on Monday morning. Your next job will get sorted then. After your long spell undercover, surely you've got a day's holiday owing to you. So take the rest of the week off. Thanks for your help. Who knows? Maybe we'll work together again."

"Okay, guv," said Rick, "I don't need to be told twice. So I'll grab a takeaway in town, get home, drink a few beers, and then fall asleep watching the tennis on TV."

"The exciting life of a single bloke," said Neil.

"Separated, Neil," said Rick. "My marriage went down the toilet eighteen months ago. My missus is a staff nurse and worked long shifts at the hospital. We rarely saw one another. That's why I volunteered for undercover work. It got me out of the empty house."

Gus sympathised with Rick Chalmers. Rick was a good detective but finding someone who understood how a case became all-consuming was never easy. You wanted to do right by your colleagues and, above all, the victims. People who wanted to share that life were thin on the ground.

"Best of luck with your case," said Rick as he made for the lift. "I'll see you."

Gus helped his team tidy the office, and half an hour later, they had everything as near normal as possible.

"Rick made me hungry when he mentioned that takeaway," said Neil. "Can we take a break for half an hour, guv?"

"Fair enough," said Gus. "I need time to get my head together after today's events. So first, I'll recap everything until last night, and then I'll hear what you learned this morning."

Alex and Lydia left the office together. They had plans to make for the coming weekend.

"Did you bring lunch today, Blessing?" asked Luke.

"Yes," she replied, "Jackie Ferris won't let me leave in the morning without finishing my breakfast and accepting a packed lunch. I must join a gym soon to lose the weight her food is adding."

"You'll have your car back tonight," said Neil. "You won't get stuck in Worton in the evenings."

Blessing hadn't shared her news with Neil about Dave Smith taking her out after returning her car. Instead, Neil would only tease her and want a full report in the morning.

Blessing went to the restroom to fetch her lunch. As she waited for the coffee machine, Gus joined her.

"A black coffee, guv?" she asked. "I'll bring it through."

"Thanks, Blessing," said Gus. "How are your parents settling in?"

"My mother rang last night," said Blessing. "Her usual midweek check that I've not succumbed to a life of debauchery. I mentioned that you were visiting a place near the village today. My parents haven't ventured deeper into the countryside yet. So my mother hadn't heard of the place. My father is still getting the trip to the University locked into his head. By September, when the students return, he should be able to get to work and home again without getting lost."

"Will you get here on time tomorrow?" asked Gus.

"I have my satnav, guv," said Blessing. "I don't plan to be late to bed tonight. It's just a drink."

"Ah," said Gus, "what's this? Have you met someone?"

Blessing explained about the Malmesbury PC who

rescued her when she broke down. Unfortunately, she omitted to describe the tall hunk with the cornflower blue eyes.

"So, I need to keep my eyes peeled for a Nissan Micra in the car park from tomorrow," said Gus.

"Yes, guv," replied Blessing. "I hope I can avoid bumping into anyone from the team while parking."

Gus carried his black coffee back to his desk. Blessing stopped to chat with Neil and Luke before starting her lunch. She thought she could eat the sandwiches before Gus wanted to restart work. But she could not finish the fruit cake Jackie had given her.

"It's for a special treat, Blessing," Jackie had said.

Blessing stared at the giant slab of scrumptiousness. It was more of a meal than a treat. It would keep for later.

Alex and Lydia exited the lift with minutes to spare. Finally, Gus was ready to begin.

"Right," he said, "who wants to start? Neil?

"I checked with Ieuan Arlett, guv. He never saw or heard a thing about Kendall gambling. He told me that it didn't sound like something with which he would get involved. As you pointed out, Ivan never had spare cash after losing the well-paid job with the builder's merchants."

"I don't suppose any high-street bookies would tell us whether Ivan held an account without a warrant, anyway, guv," said Luke.

"I think it's more likely that there's another explanation," said Gus. "What did you learn at the Dilton Marsh site, Neil?"

"The Homes and Communities Agency agreed on funding for several sites in Wiltshire around six years ago, guv," said Neil. "The scheme aimed to offer appropriate sites for travellers, with standards of accommodation equal to that of the settled population. The project helped reduce unauthorised encampments and associated nuisance, but demand hasn't been as great as first thought, and only ten more pitches were agreed upon across the county. Two of those were at the site near Westbury, increasing the present number to seven."

"That reduces the number of places where the killers could have lived," said Gus.

"Provided they stayed on one of the official sites, guv," said Luke.

"The sites contain what they term family pitches," said Neil. "Each pitch has a building that provides cooking, washing, and bathing facilities."

"The only thing the resident needs to provide is a caravan," said Luke.

"I presume the occupiers stay there under certain licence conditions," said Gus.

"Yes, guv, and they must pay rent, council tax, and a site service charge. Residents also pay for water and electric usage."

"Eddie Sinclair gave the impression that several of the families had been there some time," said Gus. "Were you able to trace anyone there in March 2014 that fits our possible attackers?"

"I spoke to a Mr and Mrs Wakefield, who have been semi-permanent residents there for years. They were reluctant to say much. It's a tight-knit community. However, they admitted that occasionally their unmarried daughter drives across from another authorised site near Corsham. She stays for a few nights at a time. I pushed them on that, and Mrs Wakefield told me her daughter's partner got into bother with the law. Her daughter didn't want to stay on the site alone while he spent seven days in the nick. I think the partner likes a drink, so the daughter escapes during spells when he's on a bender."

"So, is it possible the other family pitches could have visitors, too?" asked Luke. "If the main caravan holder paid the rent, council tax, and site fees, the council wouldn't be any the wiser."

"You must return to the site to interview the official holder of every pitch, Neil," said Gus.

"I've met with five of them, guv," said Neil. "Their caravans aren't big enough to sleep an additional two bodies."

"The killers could have split up," said Lydia, "and slept in separate vans."

"That's possible," said Luke. "The sort of men capable of what they did to Ivan Kendall would intimidate older couples. Could these men be relatives?"

"A car or van could enter the site without a caravan trailing behind," said Blessing. "What's stopping someone from sleeping in their vehicle overnight?"

"Luke will go with you in the morning, Neil," said Gus. "You can apply intimidation tactics of your own. I appreciate the community we're talking to is reluctant to cooperate with the police. First, however, we need to find these two killers, and our best bet is that they were staying on this site temporarily. That fits with Eddie Sinclair's reasoning."

"I've had a thought, guv," said Blessing. "You asked Neil to think of an activity in which Ivan Kendall could have taken an interest. Why not think of something our two killers might do? We haven't established a motive for the murder yet. Nor have we explained why Ivan Kendall travelled from Pontyclun to Westbury."

"Do you mean they agreed to block-pave his driveway, Blessing," said Neil. "Several people have got caught in that scam. We'll do it for fifteen hundred quid, mate. The homeowner's eyes light up at saving two-thirds of the usual price, and within a month, the whole thing's falling apart because the travellers skimped on preparation and materials. Good luck finding them again; they've moved."

"That's unlikely, Neil," said Blessing. "Anyway, if they did knock on his door and offered to do a job, what does that tell us?"

"Ivan Kendall met them in Pontyclun," said Gus. "Where's the nearest traveller's site?"

Luke Sherman hunted on the internet. He found the information in seconds.

"There are two authorised sites in Cardiff, guv. Other towns nearby, for example, Caerphilly, assessed the demand for pitches, but there wasn't enough to invest in schemes such as the one Wiltshire carried out."

"The sites are close enough to the village that it's feasible that Ivan met his attackers while cleaning windows," said Luke. "It depends on what services they offered while they trawled the village for opportunities."

"They could have been thieving," said Lydia.

"Nicking the lead off the church roof," said Neil.

"We need Dai Williams to help us," said Gus. "Alex, you and I will drive there tomorrow and try to put names to these rogues. Maybe they've got a record in the Principality."

"We'll continue the search for Sally and Lexie Kendall," said Lydia.

"That search should be easier now you're concentrating on a smaller area," said Gus. "Discount anywhere outside a twenty-mile radius from Pontyclun. We should consider that Sally may have remarried or reverted to her maiden name to hide her connection to Ivan Kendall. Whether or not she was mistaken, Sally hid because she feared for her life.

Alexa is twenty years old now and could be married. How valuable are the photographs we have of the pair of them?"

"Not very, guv," said Luke. "This was never a normal murder. We can't visit the victim's home to talk to his family. As you might expect, the local police collected evidence from the house, but very few family photos were among the items in the file we got from London Road. There was plenty of information on Ivan Kendall because they believed he was a missing person at the outset. When Cardiff got involved, their detectives soon learned the murder scene was eighty miles away. So why descend on the house in Pontyclun for photos of Sally and Alexa?"

"What do we have then?" asked Gus.

"A school photograph from Y Pant Comprehensive," said Luke, "showing Alexa in school uniform, together with the rest of Year 11."

"Ivan and Sally's wedding photograph from the local newspaper, guv," said Neil, "next to useless after over twenty years."

"What about the shops where she worked?" asked Blessing. "Maybe they have a photo on file. Did they have Christmas parties? We need something more recent."

"Good idea, Blessing," said Gus. "We'll follow up on that while we're in Wales tomorrow."

"If you get something usable, guv," said Neil, "the rugby club might post Sally's photo with a 'Do you know this woman?' message on their Facebook page. People often share things such as that, and if Sally is still in the region, someone could recognise her."

"It might drive her further away, Neil," said Lydia. "If Sally still thinks someone was after her."

"We must be careful," said Gus. "Let's find more recent photos of Sally if we can. We don't know whether Sally has an online presence. I think Alexa is the key. Even though the school photo is sketchy, we could get the Hub people to enhance it and produce an artist's impression of her at twenty. Then, we'll use that to aid your search for her on social media."

"Right you are, guv," said Luke.

"Do you think the dogs have something to do with the case, guv?" asked Blessing.

"I've no idea," said Gus. "Alex and I will visit the football club in the park that Ieuan Arlett mentioned. Both he and Tommy said Alexa exercised dogs, plural. There was no mention of the breed of dog. Nor confirmation of whether they belonged to a neighbour or a boyfriend. It could be another red herring, and they were unrelated to Alexa's father and his murder. What were you thinking, Blessing?"

"Well, pets are rare among people from the true Roma culture. They consider cats and dogs unclean, whereas the horse is a sacred and revered animal."

"You're suggesting that if Ivan Kendall did own dogs, our two travellers wouldn't have any interest in them," said Luke.

"If they were true Roma, I don't believe they would steal them," said Blessing.

"Don't forget the Kendall family's circumstances," said Lydia. "They were always short of money. Could Ivan afford the purchase and upkeep of dogs? Especially dogs of sufficient pedigree that someone might want to steal them. We haven't been able to ask Sally and Alexa whether these dogs were family pets. If they were, I could understand how devastating it would be if they got stolen. If he had learned where they were, Ivan might have travelled to Westbury to retrieve them. Why didn't he tell Sally why he was going out that night? Instead, Ivan left without a word. There was no mention of dogs in any statement from Sally or Alexa. No hint that someone stole them. It might be a wild goose chase."

"I agree," said Luke. "We'll find that Alexa walked the dogs for someone outside the family."

"Why didn't they come forward at the time of the murder?" asked Blessing. "Why did nobody link their dogs to Alexa? Pontyclun is a small village. After Sally and Alexa disappeared, the dog owner needed to find a replacement to give them exercise. There would be conversations in the pub, supermarket, and street. Eventually, the gossip would reach the ears of Ieuan Arlett. Yet, even four years later, he was no further forward in knowing whose dogs they were. Let alone be able to name children called, say, Megan or Max Evans as the kid that took over from Lexie Kendall."

"That's another question to add to your list for tomorrow, lads," said Gus. "Is everyone who stays on the site a true Romany? They could be Irish travellers. There are differences. Also, they could be people who live a nomadic lifestyle despite having no traveller blood. So the normal rules on pets and other cultural quirks might not apply."

"Tomorrow could bring us answers, guv," said Neil.

"It's about asking the right questions," said Gus.

# Chapter Nine

GUS and the team spent the rest of the afternoon preparing for Friday.

Much of that work continued in silence. The events of the late morning would colour everything they did in the coming days. It was impossible to shut it out of their minds altogether. One of them had a secret and didn't know what to do with it.

At five o'clock, Gus watched the others tidy their desks and make for the lift.

Luke Sherman was giving Blessing Umeh a lift to the Ferris's farm for the last time.

Alex Hardy and Lydia Logan Barre would spend the evening together once again.

Neil Davis hung around for a while longer than the others.

"A penny for them, Neil," said Gus.

"Luke mentioned the name of the guy you met this morning, guv, while we were chatting over lunch."

153

"Callum Wood? Yes, did you ever hear your Dad mention him?"

"I was only a nipper when my Dad worked here," said Neil. "I remember Callum coming to our house several times. Their boss used to have team get-togethers in the Waggon and Horses at Harrington End. Callum was single and collected Dad so that he could have a drink. Then Callum dropped him home drunk afterwards. After moving to Bath, Callum married Debbie Turner. She worked in this station too, but Callum was slow to catch on that she fancied him. It's so long ago now. Can I ask what he does these days?"

"No idea, Neil. It's above our pay grade. So get off home to Melody, and let's put it behind us, eh?"

Gus decided he'd had enough for today. He closed his computer and followed Neil to the lift. As they travelled down together, Gus asked:

"So, Phil Hounsell drank in the Waggon and Horses," he said. "Small world, isn't it?"

"Yes, guv. And Hounsell's future missus worked behind the bar. So maybe that explained why he kept taking the detective squad out there."

"Goodnight, Neil," said Gus.

"You too, guv," said Neil.

SUZIE'S GOLF was outside the bungalow. That didn't surprise Gus. She would be eager to see what shape he was in after today. His first port of call was the kitchen, but the room was empty, although there were signs of something cooking in the oven.

"I'm in the living room," she called out. "I've poured you a wee dram."

Gus walked through to see what delights lay in store.

"Just as well that I don't plan to drive anywhere until the morning," he said as he spied the twelve-year-old Macallan bottle on the side table next to Suzie.

"Make yourself comfortable, Gus," said Suzie, "have a glass with me and get it off your chest."

"No need," he replied. "I know you think us blokes keep a tight grip on our emotions rather than share our feelings with the world. But the Burnside business is behind me now. My total focus is on finding Ivan Kendall's killers."

"I'm not sure I altogether believe you, Gus Freeman," said Suzie, "but have a drink, anyway."

Gus flopped into a chair beside her and rolled the whisky around the bottom of his glass.

"The way I dealt with days like today in the past was to bury the bad stuff as deep as I could. Sometimes, a drink aided that process; on other occasions, it was a drink that allowed long-buried stuff to return to the surface. There have been dozens of dreadful days in my career. Many days were more traumatic than today. The day I returned here to find Tess dead on the kitchen floor for one. After that day, I searched for answers in several glasses but never found them. If I hadn't picked up that old book of Tess's in a suitcase destined for the dump, I would be a hopeless alcoholic by now. I threw myself into my work this afternoon. Tomorrow I'll do the same. In time, I'll bury the Burnside business as deep as the other dark days from my past. If we sit and analyse this morning's events, it will be a waste of good whisky. Let's think of something else to talk about that befits the nectar of the gods."

"I'm sorry," said Suzie. "I got it wrong, didn't I?"

"No," said Gus, "you remembered that we need something to eat if we're going to enjoy a drink. So tell me, what have you been up to today?"

WHILE GUS and Suzie contemplated life in Urchfont, Blessing Umeh was in Worton worrying about what to wear. Luke had dropped her off at a quarter to six and driven home to Warminster. Jackie Ferris had been in the kitchen when Blessing walked indoors from the yard.

"What time will your young man be arriving with your car," she asked.

"Dave's not my young man," Blessing had replied. "He's an acquaintance. I've only met him once. What if I don't like him when I meet him again?"

Jackie had laughed.

"Sit and eat your dinner and then get ready. If you had any doubts, you wouldn't have agreed to let the young man drive the car from Malmesbury. John could have driven you out there to collect it."

Jackie had put the plate of food in front of her, and Blessing gave in. Now, at a quarter to seven, she sat on her bed and gazed at the wardrobe. It was only a drink. She chose a colourful, summery blouse and slacks. There was still time to change three or four times before Dave arrived.

Blessing heard a familiar sound coming through the open window. Her Nissan Micra looked cleaner than it had for a while and sounded one hundred times better than the day she drove to Devizes from her old home.

Dave Smith climbed out of the driver's seat. Because he was so tall, it wasn't a graceful exit. Dave unfurled himself from the car, and Blessing couldn't resist a giggle. He looked up at her bedroom window and gave her a wave.

Dave wore a white shirt and blue jeans; Blessing didn't

need to change. Instead, she wanted to get downstairs to see him and check over her little car.

"Your young man's here," said Jackie Ferris, with a grin as Blessing dashed through the kitchen door.

"My car sounded great when you drove up, Dave," said Blessing. "Thank you."

"It's my brother you need to thank, not me," said Dave. "I've got the invoice here, too, so you might not be so pleased to see me after you've read it."

"I won't read it until after you've gone home," said Blessing.

"Where shall we go?" asked Dave.

"There's no rush," said Blessing. "It's a lovely evening. First, I'll show you around the farm, and then I'll drive us into Devizes. Did you know there used to be ninety pubs in the town? There are less than twenty these days, but that's still a wide enough choice for us to find a place to sit and chat."

"Ninety? Are you sure, Blessing?" asked Dave.

"I read it online," she replied. "A local historian organised a walking tour around the sites a few years ago. I don't know whether they still do it, though."

"We'll give it a miss," said Dave. "How's the job going? Any excitement you can share?"

"A team of detectives from the National Crime Agency raided us this morning," said Blessing. "I've never been so frightened."

"You've got a dry sense of humour," laughed Dave. "How can you keep a straight face when you say that?"

"I *was* frightened," Blessing insisted. Dave Smith laughed even harder.

"Alright," he said, "I'll fall for it. Who were they looking for, Lord Lucan or Shergar?"

"I don't know who or what you're talking about, Dave," said Blessing. "I'm serious. They raided offices on London Road as well. Two of my colleagues stumbled across evidence connected to one of Gus Freeman's cold cases that the team investigated before I joined them. We got told not to continue with that part of the investigation. I couldn't understand why, but that's the way things go sometimes, isn't it?"

"Blimey," said Dave, "your team gets more excitement than we do in the sticks. But, unfortunately, traffic offences and anti-social behaviour fill my days."

Blessing took Dave past the stables and into the orchard. They sat under an apple tree, and Blessing wondered whether Dave could help her.

"Do you come into contact with any travellers in the Malmesbury area?" asked Blessing.

"There used to be an illegal site with around eighteen vans fifteen minutes away from the town. They had temporary permission to stay there, but the Council was under constant pressure from locals to move them on. So they've got two authorised sites around Swindon for almost sixty vans. Why do you ask?"

"Our latest case concerns a South Wales man murdered in Westbury four years ago. We believe his killers stayed on an authorised site near the town. We haven't confirmed whether they moved there from Wales yet. I wondered what activities they could get up to that saw them cross paths with our victim."

"You must remember that travellers only represent one per cent of the population, Blessing," said Dave, "and they can get a bad rep in the media. They're not responsible for any more crime percentage-wise than the settled population, but sometimes an entire encampment gets moved on because an individual gets caught out. I'm sure you know this from working in Warwickshire, but it's a civil matter when travellers trespass on private land. We don't have powers to prevent trespass and can only act in aggravated circumstances."

"It's up to the landowner to take action through the courts," said Blessing, "yes, I knew that. But, does it seem fair to you that when those travellers move on, it's the landowner's responsibility to clear away rubbish and waste they've left behind?"

"That's the law, Blessing," said Dave. "Of course, if those travellers caused damage, or threatened someone, then the landowner only has to call us."

"Too late by then," said Blessing. "The culprits have disappeared."

"I attended a raid on an authorised site a couple of years back," said Dave. "What we found there might give you a few ideas. Your victim could have had similar items stolen. We recovered transformers, a mini-digger, and industrial tools. Over a dozen stolen vehicles got seized: lorries, vans, and cars. The biggest money-making item we recovered was a catalytic converter processing unit. Someone used it to strip the precious metals from stolen units and sell them to scrap dealers. Was your victim a farmer? Farm equipment is always a lucrative business, and travellers often siphon red diesel for their vans from farm vehicles. The site we visited had a large storage facility for illicit fuel."

"That's a comprehensive list, Dave," said Blessing. "Not one of those things connects with our victim at first glance, but who knows? One of our team thought there was a connection to dogs, but I didn't think it likely."

"I saw dogs on that site, Blessing," said Dave, "and they looked in excellent condition. You get all sorts on those sites these days. Why should the makeup be any different to the settled population? We both know how cosmopolitan that's become."

"Let's get into Devizes for that drink," said Blessing, getting up and walking through the vegetable garden to head for the farmyard. "Otherwise, the night will have gone, and you'll be searching for a taxi."

When they reached Blessing's Micra, she stopped.

"Can I have my car keys back, please?" she asked.

Dave fished them out of the back pocket of his jeans and handed them over.

"Sorry," he grinned, "force of habit. That invoice is in your glove compartment for safe-keeping, by the way."

"Jump in," said Blessing, "I'll choose the pub. You can buy the first round."

### Friday, 13 July 2018

"ARE YOU SUPERSTITIOUS?" asked Suzie.

"Am I not allowed secrets now that we live under the same roof?" Gus replied.

"I know plenty about you," said Suzie. "But this will be the first Friday, the thirteenth, that we've spent together."

"It's just a Friday. Nothing unfortunate will happen. I got that out of the way yesterday. Now, can we get up and get on with our day? I'm off to South Wales later. It's bound to rain there, it rained yesterday, and it will rain again tomorrow. The coincidence of a day of the week having a certain number doesn't influence that fact one jot."

"Are you always this grumpy after several glasses of whisky?"

Gus groaned, slid out of bed, and headed for the shower.

"You know I love you, don't you," said Suzie when she joined him two minutes later.

"How come you're as bright as a button this morning," said Gus, "yet we had the same amount to drink."

Suzie opened her mouth to speak.

"Don't answer that," said Gus.

"What time do you expect to get home," asked Suzie.

"Half-past five at the latest," said Gus, "and you?"

"The same. Are we gardening, followed by a bite to eat in the Lamb?"

"Definitely," said Gus. "Brett has his interview in Wootton Bassett today. I hope he's in the pub celebrating getting the job. It will put his Aunt Margaret's mind at rest. He'll be able to monitor Bert."

"Bert enjoys having him around anyway," said Suzie.

"Do you think a healthy breakfast will counteract the effects of the whisky?" asked Gus.

"Only one way to find out," said Suzie. "Live dangerously, have a bowl of muesli and Greek yoghurt with me."

Gus sat at the kitchen table with his first coffee of the day and wondered whether there was something to this phobia. He studied the bowl in front of him. It might be bearable if he closed his eyes and wolfed it down.

"Feeling better?" asked Suzie twenty minutes later as they stood outside by their cars at half-past eight.

"Oh yes," said Gus. "I checked the calendar. The next time we get a Friday, the thirteenth, is next September. So I can claim a legitimate excuse for not eating damp cardboard again for another fourteen months."

"You're incorrigible," said Suzie. "Please try not to get into trouble today."

Gus drove through Devizes and listened to the weather forecast on the radio. Twenty-three degrees, partly sunny, with a slight chance of a shower by six o'clock this evening. Typical. It sounded like he would bring rain back across the Severn Bridge. He and Suzie might need a change of plan for this evening.

As Gus swung the Ford Focus into his parking spot, he spotted a Nissan Micra in his rear mirror. It was Blessing Umeh reunited with her motor. Gus got out, locked the car, and waited. Finally, after three attempts, the young DC reversed her car between the white lines.

"I always struggle to do that," she sighed.

"Why not drive straight in?" asked Gus.

"I've still got to reverse out," said Blessing.

"I know," said Gus, "but at least you don't have to consider the white lines. You only need to avoid the cars behind you."

The look Blessing gave Gus told him that was something else she fretted over.

"How did last night's date that was not a date go?" asked Gus.

Gus couldn't tell whether or not Blessing blushed. So he decided not to push it.

"I got useful tips from Dave, guv," she said.

Blessing told Gus which items Dave Smith said might attract the interest of criminals from within the travelling community.

"We'll mention those in Cardiff later, Blessing," said Gus. "It might jog DI Williams's memory. Thank Dave for me next time you see him."

At that moment, the lift doors opened, and they were in the office. Everyone was working, although Blessing convinced herself they had one ear cocked, hoping to catch a juicy bit of gossip.

"Morning, everyone," she said and headed straight for her desk.

"Right. Is everyone clear on what we're after today?" asked Gus.

"Yes, guv," said Neil. "Alex is coming with me to the traveller's site near Westbury. We need to get meaningful responses this time from the residents."

"You and I will pay a second visit to Cardiff Central, guv," said Luke. "Then we'll do the rounds in Pontyclun."

"We're continuing the hunt for Sally and Alexa, guv," said Lydia.

"Don't sound so glum, Lydia," said Gus. "We'll send any improved images we find for Sally on our travels. Everyone has a valuable role to play today. So let's get started."

Alex and Neil were already on the way to the lift.

"Now Neil's out of earshot. How did it go with Dave last night?" Luke whispered as he paused by Blessing's desk to join Gus.

"A lady never tells," said Lydia, who stood right behind him.

"It cost an awful lot of money to mend my little car," said Blessing. "I don't know whether I could afford to see him again for a while."

"You want to, though?" asked Lydia.

Blessing nodded.

She could have done with a small step to reach up to kiss him for the first time last night; he was so tall. But it was worth it. Blessing had parked in the centre of town, and they visited The Bear. They had found a quiet corner and chatted as if they'd known one another forever. The barman called last orders before they knew it, and it happened when Dave walked her to her car. They kissed, and he asked to see her again the following weekend. Blessing hadn't wanted to appear too eager and told him she'd call him in the week. She'd set the reminder on her phone before falling asleep last night. Of course, she would see him again.

Luke and Gus had disappeared into the lift when Blessing stopped daydreaming.

"Alex and I are taking the ferry from Harwich to the Hook of Holland tomorrow, " Lydia said. "A thirty-minute drive takes us to Rotterdam, where we're booked into a hotel overnight. I'm hoping to meet my father for the first time."

"How exciting," said Blessing, "I expect you're nervous?"

"Just a bit," laughed Lydia. "Right, let's hunt for this blessed young woman."

"DO you think we'll be any more successful today, Neil?" asked Alex.

"We can but try, Alex," said Neil. "They're a tight bunch. We're unlikely to find seven caravans occupied. Those families that have been there for several years, like Stan Wakefield and his wife, are retired now. I expect them to answer our knock. The menfolk living in several of the other vans will be off-site grafting. If they've got a wife and kids, then it's potluck."

"We don't have a warrant, so we can't force them to answer the door," said Alex.

"When I was there the other day, one wife answered but refused to talk. I said she wasn't in any trouble; we just wanted information. She told me that if she spoke to anyone, not just the police, her husband would be mad."

"She was frightened that he would hit her, did you mean?" asked Alex.

"The woman had three kids under school age hanging on her arm or her skirt," said Neil.

Neil drove through the town of Westbury, and Alex noticed the sign for Westbury Leigh.

"Did I see that name in the Freeman Files related to this case?"

"I suppose you're playing catch-up," said Neil, "now your work at the Hub has come to an abrupt halt."

"I had a brief read through the murder file this morning to familiarise myself with the case."

"Sid Dyer, the train conductor, lived out this way," said Neil. "He found the blood in the toilets that started the search for a body. We would have liked to interview him, but he got knocked off his motorcycle not long after he retired. That was two years ago or thereabouts."

"Interesting," said Alex.

"It's the way we think, isn't it," said Neil. "Luke and Gus made the same comment in the office and added a footnote in the files. We're suspicious by nature."

"Accidents happen," said Alex, "but I'm an experienced motorcyclist, and this stretch of road doesn't fill me with dread. Visibility is good. Of course, we'd need to check the road conditions on the day. Do you recall if there were any witnesses?"

"None. The inquest assumed an HGV clipped Dyer's bike as it passed him, and the driver didn't realise. Instead, a passing motorist found the bike and Dyer's body on the grass verge."

"It's another question we can ask, Neil," said Alex. "Did

a couple of blokes stay on the site on more than one occasion? Say in 2014 and 2016?"

"Here we are," said Neil. "Half-past nine in the morning. Not much activity, is there? Someone is hanging out the washing in the corner. Let's try her first."

Neil parked the car and got out. Alex joined him, and they approached the young woman. She looked no more than fifteen.

"We're detectives, Miss," said Neil. "Are your parents at home? We want a word, nothing to worry about. Shouldn't you be in school?"

"I don't go to school, and it's Mrs, not Miss. My husband's not here. You must leave."

"How long have you and your husband lived here?" asked Alex.

"Nine months," the girl replied.

"Where were you before that?" asked Neil.

"Downton, with my parents."

The girl edged towards the caravan door.

"I've got to go now," she said and ran indoors.

"Did you notice the bump when she dropped the washing basket?" asked Neil.

"I did," said Alex, "it fits with their tradition. They marry young, and the wife's duty-bound to give birth within twelve months. She and her husband can't help us, anyway."

"Let's get back to the first van inside the gates. Stan Wakefield's wife might brew us a cuppa."

Neil tapped on the window. Thirty seconds later, a white-haired man opened the caravan door.

"It's you again," he said. "I suppose you want to come inside?"

"Yes, please, Mr Wakefield," said Neil. "This is my colleague DS Hardy. We've got follow-up questions."

"About our daughter, I presume?"

"Not at all," said Neil. "We're still looking for information that might help us solve that nasty murder in town four years back."

"I don't go into town much," said Stan Wakefield.

"Is your wife here this morning?" asked Alex.

"She's gone shopping,"

Neil realised his chance of a cup of tea had disappeared.

"Do you remember the last time I came? I asked whether you'd seen anyone visiting one of your neighbours. Someone who might have stayed for several nights on several occasions."

"I remember," said Stan Wakefield. "Maybe I saw someone, and maybe I didn't."

"Why don't you visit the town much, Mr Wakefield?" asked Alex.

"Too many people, lots of noise. I'm not too fond of the shops. It's the way the staff look down their nose at you."

"I think you know more than you're letting on," said Alex. "If we took you back to the police station and put you in a cell for a couple of hours, do you think your memory might improve?"

"I don't think there's any need for that, do you, Stan?" said Neil. "Maybe you can remember who had visitors and when they were here. What do you say?"

"Jack Ayres used to keep a van here," said Stan. "His wife died. That would be seven, maybe eight years ago now. He was in his eighties, almost blind. His nephews stopped with him now and then."

"Can you remember their names?" asked Neil.

"Jack never told me, and they weren't the sort of blokes you dared ask for details if you follow me. They were his sister's boys."

"How old would they have been, Stan?" asked Alex.

"Over forty then, closer to fifty today. How should I know?"

"Did they have their own caravan?" asked Neil.

Stan shook his head.

"Arrived in the night in an old, white van. A length of cable secured the exhaust. Nobody had washed that van for a twelve-month. No idea what they did to earn a crust. They hung around during the day and left the camp when it got dark. After two weeks, maybe three, they'd gone."

"When was this?" asked Alex. "Any way of pinning down the date?"

Stan Wakefield thought for a while.

"Just before Spring, the first time," he said.

"March then," said Neil, "the month of the murder. Good, now we're getting somewhere. That visit was in 2014, Stan, is that right?"

"I don't think so," said Stan, looking at Alex. "Jack's wife had only been dead a year the first time they came. But, then, they came back, as you said. So, they could have been here that year."

"You're saying they came in early March every year," said Alex. "Is that how you remember it?"

"That sounds right," said Stan.

"Did they always have the same van?" asked Neil.

Stan nodded. "They had the exhaust fixed one year. The van wasn't any cleaner, though."

"Where did they go for the rest of the year?" asked Alex.

"You need to ask them," said Stan.

"That's okay, Stan," said Neil. "We'll ask Jack Ayres."

"I'd pay to see that. I'll come with you," said Stan. "You'll not find his grave in the cemetery without help. There's no memorial stone yet. He died last November."

"Have you forgotten that room I mentioned, Stan?" said Alex.

"Some travellers move regularly," said Stan, "follow the fairs or the horse sales. Others stay in one spot most of the year, then take time to tour around visiting family. Men like Jack's nephews move on once they've exhausted the work opportunities. They came here in March for a few weeks to visit Jack. Then they might have spent the summer closer to their family home."

"Where was Jack's family home?" asked Neil.

"North Wales, I reckon. Jack had family all over Wales."

"What happened to Jack's caravan?" asked Alex.

"His family took everything away," said Stan. "No, they didn't set it alight. It was worth too much. A new couple of youngsters have got it now. The lad's parents bought it for them."

"I think we met the wife," said Neil.

"When was the last time you saw the nephews?" asked Alex.

"They didn't come here this March. There was no point, was there? Their Uncle Jack was dead."

"Thanks for your help, Stan," said Neil. "We'll let you get on with your day."

"The wife will be back shortly. I would have offered you a cuppa, but I wasn't sure I had enough milk for three cups."

Stan Wakefield stood by the open door of his van and watched Neil and Alex to their car. When Alex got into the passenger seat, he glanced back. Stan had closed the door.

"What about the other caravans, Neil?" he asked.

"We should have enough to work out the names of our suspects," said Neil. "Stan kept us talking long enough for the others to make their escape. Why do you think it's so quiet? Didn't you hear the vehicles creeping past Stan's van? We won't find anyone in now. Stan will have a way of notifying them that the coast's clear. Let's get back to the office."

# Chapter Ten

"IMAGINE HAVING to make this trip daily, Luke," Gus said as they crossed the Severn Bridge.

"No problem on a sunny day, guv," said Luke.

"Let's hope we learn enough on this trip that another trip isn't necessary," said Gus.

Forty minutes later, they had negotiated Reception for the second time this week and were on their way to DI Dai Williams's office.

"I thought we'd got rid of you," said Dai Williams, with a grin. "What did you forget to ask the last time?"

"We've uncovered fresh evidence," said Gus. "We now believe the killers stayed on a traveller's site near Westbury for a short period on either side of the murder in March 2014. You have two authorised sites in the city. Our suspects probably stayed at one of them and carried out work or were engaged in a criminal activity that took them north of the city towards places such as Pontyclun."

"Do you have names for these suspects?" asked Dai Williams.

"Not yet," said Gus.

"What nature of crime did you record in the first few months of 2014 that you could tie to members of the travelling community," asked Luke.

"Analysis of crime statistics by ethnicity can be problematic," said DI Williams. "Perhaps, you could be more specific. For example, what type of crime do you mean?"

"Were there thefts of industrial tools, catalytic converters, farm equipment, and quantities of red diesel?" asked Gus, referring to Blessing's tip list.

"Across South Wales, those items appear with an annoying frequency, Mr Freeman. In addition, we have anti-social behaviour and theft incidents that get traced back to residents on the sites you mentioned. However, nothing in our figures for the period in question relates to items stolen or damaged in Pontyclun."

"When travellers come looking for work in the city," asked Luke. "What work is it they're carrying out?"

"Buying scrap metal, tarmacking driveways, cutting high hedges, lopping branches from trees," said DI Williams. "They can turn their hand to most things."

"Do you have any names for us?" asked Gus.

"From our two authorised sites? There are several family names to watch for, Chapman, Cooper, Scott, Ayres, Brazil, Corbett, and Kelly. I need not remind you that most members of those families are hard-working and law-abiding. But, with every flock, there's a rare black sheep."

"When your detectives finally investigated Ivan Kendall's disappearance, did they remove any family photographs from the house?"

"It'll be on file, Mr Freeman," said Dai Williams. He searched his computer for several seconds.

"The only photos we removed were of Ivan Kendall.

We weren't interested in the wife and daughter. They weren't missing."

"That's what we thought you would say," said Gus. "We'll gain nothing by staying here, Luke. Let's drive to Pontyclun."

"Safe journey," said DI Williams.

"A fat lot of use he was," said Gus as they reached the visitor's car park.

"Never mind, guv," said Luke, "I always thought our real chance of progress lay in the village. Then, the locals might have more of an idea of what our suspects got up to in the weeks before Ivan's death."

Luke drove them away from Cardiff Central and out of the city. Gus sat quietly beside him as they headed for the village.

"Where to first, guv?" asked Luke.

"As close to the centre as possible, Luke," said Gus. "Sally worked in a series of local shops after leaving school. So we'll start at the supermarket, if they have one, and work our way down to the corner shops. With luck, someone will have a decent photo we can use."

Luke spotted a sign for a free car park and found a place to park.

"You don't see many of those these days," said Gus. "It's as if they want people to visit their shops."

"It doesn't take a genius to work out that if you ramp up parking charges in the town centre, you drive the trade to the out-of-town retail parks," said Luke.

"That Tesco outfit looks like our best bet," said Gus.

Once inside the busy little store, Gus searched for someone in authority. How did one distinguish between people clad in the same uniform? He noticed an older lady at the end of an aisle doing nothing.

"Are you the manager here?" he asked.

"I'm in charge on the shop floor today," she replied. "How can I help you?"

"Did Sally Kendall ever work here?"

"Oh, yes, Sally worked here for several years on the checkouts. Why do you ask?"

"We're from Wiltshire Police," said Gus, producing his identification. "We know Sally left the village not long after her husband's death, but we're eager to find her."

"I've no idea where she might be, I'm afraid,"

"Could I have your name?" asked Gus.

"Dilys Morgan, Mr Freeman," she replied.

"Well, Dilys, we have the technical ability to locate her, provided we get an accurate description. We need a photo of Sally that's more recent than anything we can find through the usual avenues."

"Sally Prosser was a local girl, Mr Freeman. I remember when she and Ivan Kendall married at St Paul's."

"Their wedding photograph from the local newspaper is what we have so far," said Luke. "Because Sally and Alexa left without leaving a forwarding address, there's nothing of the Kendall family's belongings to offer something more relevant. Would you have a staff photo of her?"

"It's possible," said Dilys. "I could ask the manager later. Unfortunately, she's not here this morning. It would be best if you visited the other shops where Sally worked to ask them. I can give you a list if you like?"

"That would be a great help, Dilys," said Gus.

"I know it's four years since she left the village," said Luke, "but what about social occasions? Would anyone who worked with Sally carry photos of her on their phones or computer at home?"

"We girls get together often," said Dilys, "birthdays, hen

nights, baby showers. Any excuse, not just Christmas. So, it's a distinct possibility that one of us has a photo of Sally somewhere. I'll put a notice on the board in the staff room. Then, if you give me your contact details, I'll send you anything I can find."

"Many thanks," said Gus. Luke handed over a card, and Dilys Morgan slipped it into the breast pocket of her uniform.

"I miss Sally," said Dilys. "She was a good worker. Some people thought she was quiet and withdrawn, but she was a typical shy country girl. It took a while for Sally to come out of her shell. Of course, there might be the odd photo on those social occasions where she's let her hair down and got as squiffy as the rest of us. But, it was nights like that where she seemed more like their daughter, you know?"

"Alexa was a wild child, according to the stories we've heard in the village," said Gus.

"Lexie was wild from the day she was born, Mr Freeman. Yet, Sally was always so level-headed. I could never understand what frightened them away. Have you learned why that was?"

"We haven't," said Gus. "No matter which line of enquiry we follow, there's nothing to suggest Sally had anything to fear. Ivan died eighty miles away. His killers don't appear to have any connection to Sally and Alexa. We're still trying to confirm what connected them to Ivan. Another level-headed man who kept to himself. Not a man to attract trouble."

"Did Ivan Kendall clean your windows?" asked Luke.

"No," said Dilys. "He called at houses on my street. My husband had found someone well before Ivan started his round. Who did you speak to in the village?"

"The police gave us a good deal of background," said Luke, "and we visited Ieuan Arlett up at the rugby club."

"After Ivan got made redundant, he showed a darker side of his nature," said Dilys Morgan. "Not like we'd seen in the past. You asked about the window cleaning. Ivan knocked on our door and spoke to my husband. They had often stood together, watching a match at the rugby club. Ivan wasn't best pleased when my husband said no. He worked cheaper than the competition, but Noah told him we would stay loyal to the firm we'd used for years."

"How did Ivan react?" asked Gus.

"Ivan didn't speak to Noah after that," said Dilys. "You'll find others in the village who will tell you the same. Instead, Ivan passed snide remarks in the club about knowing who your friends were. Everyone knew Ivan was struggling, but it wasn't as if we lived in the lap of luxury. Everyone's had it hard in the valleys."

"Did you hear of anything Ivan might do to get himself out of his financial hole?" asked Gus.

"Ivan had an allotment," said Dilys, "but what he grew there, I don't know. My Noah said Ivan spent a fair bit of time there instead of coming to the club to watch the games."

"Mr Arlett told us that Ivan did something different during the summer months," said Luke. "Did your husband ever learn what?"

"If I'm not working at the weekend, we get away. We own a motorhome we take to Porthcawl or as far as Tenby sometimes. So, Noah doesn't spend much time at the club in the summers. He wasn't that interested in what Ivan got up to as they weren't on speaking terms."

"We'll let you get back to your customers, Dilys," said Gus. "You've helped us a great deal already. If you uncover photos of Sally, that will be even better. We look forward to hearing from you."

"You're welcome, Mr Freeman, I'm sure. Here are the names of the four shops still open where Sally used to work."

Gus and Luke left Dilys Morgan to oversee what passed for the lunchtime rush in the village store.

"Small steps, Luke," said Gus. "The local police should have known about Ivan's allotment and his falling out with old friends who decided against becoming customers. Dilys Morgan painted a different picture of the man, didn't she?"

"We heard a slightly different description of Sally Kendall too, guv," said Luke. "When she was out with the girls, Sally was more carefree than at home. So we've gained more positives since we arrived here than we collected from DI Williams."

"Fingers crossed, Dilys was right, and her friends can retrieve those photos we need," said Gus. "We'll split up, Luke. You visit the other smaller shops. I'll walk out to the rugby club. It can't be over four hundred yards from here. Ieuan Arlett was there around this time the other day. I'll get him to explain the allotment business. I wonder why he didn't realise that was where Ivan was spending his summers. Those allotments skirt the field that contains the clubhouse."

"We couldn't see much of those allotments when we sat in his office, guv," said Luke. "And Ieuan would be busy behind the bar on Saturday afternoons."

"Maybe, Luke, but it's a village. Look at Urchfont. Everyone knew my business within hours. Whether it was the first time that Vera Butler stayed the night or the day Suzie moved in. Unless every single allotment holder is a rugby hater, someone will have mentioned seeing Ivan there."

Luke watched as Gus strode into the distance and then studied Dilys Morgan's list. His first port of call was a family-owned newsagent and general store. A young girl was on duty when he reached the counter at the far end of the tiny shop.

"Are you working alone today?" he asked, showing the girl his warrant card.

"My father's out the back," she replied. "I can get him."

"Please do," said Luke with a grin, "I don't think you worked here four years ago."

"No, I was still at Y Pant,"

"Do you remember Lexie Kendall?"

"Everyone remembers, Lexie," said the girl. "Once seen, never forgotten."

The girl disappeared through a beaded curtain and returned a minute later with her father. Luke could tell from the smell he brought with him he'd stepped outside for a cigarette.

"Mr Jones?" asked Luke.

"Martin Jones, that's right. Carys thought it was about the Kendall girl."

"Her mother, Sally, worked here, didn't she?" asked Luke.

"For a while. A few years back now," said Martin Jones.

"A good worker?"

"I had no trouble with her. She was popular with the customers. I was sad to see her leave. Honest as the day is long was Sally. Not like some I've employed since."

"Was there any reason for Sally to leave?" asked Luke.

"They paid more up the road in the big store. Money

was tight. Sally was with us when the firm Ivan worked for sacked two dozen employees. Several local families had a hard time of it after that."

"In a smaller shop such as this, do you have photos of your staff or occasions when you socialised where someone might have taken photos? We have nothing more recent than a wedding photo of Sally to help us trace where she went after leaving Pontyclun."

"Nothing like that, I'm afraid. I remember Sally telling me neither she nor Ivan had a passport. They'd never travelled outside of Wales, let alone abroad. Of course, that might have changed over the years. I wouldn't know."

"Why do you think she left the village so suddenly?" asked Luke.

"I thought she went to her mother's old house in Llanharry," said Martin Jones. "Sally was a home bird; there was no way she'd live in a big town or city."

"We heard that Sally was afraid of something, or someone, Mr Jones," said Luke. "She took Alexa away because she thought their lives were in danger. Sally believed the men who killed Ivan wanted her dead too."

"That makes no sense to me," said Martin Jones.

Luke noticed a reaction from Carys.

"What do you think, Carys?" he asked. "Lexie doesn't sound as if she'd be afraid of anything from what we've heard."

"Lexie had friends in the village," said Carys, "but she made enemies too."

"Some of these older boyfriends we've heard about were married. Is that what you mean?"

Carys nodded.

"They weren't all local guys she mixed with, either.

We've got the odd tearaway in the village, but two men I saw hanging around Lexie looked nasty. But, of course, they never came right into the village. I saw them up at the park a few times, though."

"Not at the rugby club then, Carys? You mean the large playing field where the football teams have a clubhouse?"

"That's right. In the summer, Lexie exercised the dogs at Ivor Park. Me and my mates kept out of her way. I saw that pair of rough-looking blokes watching Lexie from a distance a few times. Did you hear about her reputation?"

Luke nodded. Martin Jones waved a hand to show he was going for another smoke.

"We heard," said Luke. "Did she ever visit the shop when her mother worked here?"

"Once or twice," said Carys. "Lexie was only ten. She wasn't into boys then. Lexie used to badger her Mum for sweets and a comic."

"Why do you think this pair of older men were watching Lexie?" asked Luke.

"Well, I thought they were interested, you know," said Carys. "My mates and I gave them a wide berth and came back to the village if we ever saw them. They creeped us out."

"Have you seen them since Lexie and her mother left the village?"

"No, I haven't. Anyway, I don't go to the park now," said Carys, looking to see whether her father was on his way back. "I've got a boyfriend with a car."

"Your secret's safe with me," said Luke. "One last thing before I leave. Was there a particular reason for staying out of Lexie's way when you were at the park? Did you two not get on?"

"We knew one another, but we weren't that friendly. My Dad would have had kittens if I'd got up to the things she did. I didn't want to get tarred with the same brush. No, the dogs had to wear muzzles whenever Lexie brought them out. But they still frightened the living daylights out of me. That's why I kept my distance."

"Thanks, Carys," said Luke. "Thank your Dad for me too. If either of you remembers someone who might have a recent photo of Sally Kendall, call us on this number. Luke handed Carys a card and left the shop.

Luke walked out of the village towards the rugby club. As he approached the entrance he'd driven through the other afternoon, he saw Gus Freeman in the distance and smiled. Gus was on the other side of the hedge, talking to an older lady.

Gus would be in his element, discussing the merits of an allotment for people of a certain age. As he drew nearer, Gus saw him and pointed towards the bottom corner of the field. Luke turned left and made for the corner. A stile let him get into the allotments. Luke realised that the main entrance was from the housing estate at the opposite end.

"Luke," said Gus, "Meet Bethan Lewis, an avid gardener. Bethan's told me something about Ivan Kendall and why he rented the plot over there."

"Good afternoon, Mrs Lewis," said Luke. "Someone has worked hard on that plot in the past four years. Is that you?"

"It is, detective," replied Bethan. "I'm a cleaner over at the rugby club, and after Ivan Kendall died, I applied to the council to take over the mess he'd left behind. When I came to do my cleaning job every day, I could soon tell that his heart wasn't in it. He wasn't a gardener."

Mrs Lewis moved away to carry on working on her compost heap. Gus and Luke walked along the path towards the stile.

"I think we know now why Ivan rented it," said Luke. "Carys told me Lexie 'fetched them' rather than 'collected them' from someone."

"Bethan tells me that shed is very sturdy. Check the others on this patch of land. Most are in poor repair, or the owner substituted it for a robust plastic storage cabinet."

"Kendall needed a place to keep something other than gardening tools," said Luke.

"Something Lexie and Ivan wanted to keep from Sally," said Gus.

"Carys Jones from the newsagents told me the dogs Lexie exercised in the park had to wear a muzzle. She also told me two rough-looking men watched while she exercised the dogs on more than one occasion."

"Travellers?" said Gus.

"Maybe," said Luke. "Carys said they never came into the village itself. She only saw them on the outskirts, in wide-open places like the park and its football pitches."

"That's where we need to go next, Luke," Gus said. "Let's get back to the car."

Luke drove them out to Ivor Park. Gus imagined that as it was a Friday afternoon in mid-summer, they'd only find daisies on the football pitches. Luke parked alongside three other cars, and Gus could see several grown-ups coaching junior boys and girls in different parts of the park.

"Another example of what a thriving community they have here, Luke," said Gus.

"You haven't mentioned Ieuan Arlett, guv," said Luke. "How did he respond to your question about Ivan's allotment?"

"Arlett swore blind he'd never known that Kendall was over the other side of the hedge. I don't say I believe him, mind, but what can we do now?"

"Mrs Lewis gave you something more useful, guv," said Luke.

"That shed do you mean?" said Gus. "Yes, that ties in with what you learned from the corner shop you visited. Bethan gave me tips on how to improve my rhubarb crop too. So, it's been a good day so far."

"I gave the other shops on the list a miss, guv," said Luke. "I thought you'd want to visit this park sooner rather than later after what Carys told me. I can call in on them later this afternoon if you think it's necessary."

"Let's have a word with the adults standing on the side of the pitches first," said Gus. "I wonder whether anything went missing from here while that rough-looking pair your shop girl mentioned were in the vicinity."

"Four years ago, guv?" said Luke. "These two might have been playing then, not coaching."

"Harsh," said Gus. "What are they, in their late thirties, early forties?"

They could hear a tall, dark-haired man shouting as they got closer to the pitch. Gus wondered why the young girls, who looked nine or ten years old, gave up an afternoon playing computer games to have someone yell at them.

"Can I help you?" the man asked, turning his back on the kick-and-rush game behind him.

Gus explained who they were and what they were investigating. Luke sensed the man had something to hide.

"I remember Ivan Kendall," said the man, who introduced himself as Gethin Hughes. "It shocked a lot of people when he got killed. He was always so quiet."

"Did you know his wife, Sally?" asked Gus.

"I saw her in the supermarket if I went shopping with my wife."

"I imagine you knew Lexie better," said Luke. "She came here with the dogs, didn't she?"

"Not at first," said Gethin. "She was never interested in playing football. But then, Lexie started coming to watch matches and training sessions because there were plenty of men around. Her Dad was more interested in rugby."

"How old was she when she showed an interest in the players?" asked Luke.

"Fourteen, maybe," said Gethin. "Difficult to tell when they're not in school uniform, wearing make-up, and smoking, isn't it?"

"I wouldn't know," said Luke.

"When did you and Lexie hook up?" asked Gus. "Don't deny it. You've stood there shuffling your feet for the past few minutes."

"She was sixteen," said Gethin Hughes. "I was with Lexie the night her Dad got on the train to Cardiff. We were at the station. Lexie never told the police who she was with."

"Were you a married man four years ago, Mr Hughes?" asked Gus.

"I was; we married young," said Gethin Hughes, "there's not much to do around here when you're a teenager. After ten years, we got bored with one another. It happens. Lexie was young and always up for it. We saw one another for a month. I only met up with her twice after that Saturday night."

"Why did you stop seeing one another?" asked Luke.

"My wife got suspicious at the number of football meetings I had to attend. Also, Lexie's mother had a funeral to arrange. It was a tough time for both of them. Finally, I told Lexie we had to cool things for a while. She just shrugged and told me not to worry. They would not be around much longer, anyway."

"So, Lexie knew her mother wanted to move away not long after the funeral?" asked Gus.

"It was the end of June, beginning of July when Lexie ended things. She left school later in the month. Lexie planned to go to college in Bridgend in September, but because of her father's murder, she couldn't concentrate on her exams. As a result, I don't think she got the grades she needed."

"You seem to know a lot even though you no longer saw one another, Mr Hughes?" said Gus.

"It's a small village," replied Gethin Hughes. "Sally and Lexie were on everybody's mind because of what happened. I heard plenty of stories that summer. Lexie never found a job. She stayed at home until Sally's mother died."

"Her mother lived in Llanharry, didn't she?" asked Luke.

"That's why everyone thought that's where Sally went. She'd run away there more than once."

"Did Lexie ever give you a hint of where they might go?" asked Gus.

"Never spoke to her," said Gethin. "It was none of my business. So I wasn't that worried about where they went."

"Did you ever exercise the dogs with Lexie?" asked Luke.

"Once or twice," said Gethin. "We went to the allotments by the rugby club to collect them. They were a nightmare to control."

"What breed were they?" asked Luke.

"God knows. They were a crossbreed, I reckon. Even

though they were only twelve months old, they were so powerful. They doted on Lexie, though."

"When did you first notice the Kendalls had left the village?" asked Gus.

"I was hunting for a turkey crown in the supermarket with the wife. It was two weeks before Christmas, and Sally wasn't on the tills. So I asked the security guy when I returned our trolley to the rack in front of the store. He told me she quit her job, and Sally and Lexie moved away. So I asked where they went, and he said Sally wouldn't let on."

"What happened to the dogs?" asked Gus.

"No idea," said Gethin Hughes. "Lexie had stopped coming here after her father died."

"We'll let you get back to your game," said Luke. "One of your girls has just scored an own goal. She's the one standing in the goalmouth crying her eyes out."

Gethin Hughes turned away and trotted over to console the little mite. Gus and Luke noticed the other man walking their way.

"Everything okay?" he asked.

"We were asking Gethin what he knew about Lexie Kendall and her dogs," said Gus.

"What's it to you, then?"

Luke explained who they were.

"Oh, right. Mervyn Jessop, that's me. I train the junior boys for one week; Gethin looks after the girls, and then we swap over the next time. It was Lexie Kendall you were asking after, was it? Yes, well, Gethin knew her better than me. As for the dogs, Lexie's father bought them as pups. Heaven knows what Ivan was thinking. I watched those dogs drag Lexie around this park week after week."

"Did you notice anyone else taking an interest in the dogs, Mr Jessop?" asked Gus.

"The tinkers, you mean?" asked Jessop. "I saw them loitering when Lexie brought the dogs here."

"When would that have been, Mr Jessop?" asked Luke.

"It was four years ago," said Jessop, "hard to be accurate. The first time was in the summer, while I was creosoting the clubhouse walls and helping repair the roof. Lexie came here every weekend through the winter. We get quite a few people up here during the football season. It's not so easy to spot strangers, then. The last time I saw those tinkers was around a month to six weeks before Ivan died."

"Were they speaking to Lexie?" asked Gus.

"No, they stood beside a clapped-out white van, watching her run with the dogs. I feared for her safety, despite the loose morals she had. So, several committee members agreed to walk over with me and tell the tinkers to move on. We told them there was nothing worth nicking in the clubhouse. They gave us a few choice words and then drove away."

"Have they been back?" Gus asked.

"I've seen the van, on and off," said Mervyn Jessop. "They visit the village from time to time, looking for work as tree surgeons. You'll find their cards in everyone's recycling box."

"Where do you think they live?" asked Luke.

"There are a handful of unauthorised sites close by the village. The van's number plate showed its registration was from Cardiff in the early Noughties. The first two letters were CB. They could have stayed on one of the city's authorised sites."

"I don't suppose you took a note of the rest of the number plate?" asked Luke.

"They moved on, so there was no need. The van was so dirty it was hard to read."

"Can you describe these men?" asked Gus.

"Medium height, medium build, dark-haired, with a swarthy complexion. The pair wore ragged clothing, with jeans and always well-worn labourer's boots, regardless of the time of year."

"Anything else?" asked Gus. "How old?"

"Older than me," said Mervyn Jessop, "mid-forties, maybe. They were like two peas in a pod. Twins, I reckon."

"That's a help, Mr Jessop," said Gus. "You're very observant."

"I give my free time to community projects like this one, Mr Freeman. I'm a PCSO in my day job."

"I'm not surprised," said Gus, "have you been at it for long?"

"Only eighteen months," said Mervyn Jessop. "I was a double-glazing sales agent before that."

"That company's loss is the community's gain," said Gus. "We'll let you get back to the lads."

"I don't think I've got a future Welsh international among that lot, but it keeps them out of trouble."

"I'm sure their parents and the good folk of Pontyclun will be forever in your debt," said Gus.

Mervyn Jessop trotted off to rejoin the red-faced lads racing around the pitch.

"That was a pleasant thing to say, guv," said Luke.

"I'm sure Mr Jessop does his best, but some parents might not be so keen to learn that Mr Hughes isn't above a little underage sex if the opportunity arises."

"He told us Lexie was sixteen, guv," said Luke.

"Well, he would, wouldn't he?" replied Gus. "Mandy Rice-Davies was Welsh too, Luke, but I expect her famous quote would be before your time."

"You're right, guv. Back to the car?" asked Luke.

"I don't think you need to visit the other small shops, Luke. We've covered the period when Ivan lost his job and the years before his murder. Any photos you found would be as dated as the wedding photo. No, we'll get back across the bridge and find out what Neil and Alex have to say."

## Chapter Eleven

"WE'RE BACK," cried Gus as he and Luke exited the lift. "Sorry, did I wake anyone?"

"Someone's had a good day," said Neil.

"We didn't do so badly ourselves, Neil," said Alex.

Gus flopped into his chair.

"After a fruitless visit to Cardiff Central," he began, "we spoke to half a dozen people in Pontyclun that the local police missed four years ago. What we learned has given us plenty to work on."

"Vaughn and Shaun Corbett, guv," said Neil.

"Forty-seven-year-old twins," said Alex, "part-time tree surgeons."

"Stan Wakefield didn't have his wife to keep him quiet this morning. He described these two as regular visitors to the camp. Their uncle was a chap called Jack Ayres. He's dead now, but between 2010 and 2017, the twins stayed at the camp for several weeks at a time. Stan said they arrived on the first day of Spring each year."

"Mr Wakefield confirmed the pair were in the Westbury area at the time of Kendall's murder," said Alex.

"Stan also told us they would have been there at the time Sid Dyer had his fatal accident."

"That accident occurred after a stormy night," said Gus. "The coroner decided Dyer lost control of his bike in high winds as an HGV passed him. I'm not sure we could prove that these two were responsible."

"We've checked evidence recovered at the scene, guv," said Alex. "Stan Wakefield said the Corbett brothers' white van was always filthy. Soil samples from Dyer's clothing and the bike's pannier didn't match the grass verge. So forensics assumed it to have come from the other vehicle. There was no way to check because the driver didn't realise he'd hit anyone. Well, that's what they thought."

"We returned to the campsite after lunch," said Neil, "and collected samples from where the van would have parked. Then, after a stormy night, their van collected large quantities of grime negotiating soggy grass and a water-logged gateway."

"We're hoping the unmatched samples that forensics collected four years ago will have features that place them firmly in the campsite. It's still circumstantial, but two years ago, the police had stopped looking for Kendall's killers. They wouldn't link Dyer's tragic accident to the travellers' campsite."

"Stan Wakefield identified the Corbett brothers by name, did he?" asked Luke.

"No, Jack Ayres had a large family spread over Wales," said Neil. "He came from the North originally. We found birth records for his three brothers and two sisters. The eldest sister, Bronwen, married Keith Corbett from Tredegar in June 1970. The twins arrived ten months later."

"Excellent work," said Gus. "We know who we're looking for now. What about motive, lads? Have you worked that out too?"

"No, guv," said Alex. "But the grin on Luke's face suggests you're closer than us."

"We're almost there, Alex," said Gus. "You can read the convoluted version in the Freeman Files after Luke and I have updated our records. In simple terms, it was those dogs Lexie exercised. They were eighteen months old, fiery, and always wore muzzles. We don't think Sally was aware of their existence. Ivan kept them in a shed on his allotment and tended them during the week. Lexie exercised them at weekends and during school holidays. The Corbett brothers arrived in Pontyclun and spotted the dogs. I guess they followed Lexie to the allotments, waited until she left, and then stole them. Ivan found they were missing when he went to the allotments on Saturday afternoon."

"How did Ivan know who took them?" asked Alex.

"Why didn't Lexie tell her mother she knew where her Dad was going?" asked Lydia.

"I said we were *almost* there," said Gus, spreading his hands wide.

"Did you get any new photos?" asked Blessing.

"A helpful lady from Tesco Express promised to send photos through Blessing," said Gus. "It might be Monday, though."

"What do we do next, guv?" asked Neil.

"Based on their previous travel history, the Corbett brothers will be somewhere in Wales. I'll phone DI Williams and explain what we've learned. He can locate them and get them in for questioning. We'll continue to hunt for Sally and her daughter."

"How do we explain Alex's question, guv," said Luke. "How did Luke know who took them?"

"What do *you* think, Luke?" asked Gus.

"Lexie was at school in March, guv. The Easter holiday was weeks away. So Ivan exercised the dogs during the week. Then, perhaps, he spotted the van trailing him around the village on his window-cleaning round. The Corbett brothers might even have approached Ivan and offered to buy the dogs."

"That works, guv," said Alex. "And Lexie couldn't tell Sally a thing on Saturday night because the dogs were a secret between her and her Dad. Lexie had no idea her Dad was going to die. Later, she could have told Sally about the men staring at her at Ivor Park. That's what scared Sally into thinking they were in danger. Lexie was more at risk than Sally because she could identify the killers and knew why Ivan travelled to Westbury. Ivan made the trip to rescue the dogs and bring them home."

"There's one missing piece in this jigsaw," said Gus.

"How did the brothers know Ivan was going to be at Westbury station at a quarter to midnight?" said Neil.

"Ivan only had sixty-five pounds in his pocket," said Luke. "How valuable were those dogs?"

"Ivan kept one secret from Sally," said Gus. "What's to say he didn't keep another? Trainer and Sinclair never considered robbery as a motive. Vaughn and Shaun Corbett could have been clever, left a small amount on the body, and took the balance of what Ivan agreed to pay to get his dogs back. But instead, the brothers kept the money and the dogs. Therefore Ivan had to die."

"How did Ivan plan to get home?" asked Neil.

"I don't think Ivan planned that far ahead," said Gus. "He was naïve enough to believe that if he gave the brothers the money, they'd hand over the dogs. So Ivan was happy to sit on the station platform until he could use those return tickets."

"Ivan needed a contact number, guv," said Neil. "Where might that come from?"

"Hang on," said Gus, "I met a fellow gardener at the allotments this afternoon. I've got her number here. Don't look like that, Lydia. She wanted me to tell her how my champagne rhubarb responded to the treatment she suggested. You're never too old to learn new tricks. Mrs Lewis? It's Gus Freeman here. When you took over the patch of ground from Mr Kendall, was there anything left lying around in the shed?"

Neil and the others waited while Gus listened to Bethan Lewis.

"That's fine, Mrs Lewis. No, I won't forget to call you. Goodbye."

"Any joy, guv?" asked Luke.

"Bethan Lewis said that the council cleared the shed of various small tools and the cages where Ivan kept the dogs. There was nothing left inside except spiders."

"That's a shame," said Neil.

"We can't expect the answer to drop in our laps, Neil," said Gus. "We're not in a TV drama where the detectives must solve the case in fifty-two minutes. This is real life."

"Mervyn Jessop, the PCSO made a telling remark, guv," said Luke.

"Ah yes, the business cards. The Corbett brothers counted arboriculture among their skill sets. Jessop said that at the appropriate time of the year, the recycling trucks in Pontyclun included hundreds of discarded flyers. I imagine them driving around the estates, noting houses with trees and shrubs in need of TLC. Then they dropped a card through the door when the homeowner was at work. If we can confirm that Ivan Kendall ever had a card in his possession, we will have squared the circle."

Gus's phone rang again.

"That was quick, Mrs Morgan. Bless you. Send them through now, and we'll get started."

Gus looked at the clock on the far wall.

"We're getting close to unlocking the secrets of this case," he said. "I can feel it. Dilys Morgan from the supermarket has a file of two dozen photos from Christmas 2013."

"I don't mind staying on, guv," said Blessing.

"If Geoff Mercer were in his office, I'd call him and get clearance for overtime," said Gus.

"The ACC will still be at London Road, guv," said Neil.

"The ACC might say no, Neil," said Gus. "No, I'll take an executive decision. We'll stop at five as usual tonight. I'll get Dai Williams to start the ball rolling. Alex and Lydia, you have a busy weekend ahead. I don't wish to stand in the way of that. We look forward to hearing all about it on Monday. Can either of you two lads help Blessing and me tomorrow morning?"

"Count me in," said Luke.

"Me too, guv," said Neil.

"Well done," said Gus. "If the ACC thinks I overstepped the mark, I'll sort out time off in lieu. If we can tie up loose ends before Monday's meeting, it should soothe his fevered brow."

Gus checked his computer for a new item in his inbox.

"Here we are, Blessing. Plenty of shots of the supermarket staff having a splendid night at the Indian restaurant. Dilys Morgan has identified which reveller Sally is on the first one. She appears in every single photo. We should find her from these."

"I've added Sally's maiden name to the search, guv," said Blessing.

"Right, get everything set up for the morning, Blessing. I suggest the rest of you update your digital files in the forty minutes left today. I'll make that call to Cardiff Central now."

At five o'clock, Alex and Lydia made their way to the lift. They were excited and nervous in equal measure.

"See you on Monday," called Neil. "Good luck."

"Thanks, Neil," said Lydia. "I'll discover tonight whether I inherited my father's sea legs."

After they left, Neil puffed out his cheeks.

"Blimey, I don't think I could spend the best part of eight hours on a ferry."

"I was sick on the switchback ride at the fair," said Blessing.

"Time to go," said Luke. "Come on, Neil. Let's help Blessing escape the car park without putting a dent in her newly refurbished Micra."

"Cheeky," said Gus as he tidied his desk.

"I parked between Neil and Luke first thing this morning, guv," said Blessing. "Better for them to err on the side of caution."

"I'll see you at nine o'clock," said Gus as the trio headed for the lift.

Alone in the office, Gus called Suzie at London Road, but there was no reply. She must have left for home already. Gus left her a message on the landline. He wanted everything he had collected updated before they started work in the morning. Another thirty minutes should do it, and the

Lamb was open until late. After that, there was plenty of time to catch up with Brett Penman.

Gus drove into the gateway of the bungalow a few minutes after six.

Suzie met him in the hallway. She had changed into her gardening clothes.

"I got your message," said Suzie. "You've had a busy day."

"Several pieces of the jigsaw fell into place," said Gus. "Dai Williams has people searching for the Corbett brothers that I mentioned. The twins battered Ivan Kendall to death in the station toilets. Of that, I have no doubt. Why the dogs were so important, I don't yet understand. A chap called Gethin Jones thought they were a crossbreed."

"Fighting dogs?" asked Suzie.

"I don't profess to know much about the matter," said Gus. "We won't know the full story until we locate Lexie Kendall. I'd like to think we'd find both mother and daughter tomorrow morning. Now that we have better photos at our disposal."

"Have a shower and get changed. Let's spend an hour at the allotment and then drop by the Lamb. If Brett's celebrating, we'll eat there and drink with him. If you need to be bright-eyed and bushy-tailed tomorrow, you must rein yourself in. I'll go riding as usual. Do you expect to work through, or will you get home at lunchtime?"

"No promises, Suzie," said Gus. "You know how these things go. With luck, I can avoid another trip to Wales. Luke and Neil can do the necessary while I work with Blessing in the office. The lads can call me later if they've put the finishing touches on the case. I'll tie the lot in a neat bow on Monday morning and drop it on the ACC's desk when I get to London Road for our scheduled meeting."

"Ever the optimist," said Suzie, pushing Gus toward the bathroom.

Gus and Suzie arrived at the allotment at twenty to seven. There was no sign of Bert Penman. Clemency Bentham was cleaning her tools and would soon get ready to cycle home.

"Hello, you two," she said. "You don't have much time to work on the land this evening."

Gus looked at the rain clouds gathering behind the church clock. He remembered the forecast from first thing this morning—curses foiled again.

"It's the thought that counts," he said. "Have you heard any news from Brett today?"

"I've been visiting my sick parishioners," said Clemency. "My sturdy bicycle and I have travelled miles today. I'm hoping to see the benefit on the scales when I get home."

"Does that mean you won't be in the Lamb tonight?" asked Suzie. "I thought you were keen to hear how Brett's interview went."

Clemency wiped a lock of hair from her brow.

"Irene's got a bad back," she said. "I don't like entering the bar alone if I can avoid it."

"That's easily solved," said Gus. "Drop by the bungalow when you're ready, and we'll provide an escort."

Clemency blushed.

"Gosh, I don't want Brett to think I'm desperate."

"You can always chat to Bert," said Suzie. "He's bound to be there."

"Take the plunge, Reverend," said Gus. "Remember those boyfriends in Dorchester and up at Oxford? It might be five years since your last date, but it's also been a while for Brett."

"Was that the first spot of rain I felt?" said Clemency.

"Don't change the subject," said Suzie. "I'm afraid you're right, though."

"A light shower won't stop me," said Gus. "You two get off home. We'll see you at around half-past eight, Reverend."

Clemency was soon scooting off on her bicycle, with Suzie jogging behind her. Gus carried on checking his rhubarb. Another month and it should be at its best. He couldn't wait to try out Bethan Lewis's ideas next year. It was no good; the light shower was growing in volume. If he didn't move soon, he'd get soaked dashing back to the bungalow. If the Gods smiled on them in the morning, he could return after lunch. With any luck, the storm would have passed.

Suzie was in the living room when he reached home. He grabbed a towel from the bathroom to dry his hair.

"Clemency was right," said Suzie. "Never mind, you can ask me how my day went."

"I always love hearing different aspects of police work," said Gus. "The daily grind of murder cases can be so wearing."

"I trust you're not being facetious, Gus Freeman," said Suzie, "we received good news today. We will soon be able to apply to magistrates for Stalking Protection Orders to help safeguard victims. It would require the respondent to notify the police of their personal details within three days of receiving the order, and anyone breaching the requirements could be in jail for five years."

"Anything that provides victims with more protection from the outset is positive," said Gus.

"My role is to continue to raise awareness of stalking as a criminal offence," said Suzie. "And to encourage victims to feel safe in reporting their concerns."

"Police forces across the UK are recording significant increases in the offence. That increase in reporting results from officers raising awareness and improvements in crime recording. Wiltshire is at the forefront of that initiative."

"Victims must be at the heart of everything we do, Gus. I want to help the most vulnerable victims across our county through the criminal justice process."

"How long will these protection orders stay in place after our officers applied for them?" asked Gus.

"At least two years," said Suzie. "That's a reasonable period. Stalking is a serious crime with a devastating effect on the lives of victims and those around them."

"I know I can rely on you to do what you can to bring offenders to justice and safeguard victims, Suzie. It's a subject you're passionate about, I can tell. I think you could establish something that will significantly impact the victims. It's one more step on the journey to you making Chief Constable."

"Just when I thought you were serious," said Suzie.

"Hang on," said Gus. "I remember that speech you gave after the raid on the cannabis factory above the village. The camera loved you."

"You're too kind, but looks alone won't win me a position like that. I'm not 'woke' enough."

"What do we need to do to get ready?" asked Gus.

"A change of clothes for both of us," said Suzie, "and then you must try to do something with your hair. You look as if you've been dragged through a hedge backwards."

"People pay a fortune to get this look," said Gus.

He ducked as a cushion headed his way.

Suzie was still getting ready when Clemency rang the front doorbell.

"Do I look decent?" she asked.

"Laura Ashley would have been proud, Reverend," said Gus. "An English rose if ever I saw one."

"The rain has stopped, thank goodness. Oh, and the scales gave me a boost to my confidence. Another pound lost."

Suzie emerged from the bedroom. Gus had never met anyone who could turn smart-casual into something that took your breath away like Suzie. He made a note to show her later how appreciative he was.

"There weren't many cars in the car park when I raced home earlier," he said.

"Not the silence of the Lamb joke again, Gus, please," said Suzie.

Gus followed Suzie and Clemency outside and locked the door behind them.

Suzie had to agree that Gus was right for a change. It was a quiet Friday night in the Lamb.

"That's Friday the thirteenth for you," said Suzie.

"Not in front of the Reverend, Suzie," said Gus.

"I can't see Bert or Brett," said Clemency.

"Let's order anyway," said Gus. "I don't think the Reverend will settle for a Chinese takeaway after closing time."

"It wouldn't be the first," said Clemency. "But now that I've got my weight moving in the right direction, I want to keep going. A small portion of something healthy from the menu will suffice."

By half-past nine, they had eaten and were settling in for a good natter over their usual variety of drinks—an elderflower cordial for Clemency and a large glass of Chardonnay for Suzie. Gus deferred to the sensible option of a bottle of lager, given his spot of overtime tomorrow.

Brett Penman came through from the car park at a

quarter to ten. He collected a gin and tonic at the bar and came over.

"May I join you?" he said.

"We thought you might have been here when we arrived," said Gus. "Is Bert not with you tonight?"

"We had a meal in Swindon earlier. I was driving, so I stuck to a non-alcoholic lager. Grandad was in the mood for a party, so I let him drink as much as he wished. He was asleep in the chair when I came out."

"Don't keep us in suspense," said Gus. "How did the interview go?"

"I think they'd made their minds up before I got there," said Brett, looking glum.

"Oh, dear," said Clemency.

"I start on the first of next month," laughed Brett. "Shall I get four glasses of bubbly?"

Gus glanced at Clemency Bentham.

The look on her face was something to behold.

### Saturday, 14 July 2018

"WAFFLES OR A FRIED BREAKFAST?" asked Gus.

"You carry on," said Suzie, "I need to catch up on my beauty sleep."

"What do you think happened after we left the pub last night?"

"We were a touch obvious," said Suzie, "leaving the two of them alone in the bar."

"I didn't hear the Reverend collect her bicycle," said Gus.

"I'm not surprised, considering, you know," said Suzie.

"I was eager to show my appreciation."

"You were certainly eager."

Gus had a look outside the door.

"Her trusty steed has gone," he called out.

"Her knight in shining armour didn't carry her home then."

"I'm having waffles," said Gus, "can I prepare Madam's muesli and yoghurt?"

Suzie strolled through from the bedroom.

"You won't stop until I get out of bed, will you?"

"Can you see that sun peeping through the clouds? You'll have fine weather for your ride, and we can have a picnic to fortify us at the allotment this afternoon. I'll call you from the office to let you know whether our fun starts early or late afternoon."

"I hope you finish the case without mishap," said Suzie. "I'll call Clemency later at the rectory for a progress report."

Gus left Suzie with her bowl of damp cardboard and a cup of coffee. He showered and dressed. When he returned to the kitchen, Suzie was clearing the breakfast things.

"I'll get going," said Gus, "I can get a few things done before the others arrive."

"Have an arresting day," said Suzie.

"I'm hoping Dai Williams will do that part this weekend. Our job is to give him the ammunition to send Vaughn and Shaun Corbett away for a long stretch."

A Saturday morning drive through Devizes and on to the Old Police Station wasn't a regular occurrence. Thank goodness, Gus thought. There was less traffic, that was true, but you only needed a couple of weekend drivers or the dreaded holidaymaker heading for the coast to slow progress to a crawl.

Forty-five minutes after leaving the bungalow, Gus entered the lift on the ground floor. Luke had arrived before him. Neil and Blessing should be less than ten minutes away.

"The search for Sally and Lexie is paramount this morning, guv, isn't it?" said Luke.

"Yes, Luke. Blessing's our expert today, in Lydia's absence. That change of surname might prove to be key. We've stuck with Kendall throughout the investigation to date. But, if Sally wanted to stay hidden from the Corbett twins, then a name change helps."

"A change of look too, guv?" asked Luke.

Gus heard the lift descend to the ground floor.

"I spotted that, Luke," said Gus. "Sally opted for highlights at Christmas 2013. A distinct change from the mousy colour hair she had in their wedding photo. Might she go darker to hide the increasing number of grey hairs? Or make a total switch to blonde?"

"Morning, all," said Neil. He had Blessing Umeh with him.

"I'm parked on the end of the row, guv," said Blessing. "Neil told me to leave a space between you and me."

"Very wise," said Gus. "Right. Are we ready to start?"

"Neil and I discussed things in the lift, guv," said Blessing. "I'll concentrate on Sally Kendall or Prosser. Neil will look for Lexie. As soon as I find a likely location for Sally, I'll advise him. Can Luke help me, guv?"

"Sure, whatever works best, Blessing," said Gus. "I'm going to read through each of the team's updates from yesterday to see if we missed anything. You will be busier than me, so just this once, I'll tackle the Gaggia at ten. We'll review what we've discovered over coffee and alter our parameters if necessary."

"Got it, guv,"

"At ten to ten, Gus looked up from his computer screen. He was bang up to date. He couldn't fault what they'd done so far. There were no significant flaws in the strategy they'd adopted.

Gus sensed Blessing and Luke were checking their facts before committing themselves.

"Do you have something?" he asked.

"Why don't you and Neil come and see guv?" asked Luke.

The mature woman with short, dark hair smiling at the camera was Sally Kendall.

Now called Sammy Prosser, she was a Sales Negotiator for an estate agent in Crickhowell, in the Brecon Beacons.

"How far is that from Pontyclun?" asked Gus.

"An hour's drive, guv," said Blessing.

"Did you get that, Neil?" asked Luke.

"Crick something," said Neil. "That could help things along. I've got the enhanced school photo of Lexie as she could look aged twenty. I've searched and searched online, but she's not in the obvious social media places."

"Did you check for Lexie Prosser and Kendall?" asked Blessing.

"I tried every combination of first name and surname," said Neil.

"What if she's married?" asked Luke.

"I can't find a marriage registered anywhere in South Wales," said Blessing.

"Right, Neil," said Gus. "Call the estate agents where her mother works. Someone might be in the office this morning. Get a contact number, and then you and Luke can drive to Wales to interview her. Surely, she will know where her daughter's got to. Any questions?"

"No, guv," said Luke. "We know what to ask."

"Blessing and I will continue to search for Lexie. I'll call you if we find further information while you're en route. Who's driving?"

"Me, guv," said Luke. "We should reach Crickhowell at around eleven o'clock. Neil can keep his phone handy."

"Good," said Gus. "I don't expect to be here this afternoon. So, whatever you learn, call me on my mobile."

"Ms Powell isn't in the office today, Guv," said Neil ten minutes later, "but her manager provided a home number. Sally lives on Oakfield Drive. I think my call came as a shock, guv. She wasn't keen to speak to us, but I insisted. I told her a quiet chat over a cup of coffee was preferable to going to the police station for a formal interview."

"You nicked a line from my playbook, Neil. You're learning," said Gus. "Off you go then, you two, and good hunting."

After Neil and Luke left the office, Blessing took over the search for Alexa or Lexie.

"Why wouldn't she be on the usual social media sites?" she asked.

"Remember what Luke said after we returned from talking to Ieuan Arlett," said Gus. "Luke wondered whether we needed to look for a Sexy Lexie online. Alexa left school with fewer qualifications than she had hoped. That scuppered her dreams of a college education. Gethin Hughes told us his ex-girlfriend never found a job before leaving the village. Maybe, we need to delve into the murkier parts of the internet to find Lexie."

"If Lexie's a working girl," said Blessing, "this Hub version of the school photo won't be much use. Even if some men get turned on by the school uniform."

Gus thought of Gethin Hughes.

"What happens if you crop the photo to produce a headshot?" asked Gus.

"The resolution wasn't great anyway, guv," said Blessing. "It gets even more blurred if we concentrate on a tiny part of the original school photo. Look."

Gus had to agree. No wonder the search routines weren't giving meaningful results.

"Did you and Neil use the same search parameters?" he asked.

"We agreed that as Sally Kendall was a home bird, she'd live within a twenty-mile radius of Pontyclun, guv," said Blessing. "It took longer to find her because Crickhowell is forty miles away."

"So, Neil's social media searches only extended twenty miles from Pontyclun?"

"No, guv, Sally had zero social media presence. So I checked for photos of her in any capacity. That's why I hit on a newspaper advert for her estate agency that featured staff members by name. Neil trawled for Alexa or Lexie, with Kendall or Prosser as a surname, and found nothing on Twitter and Facebook. According to his notes, Neil also looked at the other popular sites without luck."

"Do you know where else we might check?" Gus asked.

"There are adult services adverts we could look at, guv," said Blessing.

"As a young copper in Salisbury, I saw women looking for business on street corners and moved them on," said Gus. "We cleared their cards from telephone boxes, too, if we received complaints from shocked senior citizens."

"You can find whatever you're looking for online now, guv," said Blessing, "and check the reviews before you buy. My father would have a fit if he knew what I've had to deal with since I've been a detective."

"I'll get us a coffee, Blessing. I can't help, I'm afraid," said Gus. "You know better than me where to look. Sorry if that came out wrong."

Gus went to the restroom while Blessing made a start. He returned five minutes later with their drinks. Blessing was concentrating so hard on her screen that Gus didn't want to interrupt her.

"Your coffee will get cold, Blessing," he said ten minutes later.

"No luck, guv, and that could be good news. Nobody called Lexie or Alexa is advertising anywhere across South Wales. I've checked ads for massages in the comfort of your home, the lot."

"You might have stumbled on something there, Blessing," said Gus. "We had a case in Swindon that centred on a massage parlour. None of the girls used their proper names; they chose something exotic. I'll call Neil and ask him to press Sammy Prosser on Lexie's whereabouts and what she does for a living."

Gus called Neil.

"Hi there, guv. We're just crossing the Severn Bridge. Have you found anything?"

"Not really, Neil. We wonder whether Lexie works in adult entertainment or at a massage parlour using an assumed name. Tread carefully with her mother. They could have lived separate lives for some time."

"Got it, guv," said Neil.

He ended the call and tutted. As if Sally hadn't suffered enough.

# Chapter Twelve

ON THE WELSH side of the Bridge, Luke and Neil were soon entering the bustling small town of Crickhowell. Luke negotiated the narrow streets and found Oakfield Drive. As he parked the car, Neil nudged his elbow.

"That's four curtains that have twitched already, Luke. Sammy Prosser can't get many visitors."

Luke knocked on the front door. Sammy Prosser answered at once and stepped back to allow them to enter.

"Come into the living room," she said. "How did you find me?"

"We asked people at the rugby club, at Ivor Park, and in the shops where you worked," said Luke. "Nobody had a clue where you were. Then, yesterday, one of your former colleagues sent us photos from a Christmas party just before you left the village. That helped us find you. The change of name and hairstyle might fool the locals, but we soon realised you were Sally Kendall."

"We've identified the men we suspect murdered your husband," said Neil. "They'll get arrested in the next twenty-four to forty-eight hours. So you needn't hide away any longer, Sally. Neither does Alexa. I'm sure you want to call your daughter to give her the good news."

"I prefer Sammy," she replied, "and Alexa and I don't talk these days."

"That's a shame. When did Alexa tell you about the dogs?" asked Luke.

"The day after the police discovered Ivan's body," said Sammy.

"Tell us about that weekend," said Luke.

"Ivan was quiet and withdrawn that Saturday evening. I knew something was up for weeks. I thought Ivan had another woman, but there were no signs on his body or clothes. Then Ivan left without a word. Alexa came home around ten and said she saw her father at the station boarding the Cardiff train. He wasn't there when I woke up the next morning. After lunch, I called the police. They didn't seem worried because only a few hours had passed since he'd gone. I kept telling them it was out of character, but nobody listened. They turned up the next day with a policewoman with a face like a wet weekend. I knew what the detective had to say before he opened his mouth. Alexa came downstairs when she heard me cry out. After they left, she told me everything."

"Ivan had bought two young pups and kept them in a shed at the allotments," said Luke.

"Not quite," said Sammy. "Ivan was on his window-cleaning round on a Saturday morning, and someone said they couldn't afford to pay him. They had to get rid of their pets because money was so tight. Ivan took two pups in payment, and Alexa helped him look after them. I under-stood why they kept it a secret. I'm not too fond of dogs.

They frighten me to death. I wouldn't have had them in the house."

"So, they cared for the dogs for a year without your knowledge. What did Ivan intend to do with them?"

"Alexa said her Dad reckoned the chap who handed over the pups did not understand how valuable they could be to the right buyer. Ivan planned to sell them when they were fully grown."

"Which would have been around fourteen to sixteen months," said Neil. "Did Alexa mention the travellers?"

"Not straight away. Alexa told me someone stole the dogs from the shed and her Dad went to get them back. After the funeral, Alexa mentioned the men turning up at the park when she exercised the dogs. She was scared they would come back for her. I told her not to be daft, but she said they visit the village yearly. They'd recognise her eventually. My mother died in November, and I knew that was our chance to start a new life. I sold Mum's place, changed my name and appearance, and kept out of the limelight. I thought I'd left it behind me. Then you called this morning."

"How did Ivan plan to get the dogs back?" asked Luke. "Did he agree on an amount?"

"Alexa wouldn't tell me how much that was or how Ivan got the money," Sammy replied. "We were broke."

"We believe Ivan took whatever sum they agreed to Westbury that night, thinking the men who stole his dogs would do the honourable thing and hand them over," said Luke.

"Ivan did it for your daughter," said Neil. "Alexa doted on those dogs. So even if it cost Ivan the money he hoped to earn from selling them, he thought it worth it."

"Why did they have to kill him?" asked Sammy Prosser.

"We may learn that in time," said Luke. "Officers from Cardiff Central will interview his killers over the coming days. Do you have an address or contact number for Alexa? We want to speak to her. We have several questions to put to her."

"Alexa left home eighteen months after we moved. This place was too conservative for her. She moved from one minimum wage job to another and never stuck at anything. As soon as she hit eighteen, she moved to Bridgend and now my daughter dances for a living."

"In a nightclub?" asked Neil.

"You're a police officer. You don't need me to draw you a picture. Ivan would be heartbroken. I'm heartbroken."

"We'll find her," said Luke. "We're sorry you two are estranged. When my boss and I talked to people at the supermarket, they told us how fond they were of you. Without Dilys Morgan's help, we would never have found you. Now that any danger has passed, perhaps you might be ready to get in touch again. I'm sure Dilys would like that."

"Maybe, but everyone would ask about Alexa. I don't know if I could stand the shame. Is that it, then? Will you go to Bridgend to find Alexa now?"

"Yes," said Neil. "We can give her a message if you wish?"

"Just tell her I love her."


"WHAT GUS SAYS IS RIGHT, isn't it?" said Luke as they drove away from Oakfield Drive.

"Usually," said Neil. "Which saying do you mean?"

"Ivan died four years ago, yet the repercussions echo through his family."

"I'm sure there were more questions we should have asked," said Neil.

"I thought it kinder to ease off on the poor woman. We need to get the answers from Lexie," said Luke. "Her mother didn't know where the money came from or how much it was. Lexie will know. Also, Lexie's more likely to know how Ivan contacted the Corbett brothers to arrange the meeting."

"It shouldn't take long to find her in Bridgend," said Neil. "Even with a population of over one hundred thousand, there can't be that many strip clubs, can there?"

Neil was right. An hour later, they sat opposite Alexa Kendall, or Satin, as the glossy photos in the foyer had styled her.

The young woman didn't want to talk to them, but Luke had described the alternative.

"What time do you start work?" asked Luke.

"Five o'clock," she replied. "Why? Were you thinking of staying?"

"We're on duty," said Neil. "We've just come from your home in Crickhowell."

"What are you after, anyway?" asked Lexie.

"We set out this week to find your father's killers," said Luke, "and in that regard, we've succeeded."

Lexie's eyes narrowed, but she didn't comment.

"Yes," said Neil, "Vaughn and Shaun Corbett, the travellers who frightened you when they kept pestering you at Ivor Park, will soon be in custody. You have nothing to fear now."

"Did they ever come to the house?" asked Luke.

"No," said Lexie. "I only saw them at the park or near the rugby club. They watched where I took Bubble and Squeak."

"Odd names for Staffordshire bull terriers," said Luke.

"They were a Staffie cross," said Lexie. "Different things get thrown together. Dad thought it suited them."

"Why didn't you tell your Mum on Saturday night that you knew where he'd gone and why?" asked Neil.

"Dad said always to keep the dogs a secret from Mum. So I knew he would do something daft after we found someone had stolen them that afternoon. But it was still a surprise to see him at the station."

"So, what happened?" asked Neil. "You went to take them for their exercise, and they had gone."

"Yeah, I ran back and found Dad. He was still collecting money from people on his round. Dad said he guessed it was those two tinkers and was going to call the number on the card."

"Where did the card come from?" asked Luke.

"Those men went to the rugby club on Wednesday while Dad cleaned their windows. The tinkers told him they wanted to buy the dogs. Dad said they weren't for sale. They left the card under the windscreen wiper on his van and told him to call if he changed his mind."

"How much did they offer?" asked Luke.

"Five hundred," said Lexie.

"When did your Dad call the Corbett's," asked Neil.

"Two o'clock, maybe, no later. We used the public phone in the village."

"Where were the Corbett's then?" asked Luke.

"They must have been driving back to England," said Lexie. "Dad kept shouting down the phone that he wanted the dogs back. I was crying. When Dad ran out of coins, he said they wanted one thousand pounds, and he had to fetch Bubble and Squeak."

"The Corbett brothers agreed to meet your Dad at

Westbury station that night to hand over Bubble and Squeak in return for one thousand pounds in cash," said Neil. "Is that right?"

"That's right," said Lexie.

"Where did the money come from?" asked Luke.

"Dad didn't have it. He was crying, the same as I was. He didn't know what to do. We were desperate. I told him a secret I'd kept for years. Dad told me to go home. I'd already gone out to meet my boyfriend before he got home, so I never spoke with him again. When I saw Dad at the station, I knew that he must have persuaded the pervert to hand over enough cash to pay for the dogs. Although I was glad we would get them back, I knew that nothing would be the same again once the story got out. Then those men murdered my Dad, and it wasn't the same again, anyway."

Luke thought back over the past few days, and the pieces dropped into place.

"Dad went to chat with Martin Jones, didn't he?"

Lexie nodded.

"Carys said you used to drop by the shop and ask your Mum for sweets or a comic when you were ten years old. Mum couldn't afford to buy them for you after Ivan lost his job. Your family was still short of money three or four years later when you went to the same shop for a teen magazine or maybe a packet of cigarettes."

"Mr Jones caught me shoplifting," said Lexie. "The first and only time I'd done it. He threatened to call my parents and the police. Then he said maybe we could come to an arrangement. I didn't know what he meant. I soon found out."

"How old were you?" asked Luke.

"The first time he touched me was the week after my fourteenth birthday."

"Does your mother know?" asked Neil.

"I couldn't tell her," said Lexie. "Dad must have gone to Martin Jones that afternoon and told him that unless he handed over the money, he would tell the police what he'd done."

"You know we can't ignore what you've told us, Lexie," said Luke.

"You shouldn't have had to experience that," said Neil.

Lexie burst into tears and ran to the Ladies.

"Didn't see that coming, did we?" said Neil.

"It seemed odd to me when Martin Jones went outside for a cigarette as soon as Carys started talking about Lexie. He'd only just come back from a break. I didn't put two and two together until just now."

"What a mess," said Neil.

"Solving the murder case has opened up a world of hurt for Sammy and her daughter. Carys Jones has a nightmare ahead when she learns her father is a paedophile. Gus wanted to check the exact date when Gethin Hughes and Lexie got together too. Hughes swore blind Lexie was sixteen, but who knows? Were there others before him? People accused Lexie of being a wild child, but we know now that at least one person took her innocence against her will."

"The job she does here only perpetuates the cycle of self-loathing," said Neil. "Lexie believes this is all she's good for. What can we do to break the cycle?"

Lexie soon returned from the Ladies. She'd refreshed her makeup.

"I'm okay now," she said. "Does Mum need to know everything?"

"She does," said Neil.

"Your Mum told us to tell you she still loves you, Lexie,"

said Luke. "Do you know what I think the best thing is to do? We'll take you home. You'll need one another in the weeks ahead as much as you did after your Dad died. Neither of you should be alone."

Later that afternoon, Neil called Gus as they drove away from Oakfield Drive, Crickhowell, for the second time.

"It's a beautiful afternoon here, Neil," said Gus. "Suzie and I are having a picnic at the allotment. How did it go?"

"A light shower here, guv," said Neil. "We got everything we needed and a little more than we wanted."

"You'll have to explain that one, Neil," said Gus.

So, while Luke drove them through light drizzle towards the second Severn crossing, Neil did just that.


"IS THAT IT? DONE AND DUSTED?" asked Suzie when Gus ended the call.

"Pretty much," said Gus. "The brothers approached Ivan and offered to buy the dogs. He refused. Three days later, when they left the area to visit Uncle Jack in Westbury, they stole them. Ivan contacted the brothers and agreed on a price. The Corbett brothers met him at the station, having decided what *they* were going to do. They took the weapons with them. It was a premeditated murder."

"It sounded more than that in your conversation with Neil," said Suzie.

"Why spoil a lovely afternoon?" said Gus. "Monday morning will be time enough to get the grubby details into our files. Neil told me that he and Luke reunited mother and daughter this afternoon. Who needs social workers when your police officers have hearts as big as those two?"

# Epilogue

## *Monday, 16 July 2018*

THE FIRST SIXTY minutes of the working day can often set the tone for the week ahead.

As soon as the team arrived in the office, everyone sensed today was special.

DI Williams called Gus to confirm that Vaughn and Shaun Corbett were in custody. He listened to Gus's summary of Saturday's events and agreed they had enough evidence to proceed with the murder charge. His officers would also follow up on two residents of Pontyclun whose actions contributed in part to the events of March 2014. Gus asked what had happened to the dogs. Dai Williams promised to find out and let him know. The Corbett brothers had no dogs with them when apprehended.

AS PROMISED, Gus called Eddie Sinclair in Shaftesbury to tell him the Kendall murder case was now closed. While

Eddie was telling Gus how grateful he was, Neil Davis received the forensic report comparing samples collected at the roadside after Sid Dyer's death and the Dilton Marsh site. Gus saw Neil give him a thumbs up. Gus was about to make Eddie's day even better.

ALEX AND LYDIA knew the news they brought back from Rotterdam could wait. Wrapping up the Kendall case was more important. After that, the Crime Review Team needed to concentrate on collating the information Gus Freeman wanted to deliver to the ACC.

BLESSING UMEH CREPT across to Gus's desk and sat beside him. She couldn't keep her secret any longer. She leaned closer so the others wouldn't hear.

"You'll think I'm a hopeless case," she whispered. "No matter how I try to excel at things, something always trips me up. Do you remember I mislaid the Freeman Files, and Lydia had to set me up again? I found a folder with a heading I couldn't remember creating."

"Did it contain that missing file?" asked Gus. "The NCA goons missed it?"

Blessing nodded.

"I could kiss you," said Gus.

Gus rang Kenneth Truelove at London Road and asked for their meeting to be delayed until eleven o'clock. He needed to secure the contents of that file. Gus couldn't act yet, but he didn't plan to retire with an open cold case against his name, regardless of the obstacles.

# All Things Bright: Chapter One

*Monday, 16 July 2018*

The first sixty minutes of the working day can often set the tone for the week ahead.

As soon as the team arrived in the office, everyone sensed today was special.

Gus had hardly had time to get comfortable at his desk when the phone rang. It was DI Dai Williams from Cardiff Central.

"Good morning, Dai," said Gus, "I'm praying it's good news?"

"It is, Gus," said Dai. "I don't like Mondays, as a rule, but this feels a decent start to the week for us both. We found Vaughn and Shaun Corbett yesterday evening. They were in Tredegar making a nuisance of themselves knocking on doors just when good folk were on their way to chapel."

"I can update you now on my team's visit to South Wales on Saturday, Dai," said Gus. "After chatting to people in the village who knew Sally Kendall well, we received copies of more recent photographs, which helped us locate Ivan's widow in Crickhowell. But, as you suspected, Sally hadn't strayed far from her roots. She was now Sammy Prosser, a change of name and hair colouring, and handling a responsible job with an estate agent. When questioned, Sammy admitted that their daughter, Alexa, or Lexie, had told her about the two Staffie cross puppies on Sunday afternoon, the day after Ivan disappeared."

"Why on earth didn't she tell us that?" asked Dai Williams. "It would have helped us concentrate our attention further afield from the start."

"Maybe," said Gus, "but Lexie only mentioned it after your officers had left. So, unless you found someone in the village who had seen the Corbett brothers trailing Lexie Kendall and her dogs or conversing with Ivan, you wouldn't have been any closer to linking the matter to Westbury. Certainly not before Monday morning, when police found Ivan's body. I won't deny it would have been vital information in the twenty-four hours that followed, but what's done is done. But, unfortunately, we can't turn back the clock."

"So, mother and daughter moved to Crickhowell?" said Dai. "It's amazing how parochial villages like Pontyclun can be. Mrs Kendall only moved twenty miles away, and yet she may as well have flown to the moon. People from your side of the Bristol Channel have no appreciation of how insular the valleys' old mining communities were. So many houses were tightly packed together, as close as possible to the industry they served. Disease and gossip spread like wildfire, men faced death underground with every passing minute, yet the spirit of the community remained greater in those areas than anywhere else in the world."

"I'm beginning to understand their history," said Gus. "Sally Kendall told my detectives it was her fear of dogs that prompted Ivan to house them in a secure shed on the allotment near the rugby club. That was one secret that came to light after his murder. Lexie revealed another on Saturday afternoon. It caused Ivan to appear quiet and distant in the hours before he left home. The Corbett brothers wanted to buy the puppies. They had offered Ivan five hundred pounds at the rugby club the previous Wednesday when Ivan cleaned its clubhouse windows. He refused their offer. While her father was on his usual Saturday morning task, collecting money from customers, Lexie went to fetch the dogs for their run in the park. They were gone. Lexie found Ivan and got him to call the mobile number on the business card the brothers had left. They were already across the Severn Bridge with the puppies in their van. Lexie was desperate to get them back. The brothers weren't prepared to return them. If Ivan wanted them, he could collect them from Westbury station in return for one thousand pounds in cash."

"Why didn't Ivan report the theft to the police?" asked Dai Williams.

"Because he'd acquired them from a customer who couldn't afford to pay their bill and kept them secret from his wife for a year, I suppose he thought that was out of the question," said Gus. "He hoped to get them back without Sally being any the wiser. But then, Lexie dropped a bomb-shell as she cried by the phone box after her father heard what it would cost to get the puppies back. She admitted that Martin Jones, who owns the newsagents, had sexually abused her from the age of fourteen to fifteen. In addition, Jones caught her shoplifting, and you can guess the rest."

"I've made a note of the name," said Dai Williams. "You can rest assured that we'll call on Mr Jones before the day's out. What a mess."

"There's more," said Gus. "Lexie moved to Crickhowell with her mother but never settled. She left after her eighteenth birthday and moved to Bridgend. My lads found her in a night-club, where she appears as Satin, an exotic dancer. Your officers believed her to be a 'wild child' who was always in trouble. Martin Jones and several others may have played a part in the persona Lexie portrayed. If your pen is still poised, you might wish to speak to Gethin Hughes. He's the boyfriend who was with Lexie at the station in Pontyclun on Saturday night when Ivan left the village. Whether they had sex before her sixteenth birthday is debatable. In an interview under caution at Cardiff Central, Hughes might provide you with names of other men who knew Lexie before he got involved with her."

"Knew her in the biblical sense, you mean," said Dai Williams. "I've heard that name before. I'm sure Hughes used to play football for a local team. He must be in his mid-thirties now."

"There was a pattern," said Gus, "as my lads discovered when they spoke with Lexie. She ditched her ambitions to be a hairdresser when she left school. Jones, Hughes, and others made her believe that the job she did in Bridgend was all she was good for."

"A sad outcome," said Dai Williams, "does that mean the mother and daughter are no longer in contact with one another?"

"My lads believed that to break the cycle of self-loathing her lifestyle perpetuated, it would benefit Lexie if they reunited her with her mother. The whole sordid story will come out in time. They persuaded Lexie to return with them to Crickhowell."

"We'll do everything in our power to help them through the inevitable trauma that a case such as that attracts," said

Dai. "I can't promise they'll come out unscathed, but it won't be for lack of trying. We didn't do a great job in 2014, but we have an opportunity to put matters right. Thanks, Gus. I'm sure I'll be in touch again soon. We've got enough evidence to proceed with a murder charge. Leave it with us."

"One final question, Dai," said Gus. "Did your officers learn anything further about those dogs?"

"The Corbett brothers had no dogs with them when apprehended," replied Dai Williams. "We'll learn more when we interview them. I don't hold out much hope of Lexie Kendall seeing them again. Ivan Kendall took them to settle a debt, but we would be naïve if we thought it was a selfless gesture. Ivan realised that those dogs would fetch a sizeable sum in several areas close to Pontyclun. The Corbett brothers knew that too, and they might have engaged in the murky world of dog fights. The odds are stacked against those puppies surviving four years and more. I'll update you in due course."

Gus thanked Dai Williams for his help and ended the call. He wondered who he could talk to with inside knowledge of the dogfighting business. It was light years away from the world that Mark Malone frequented in one of their earlier cases. The sad fact was that man's best friend was used to smuggle drugs into the country on that occasion. Now, the nation's favourite pets were getting torn to bits in illegal meets for entertainment. When you thought that criminals couldn't stoop any lower, they proved you wrong time and time again.

Gus picked up the phone. He remembered he'd promised to call Eddie Sinclair in Shaftesbury with any news.

"Eddie?" said Gus, "We finally got your men in the Ivan Kendall case."

"That's great news, Gus," said Eddie, "Was it someone from the traveller's site that I pointed you towards?"

"It was," said Gus. "Vaughn and Shaun Corbett visited an uncle, Jack Ayres, every spring. Ayres came from North Wales, but the family tree had branches everywhere. The brothers spent much of the year in and around Cardiff. That's where they spotted Ivan Kendall's daughter exercising two potentially valuable dogs. At first, they tried to buy them from Ivan, then they grabbed them and brought them to the site near Westbury. To cut a long story short, Ivan travelled to Westbury station to collect the dogs. The brothers demanded one thousand pounds for their safe return. Ivan raised the cash, and when he reached Westbury at midnight that Saturday night, the brothers met him with a different outcome in mind."

"They bludgeoned him to death in the toilet and dropped his body in the fishing lakes," said Eddie Sinclair.

"They kept the dogs and the cash, leaving an amount in Kendall's pockets to confuse you. Why would you think it was a robbery if Kendall still had over sixty quid on him? No wonder you couldn't establish a motive."

"We didn't cover ourselves in glory, that's true," sighed Sinclair. "At least you got them; that's one more case that won't keep me awake at night. Thanks, Gus."

As Eddie spoke, Gus spotted DS Neil Davis giving him the thumbs up. In his other hand, he held the folder relating to the samples he'd collected from the Dilton Marsh traveller's site.

"I might be able to help you sleep even better tonight, Eddie," said Gus. "One of my lads was a motorcycle pursuit rider before he joined the Crime Review Team. He queried how Dyer's accident happened at the point it did. Even in inclement weather, the lorry driver should have been aware of contact with the 125cc motorcycle. The forensic report on samples collected at the roadside after the accident couldn't help identify the vehicle. We knew where the Corbett brothers parked their van during their visits, so another colleague asked forensics to compare samples from the caravan site with material believed to have transferred in the collision to the motorcycle and Dyer's clothing. We've just got confirmation that forensics found a match. Your former colleagues at Westbury can follow up on those findings. It seems clear that the Corbett brother's van forced Sid Dyer off the road that morning. Sid Dyer's local knowledge pointed you towards the fishing lakes far sooner than they had hoped. On their next visit to the area, the brothers took their revenge."

"Another cold-blooded murder solved," said Eddie Sinclair. "D'you know, I'm tempted to call Clive Trainer with the good news, but on second thoughts, I reckon I'll enjoy it alone for a while."

Gus smiled to himself. He wished Eddie Sinclair 'Sweet Dreams' and ended the call. This morning, his team's essential task was to complete the Freeman Files work on the Kendall case. They needed to collate the information Gus wanted to deliver to the ACC.

Blessing Umeh crept across to Gus's desk and sat beside him. She couldn't keep her secret any longer. She leaned closer so the others wouldn't hear.

"You'll think I'm a hopeless case," she whispered. "No matter how I try to excel at things, something always trips me up. Do you remember I mislaid the Freeman Files, and Lydia had to set everything up again? I found a folder with a heading I couldn't remember creating."

"Did it contain that missing file?" asked Gus, "and the NCA goons missed it?"

Blessing nodded.

"I could kiss you," said Gus.

Gus rang Kenneth Truelove at London Road and asked for their meeting to be delayed until eleven o'clock. He needed to secure the contents of that file. Gus couldn't act yet, but he didn't plan to retire with an open cold case against his name, regardless of the obstacles.

Lydia Logan Barre and Alex Hardy had joined the rest of the team at the start of the new week with plenty to tell them after a weekend in Rotterdam. Somehow, they had to curb their enthusiasm; work came first. While Gus Freeman dealt with DI Williams in Cardiff and DCI Sinclair in Shaftesbury, they updated their copies of the Freeman Files. They ensured that everything relating to the Kendall case was watertight. The files Gus passed to the ACC later that morning must offer the Crown Prosecution Service every chance of a successful outcome.

Lydia and Alex left Chippenham early Friday evening to drive to the port of Harwich. Tucked away on Essex's east coast, Harwich is one of the county's most historic towns. The 'Mayflower' set sail from there in 1620 across the Atlantic to the New World.

They were tired after a journey that took four hours with the high volume of summer traffic on the motorways. Ahead of them lay another seven hours aboard the car ferry that delivered them to the Hook of Holland. Alex was asleep within minutes of the ferry leaving port. Lydia dozed for a while, but it was difficult not to think about why she was there.

It had taken several years to find her birth mother,

Eleanor Scott, and they now enjoyed a warm, friendly relationship. Neither demanded too much from the other. Lydia
would always consider Mr and Mrs Logan as Mum and
Dad. They had adopted her within weeks of Lydia's birth.
Nothing could weaken that bond. Lydia accepted Eleanor's
reasons for giving her up for adoption, and they were
moving forward.

On the occasions they met after initial contact through a
mediator, Eleanor gradually told Lydia more details about
her father. Chidozie Barre. He was twenty-one, a sailor from
Yaba, near Lagos, Nigeria. He'd wandered into the gift shop
in George Street, Edinburgh, searching for a souvenir for
his mother.

Eleanor and Chidozie had two days together before he
sailed from the port of Leith. The handsome young man
who stole Eleanor's heart had no idea that their brief liaison
produced a bonny baby daughter that Eleanor called Lisa
Marie nine months later.

As soon as she learned her birth father's name, Lydia
wanted to discover where he'd gone after leaving Edinburgh. With Alex's help, they'd traced him to Rotterdam.
When the ferry landed in the Hook of Holland, the A20
highway would take them into the city within half an
hour.

Alex had booked them into a floating hotel on Bierstraat, only a five-minute walk via Wijnhaven from the
'Lady Eleanor' where her father lived and worked. Chidozie
Barre opened a bar in April 2016, just around the corner
from the Maritime Museum in Leuvehaven.

Lydia knew that sometime on Saturday, she would meet
her biological father for the first time. Alex had warned her
not to expect too much. They hadn't given Chidozie any
indication they were coming to Rotterdam. He didn't know

he had a daughter of twenty-five. He might not want to know.

Lydia listened to Alex's words, but she had made up her mind. She was curious to see the face of the man whose DNA determined the way she looked. What similarities were there in their physical make-up? Eleanor said he was tall. That was something they had in common. Chidozie had a smile that lit up the room, too. What kind of person was he now, after the trauma he'd suffered in the shipwreck? Was he quiet, loud, moody, or full of life?

Lydia wanted to ask why he never came back to Edinburgh. Was it a deliberate act to stay away or just chance? She needed to understand and allow him to explain himself. It was important to hear his side of the story. Everything she thought she knew came from Eleanor. If he'd realised he'd fathered a child, how would he have reacted? Would he have been like Eleanor and thought he wasn't ready for the responsibility then?

Lydia had never held a grudge against either of her birth parents. After meeting Eleanor and realising that it was enough to be friends, she redoubled her efforts to find her father. Lydia wanted to show Chidozie that there was nothing to forgive. After such an extended period, they couldn't have a genuine father-daughter relationship. Still, she hoped there would be the possibility of developing a similar understanding that now existed between her and Eleanor.

Most of all, this weekend was for closure. Lydia didn't want to look back in years to come and regretted not taking this final step. Sleep claimed her at last, and they were only minutes from the port when Alex woke her.

"Excited?" he asked.

"Nervous," she'd replied.

"You needn't worry whether you inherited your father's sea legs," said Alex.

"I had a lot on my mind," said Lydia, "before I dropped off to sleep. I know one thing, I'm starving. It's ages since we had a bite to eat."

Alex drove the car on the last leg of the journey. He'd ridden his motorcycle on holidays abroad, so Lydia was happy to let him cope with the traffic and drive on the right.

"I thought the M25 was bad," she groaned," this is a nightmare."

"We can turn off the main drag and find a place to eat," said Alex. "It's always this busy, but you'll be in a better mood once you've had your first cup of coffee and bacon and apple pancakes."

Alex was right, as usual. However, they both felt more human when they arrived in Bierstraat and parked near the hotel.

"What time do you think our room will be ready?" asked Lydia.

"Why, what did you have in mind?" asked Alex.

Lydia thumped his arm.

"I was wondering whether we could drop off our bags and take a walk to the Maritime Museum. However, before venturing inside, I want to check out the area and walk past the bar. What time does the 'Lady Eleanor' open?"

"Ten o'clock," said Alex, "according to the information I found online. The bar closes at one in the morning."

"That's a long day," said Lydia. "Chi-Chi couldn't possibly cover the whole day. I wonder which half of the day he works?"

"If we're right in our assumption that he chose the bar's location because of its proximity to the Museum, then he'll be there in an hour. You will see him raising the shutters."

"What do you think we should do first?" asked Lydia.

"You wait in the car. I'll go across to the hotel and check on the room."

Lydia sat and waited.

She had done her homework, too, just like her father. Rotterdam has evolved from a down-at-heel port city into one of Europe's favourite getaways.

Lydia smiled as she saw Alex trotting back to the car. She'd seen his face when he looked at the bill in the café earlier. Some things were far more expensive here than back in the UK. Yet, the online reviews she had read thought Rotterdam offered value for money. It certainly had plenty of museums and galleries to visit, only a ten-minute walk from where she sat if the weather was poor. They didn't have to worry on that score today.

"Three o'clock," said Alex, "but they have agreed to store our bags for us. Let's take advantage of that and then return to get checked in this afternoon."

Ten minutes later, they were on their way.

## All Things Bright: Chapter Two

"There," cried Lydia, grabbing Alex by the arm. "Can you see anyone inside?"

Alex knew the feeling would return in his arm in time.

They had turned the corner to enter the street where Chidozie had his bar. The 'Lady Eleanor' was on a narrow side street off Wijnhaven. Parked bicycles littered the pavement on either side of the bar. A loading bay for two vehicles was empty in front of the modern, bright-looking bar.

Alex and Lydia strolled along the pavement on the opposite side of the street. Three four-seater stained wooden benches sat outside the large plate-glass window. The interior blazed with light. The colour scheme of red, white, and black was nothing like Lydia's image in her head since she learned that Chidozie was living and working here.

"It looks so smart and clean," said Lydia.

"What did you expect," said Alex, "ye olde Smuggler's Tavern? Look around us. The entire district has that sleek, industrial-chic look. It's only the bikes that make the place untidy."

"I can't see him inside," said Lydia. "Not that I know what he looks like. Perhaps he's upstairs in the flat, looking at us."

Lydia stood back from the pavement's edge and peered up at the windows on the upper floors. She saw nothing.

"It's still early," said Alex. "Let's tour the Museum Park and the other attractions. Then, we can come back around lunchtime."

"I downloaded a suggested route onto my phone before we left Chippenham," said Lydia. "We can reach Central Station in ten minutes. It's one of the coolest stations in Europe, and it's supposed to set the artistic mood for our day. I'll admire the beautiful architecture while you grab us a coffee."

"You've got it worked out, haven't you," said Alex.

"If only," said Lydia. "I'm so nervous now. I can't remember what I wanted to ask or say to him. What if he doesn't even speak to me? What if we picked the only weekend in the year when he's flown away on holiday?"

"We'll follow the route on your phone and take your mind off your Dad by seeing the sights this city offers."

The station was everything Lydia hoped it would be, and the coffee was delicious.

"The next place on this quick tour is one I'm dying to see," she said as they left the station.

Alex walked beside her, and as they turned the corner, he had to admit it impressed him.

"Wow! A yellow pedestrian bridge connecting the two sides of the city,"

After exploring the Luchtsingel pedestrian bridge, they returned to the roundabout and walked south.

"This is a busy district," said Alex, taking in the sights. "With cafes, restaurants, and shopping malls on both sides of the street. I love the canal here."

"If we follow these canals, we'll soon return to Leuve-haven and our hotel. The Maritime Museum is just over there. We ought to visit it. I wondered whether it played a part in the bar's location."

One look at the variety of exhibits on offer on the notice boards outside the Museum meant that they wouldn't do it justice unless they spent several hours inside.

"Perhaps we should add it to our list of things to do tomorrow?" asked Lydia. "We might have a free day if things don't go to plan."

"Don't give up just yet," said Alex. "Who's that man explaining something to a group of visitors waiting outside?"

Lydia spun around. Through the crowds, she spotted a tall, handsome man. Lydia tried to remain calm as she studied the man's face, hair, and eyes. The way he stood looked familiar, and he had flecks of grey at his temples. The man could be in his late forties or early fifties. His eyes shone as he spoke to the visitors. The subject was clearly something he enjoyed. One child in the group asked a ques-tion or passed a comment. The man threw back his head and laughed. The smile that followed was just how Eleanor described it.

Lydia studied the man's clothes. She was convinced this was Chidozie Barre. The years he'd spent at sea had kept him fit. Chidozie was still lean and muscular. His quarter-zip navy blue sailor's sweater and navy slacks oozed class. Lydia smiled. Forget Idris Elba as James Bond. Chidozie Barre would slip into the role like a hand into a glove.

As she daydreamed of her father starring on the big

screen, he looked over the heads of the visitor group and stared straight at her.

"There's nothing for it, Lydia," said Alex. "You have to walk across and talk to him. He looks as if he's seen a ghost."

Lydia made her way through the queuing tourists, followed by Alex.

"Je gezicht komt bekend voor," said the man.

"I'm afraid I don't speak Dutch," said Lydia.

"Your face looks familiar. I recognise your accent too. You are from Scotland."

"I am. My mother was born in Edinburgh, and so was I."

Alex stepped forward and steadied a shaky Chidozie Barre as realisation dawned.

"We should find a café," said Alex. "You need to sit. You've had a shock."

Chidozie pointed behind Alex but didn't speak. He continued to stare at the beautiful coffee-coloured face of the girl with the shock of red hair. Her voice had just transported him back twenty-six years to a time he would never forget.

When Chidozie and Lydia had sat down, Alex went inside the café to order drinks.

"Is that your husband?"

"Not yet," said Lydia, "we're work colleagues back in England."

"I don't understand how you came to be here today. What are you called?"

"The family that adopted me named me Lydia,"

"The beautiful one," said Chidozie. "They chose well."

"I've searched for you for several years," said Lydia. "As

soon as we learned that you opened a bar and called it the 'Lady Eleanor', I knew I should come to meet you."

"Why didn't I know of you? Why did Eleanor not look for me?"

Lydia explained the eighteen-year-old Eleanor Scott faced problems because of her family's reaction after learning that she was pregnant. They refused to take in a baby fathered by a black man. Eleanor didn't know the ship's name and couldn't support a baby alone. So she gave her baby up for adoption.

"We left the port of Leith twenty-four hours after the last time I saw Eleanor," said Chidozie. "I was at sea for five months before I took the presents I'd bought in her shop to my mother back home in Yaba. I thought of Eleanor every day and told my mother that I'd met a beautiful Scottish girl. She said that the memory of my first love would always stay with me. Of course, because I had chosen a life at sea, there would be other girls in other ports, but in Yaba, there were girls from families that my parents knew who would be more suitable for marriage."

"Did you marry a local girl?" asked Lydia.

Chidozie shook his head.

"I never married. I was the youngest in the family, and my three older sisters married and gave my parents a dozen grandchildren between them. Although my father wished for a son to carry on the family name, he never pressured me into an arranged marriage. Both my parents are dead now. I haven't returned to Nigeria since I attended their burials."

"Why didn't you return to Scotland to find Eleanor if she was the only one for you?" asked Lydia.

"I've asked myself that question many times," sighed Chidozie. "We never spoke of love in the two days we spent together. After we made love in the park that night, there was no understanding that it was a commitment to a lasting relationship. It was just a moment we shared. It felt inevitable we'd never meet again. How could we? My ship would unlikely return to Edinburgh for a year, maybe more. As it was, circumstances with the shipping company I worked for meant that we only landed at a British port on two more occasions, years after we first met. America, Asia, and Africa were places I visited far more than in Europe. As the years passed, I accepted that a girl as pretty as Eleanor would have found someone else. What a fool I would look if I flew to Scotland and visited the gift shop with a bunch of red roses to learn that she had left ages ago to get married. How on earth did you ever find me, Lydia?"

Lydia explained how she had traced her birth mother and that she and Eleanor were friends.

"I spent so many years with the Logans that they will always be my Mum and Dad. As I got to know Eleanor, my birth mother, I asked her to tell me about my father. She told me you were a merchant sailor from Nigeria and that your friends called you Chi-Chi. We traced the details of the reefer you worked on through maritime records in London. Alex and I then followed your career at sea right through to the time of the shipwreck."

"The typhoon was too powerful," said Chidozie. "I'd never experienced such winds. We didn't stand a chance. The Coast Guard was so far away that I had given up any hopes of rescue. The authorities in Manila believed that everyone perished. I prayed that night as I'd never prayed before. Then a freighter battled its way through treacherous seas to reach us. They had seen the final distress signal that I sent, and although they were searching for a needle in a haystack, they arrived just as we were preparing to face death. They plucked twelve of us from the waves as we clung to the two life rafts we had roped together."

"We learned from your former shipping company that after that dreadful ordeal, you never went to sea again," said Alex.

"The freighter that rescued us carried us into the port of Da Nang," said Chidozie. "I went with my colleagues to the hospital to see if they were getting the care they needed. Then, exhausted but uninjured, I flew as far away from the South China Sea as possible to spend a month in Dubai, recuperating. Then, I thought I'd try my luck in America."

"That's when we picked up the trail again," said Lydia, "after a lifetime at sea and reaching the senior position of First Mate, you suddenly became an expert cocktail maker. Where did that talent come from?"

Chidozie threw his head back and laughed again.

"I needed the money to live," said Chidozie, "I don't drink alcohol, but mixing drinks to a recipe isn't rocket science. I learned fast, and because I stayed sober, I avoided the muggers and racists I bumped into when I walked home to my apartment. The move to Hamburg came at the right time. The same problems existed, but life was more relaxed than in New York. When you're a single man, if you don't drink or gamble, it's possible to save to afford your own business. So I kept my eye on properties in Hamburg and here in Rotterdam. When the right place became available, I made an offer and moved here, changing the bar's name from 'The Hideaway' to 'Lady Eleanor'. It was the right choice because it helped you find me. I have a daughter now. It feels strange, but I love it."

"We walked by the bar earlier this morning," said Alex. "I knew it was you as soon as I spotted you outside the Museum. Do you work there?"

"I volunteer my time," said Chidozie. "It's the least I can do. The sea is still important to me, despite how my career ended. I'm here whenever they need me from eleven o'clock until three. I work in my bar in the evenings. How long are you staying in Rotterdam?"

"Our ferry leaves the Hook tomorrow evening," said Lydia.

"Where are you staying tonight?"

"At one of the floating hotels a few minutes' walk from here," said Alex. "Check-in is at three. We're going to have lunch and then spend an hour resting at the hotel. Neither of us slept much on the ferry last night."

"Will you come to the 'Lady Eleanor' this evening?" asked Chidozie.

"Of course," said Lydia.

"I'll get a staff member to cover for me later. I will take you to dinner tonight. On this trip, there won't be another opportunity."

"That would be great," said Lydia.

"I have questions to ask, Lydia," said Chidozie. "but I should get back to the Maritime Museum. This is strange and new to me. What do we do now? Shake hands or hug?"

Lydia hugged Chidozie. The two men shook hands.

"What is your name?" asked Chidozie.

"Alex Hardy, sir," said Alex. "Detective Sergeant Alex Hardy. Pleased to meet you at last."

"Until tonight, then, Lydia," said Chidozie Barre.

"I was Lydia Logan until I met Eleanor and learned my birth father's name," said Lydia. "When I travelled south from Scotland to work with the same team as Alex, I made it official. I'm Lydia Logan Barre now."

"That's wonderful," smiled Chidozie, "even your name is beautiful."

With a wave, her father eased his way through the customers waiting to enter the Museum and started back to work. Lydia and Alex set off on a ten-minute walk that would bring them to the Market Hall.

"The building is enormous," said Alex, "and another must-see place in Rotterdam. We'll find food stalls, restaurants, and shops galore. There's bound to be somewhere that we can get lunch. In the Square in front of the Market Hall are the yellow Cube Houses, an icon of Rotterdam architecture."

"I was thinking of those yellow houses earlier while you were in the hotel," said Lydia. "They're on my list of things to visit. Perhaps we can look inside one after we've eaten?"

"Breakfast seems a long time ago," said Alex, "and all this walking is telling on my leg."

"We've got until three o'clock, Alex," said Lydia, linking her arm through his. "Lean on me, and we'll cross the Erasmus Bridge and admire the Mass River and the Rotterdam skyline as we eat our meal."

Ninety minutes later, the couple was ready to tackle the next stage of their tour of the best attractions. Lydia wanted to see as much of her father's home town as possible this weekend, but she didn't want Alex to get overtired.

"Let's save our legs for a while," she said. "we can take a water taxi to get us around in comfort. That will be the best way to fill the final ninety minutes before check-in at the hotel."

They returned to the floating hotel and stowed their gear in their room.

"What now?" asked Alex.

"I'm shattered," said Lydia. "Set the alarm on your phone for six-thirty. The last one asleep is a sissy."

Alex was first to wake up and slipped out of bed and into the shower. Lydia joined him minutes later.

"Chidozie told us he never married," said Lydia. "That's so sad. I hope he isn't lonely."

"When we saw how he was with the line of Museum visitors, I think he's the gregarious type, don't you? I'm sure his bar will be livelier when he's in there, and who knows, he might have met someone special here in Rotterdam."

"Maybe his late mother was right," said Lydia. "He had a girl in every port. Perhaps he's left a long line of broken-hearted females in cities worldwide."

"I don't think you should ask him that this evening," said Alex. "You don't want to push too hard."

"Okay," said Lydia. "I prepared a long list of questions before we left home, and this morning most of them flew away on the breeze. I dreamt of Chidozie telling me that Eleanor was his first love and he never forgot her. That romantic idea was in my head before we learned about the bar's name. While listening to Eleanor telling me how they met, I imagined them finding one another again after so many years and everything being sweetness and light. It was unrealistic, but they were the exact words he used this morning. He even said that naming the bar 'Lady Eleanor' had helped me find him."

"You must remember how Eleanor spoke about him," said Alex. "She made a life without Chidozie Barre and was happy with her lot. The two of you have moved forward as friends, which works for you. When we get home, talk to your mother, better still visit her, and speak about this week-end. Eleanor might decide to come here to renew their acquaintance, or she might get in touch by phone or letter. After so many years, Eleanor might be happy to learn Chi-Chi's alive and well but not want contact with him."

"You're right. It's Eleanor's choice," said Lydia. "I need to rein in my enthusiasm. I'm letting my imagination run wild."

"The most important thing tonight, and for what free time we have left tomorrow, is for you and your father to agree on what relationship you can have in the future. Once that's sorted, you can worry over what Eleanor and Chidozie want to happen."

"I'm so lucky," said Lydia. "I have a father in Aberdeen, another in Rotterdam, and if they can't offer me enough wise counsel, then I can rely on you to keep me on the right path. I love you, Alex."

"I love you too, Lydia. Now, this shower is running cold. I vote we dry ourselves and get dressed. We must try to look as elegant as your father if we're dining with him tonight. I know you brought enough clothes for a week, but I'm a smart-casual guy when I'm not at work. I leave my suits in the wardrobe when I go on holiday. You must decide which shirt looks the smartest from my limited selection."

The view that greeted them differed from this morning when they stood across the road from Chi-Chi's bar at seven-thirty. Someone sat on every seat on the benches outside, and couples and small groups congregated on the pavement. Conversation and laughter filled the air. Through the crowd, Lydia could see the bar was busy inside too. The various male and female staff members scurried from table to table, taking orders or delivering food and drink to eager customers.

Chidozie favoured a simple uniform of crisp white shirts and black slacks, regardless of gender. Lydia searched for Chidozie, but she couldn't see him at first.

"Fancy a beer?" asked Alex. "Let's get a cold one and stand outside on the pavement. It will be too warm indoors.

We'll tell the bar staff we've arrived. Chi-Chi could be upstairs getting ready or dealing with customers at the back of the room. We can't see every dark corner from here."

Alex and Lydia crossed the road and went inside the 'Lady Eleanor' for the first time. Lydia looked for a senior member of staff. Most staff working this evening were teenagers, but a middle-aged, blonde-haired woman was hovering by the bar, keeping her eye on everything. Lydia heard her issuing orders to her charges as they rushed past. Her accent was Dutch.

"Excuse me," said Lydia, "we're meeting Chidozie here. Has he arrived yet?"

"You must be Lydia," said the woman, "I'm Rosa. He's still upstairs in the apartment. He won't be five minutes."

Alex arrived with two cold lagers.

"We'll be outside," said Lydia. "It's too nice an evening to stay indoors."

Rosa smiled and resumed her vigil.

While Rosa was on deck, Alex reckoned the 'Lady Eleanor' was a well-oiled machine that maximised Chidozie Barre's profits.

"Your father chose an ideal location," said Alex when they were back outside. "With these narrow streets, most traffic will be on foot or two wheels. The four-wheel commercial transport will be early morning waste collection and morning deliveries to the restaurants and bars. The bar's sheltered from the wind too."

"Did you catch what Rosa said?" asked Lydia. "He's still upstairs in *the* apartment."

"You're jumping to conclusions again," said Alex.

"Do I look alright?" asked Lydia. "I'm nervous. What if Chidozie thinks my skirt is too short?"

"It looks fine from where I'm standing," said Alex.

"You've got great legs, Lydia. Even Gus Freeman couldn't object to what you're wearing tonight. It might be too much for the Crime Review Team office, but it's perfect for an evening in town."

Lydia tugged at her black leather skirt and tried to convince herself that it was decent. Her loose-fitting bright-orange, brown and yellow top drew most men's attention away from her skirt in any case. Not for the first time, she was the only girl in the vicinity with corkscrew curls of ginger hair.

Alex felt happy with Lydia's choice of a pale blue shirt with a button-down collar. He was thankful she hadn't opted for his white shirt. He would never have escaped the 'Lady Eleanor', although the tips from waiting on tables would have helped pay the eye-watering prices for two bottles of lager.

There was a sudden hush on the pavement behind them. Something had caused the conversation level to drop. Lydia turned to look over her shoulder. It was her secret agent emerging from the bar's interior. Chidozie left any Western suits he possessed in the wardrobe. His navy blue outfit was stylish and based on a traditional agbada. The top was wide-sleeved with elaborate gold embroidery that covered the shoulders. The undervest was a loose, round-neck, sleeveless smock, and his trousers were close-fitting, ankle-length, and narrow-bottomed.

"He knows how to make an entrance," said Alex.

"I don't think his regular customers have seen him in anything resembling his national dress before," said Lydia.

Chidozie Barre kissed Lydia on both cheeks and shook Alex by the hand.

He stood back to admire his daughter's outfit.

"I can see now why I needed to adjust my kiss to land on your cheek," he grinned.

"Four-inch heels, Chidozie," said Alex, "I need a step."

"My apologies for keeping you waiting," said Chidozie. "Rosa will look after things here while we go to a favourite restaurant of mine. Our Uber Netherlands vehicle will be here in one minute."

"Rosa seems very efficient," said Alex.

"She worked for 'The Hideaway' when I bought the place. The previous owner advised me I wouldn't find a more honest, hard-working employee in the city. So, I took her on. I wouldn't be without her."

The taxi arrived, and Chidozie didn't expand on the comment. After a delicious meal, they returned to find the 'Lady Eleanor' packed with customers.

"Is it always this busy?" asked Lydia.

"We offer value for money," said Chidozie, "a wider selection of beers than most places in the area, plus our chef prepares the best fresh fish dishes in Rotterdam. In high summer, the number of tourists swells the customers. Trade will drop off in the autumn when we take our annual holiday. Everyone needs to refresh themselves before the Christmas and New Year mayhem."

"Where do you spend your holidays?" asked Lydia.

"Dubai," said Chidozie. "It was my refuge after the shipwreck, and I return there every autumn to give thanks."

"I'm sorry if I asked a lot of questions of you this evening," said Lydia.

"It's only natural," her father replied. "Where's Rosa? I want to tell her we'll be upstairs in the apartment. There's nowhere for us to have a quiet conversation here tonight. People will drift away in an hour, but we get a regular influx of late-night drinkers that finish work at nearby businesses and then drop in for a drink and a chat."

Alex and Lydia waited by a door marked 'Privaat', which was self-explanatory. Chidozie talked to customers at tables as he made his way towards the back of the bar.

"He's popular, isn't he?" said Alex. "Half the people in the restaurant knew him too, not just the management."

"I learned superficial things this evening," said Lydia, "and he steered the conversation in such a way that it was two-way traffic. I thought with the experience I've gained working with experts such as Gus and the rest of you. He'd be putty in my hands."

"Now there's something we've discovered without asking questions," said Alex, nodding to the other side of the bar.

Rosa and Chidozie were deep in conversation. Her hand rested casually on his upper arm, and the look between them suggested their relationship was a million miles from employer and employee.

Chidozie leaned forward to kiss Rosa on the lips and then started back across the room.

"I've promised Rosa we will return when the rush is over," he said, "I will introduce you properly then."

When they reached Chidozie's apartment, Lydia could tell from the living room and kitchenette that this wasn't a bachelor pad. The furnishings and the overall ambience confirmed what they'd seen downstairs. Chidozie and Rosa were a couple.

"I have never been a hermit," said Chidozie. Nevertheless, he spotted how Lydia analysed the set-up within seconds of entering the room.

"I hope that doesn't shock you, Lydia. Rosa isn't the first woman I lived with over the years. It's true that I never married and that I have never forgotten Eleanor. I wasn't trying to deceive you."

"You don't need to apologise," said Lydia. "We're still strangers. If we continue meeting and talking, we will learn more about each other. My first few conversations with Eleanor were the same. Nothing we disclosed ever displeased or upset us enough to stop meeting. We came out the other side as friends. You and I have taken the first tentative steps on the same journey. So far, nothing makes me wish I hadn't come here this weekend."

"I'm glad you did," said Chidozie. "It was a shock for me and Rosa too. She understood that I had lovers in my past; she was no innocent when married as a young woman. After her divorce, she moved from Amsterdam to work at 'The Hideaway', and she was alone when I arrived. We hit it off within a month of me opening the 'Lady Eleanor', and we've lived together ever since. Rosa will need time to adjust to the fact that I have a daughter too. Now, let me get you a drink. What will it be?"

"We heard that a jenever was popular," said Lydia.

Chidozie laughed.

"We serve it straight from the freezer downstairs. Some prefer it straight from the bottle, like drinking vodka, but most customers mix it with vermouth and other ingredients to make it less lethal."

"Perhaps we should have a coffee instead," said Alex. "You don't drink alcohol, Chidozie, and Lydia and I already had several glasses of wine with our meal."

"I understand," said Chidozie, "you've had a long day. No doubt you want to return to your hotel before this place closes."

"I'm only twenty-five," said Lydia, "and although Alex is ten years older, we can still keep pace. We intend to be here when the shutters close. I've waited a long time for this weekend."

"Rosa enjoys a quality brandy," said Chidozie, checking the drinks cabinet, "so, two Coffee Royale's it shall be, and an Americano for me."

Chidozie prepared the drinks, and Lydia and Alex relaxed on the large sofa as Chidozie told them how he had learned his trade in the cocktails bar in New York. He had an unlimited supply of funny stories. Lydia wasn't sure after the second drink, whether it was the memories that made her giggle or the generous measures of brandy that Chidozie added.

"It's after midnight," said Alex. "We should get downstairs, or Rosa will think you've abandoned her."

"There should be more room now," said Chidozie, "the mad rush is at an end."

When they got downstairs, Rosa was behind the bar. The waiting staff had gone home, and the chef sat at the end of the bar reading a newspaper. His empty glass suggested he would soon be on his way.

No customers sat outside, despite the warm night, but the bar still contained a healthy number of people enjoying a late-night drink. Alex and Lydia sat on stools by the bar as Chidozie joined Rosa.

"Did you both enjoy your meal?" asked Rosa.

"It was excellent," said Alex. "I'm sure you know the restaurant well?"

"It's our favourite here in Rotterdam," said Rosa, looking at Chidozie. "Although, he would say the restaurant in Dubai is a touch better."

"When you eat at a five-star restaurant, it's not worth comparing," laughed Chidozie. "They each have their minor differences, but why split hairs trying to choose which one is better than the other?"

The chef folded his newspaper and eased himself off his stool.

"I'm away to my bed, boss," he said. "I'll see you tomorrow."

"Good night, Lucas," said Chidozie. "You put in a good shift today: thank you, my friend. I got great feedback from the tables as I walked through this evening. The seafood platter was a firm favourite."

Lucas nodded and left the bar.

"Perhaps we can taste how good his food is tomorrow," said Lydia.

"We're lucky to have him," said Rosa. "I don't think we'll be able to match the salary a bigger outfit could offer Lucas."

"Let's not discuss our chef, Rosa," said Chidozie, "Lucas Romeijn will leave us when he's ready. I'll not stand in his way. Let me make the introductions. Rosa de Vries, I am pleased to introduce Lydia Logan Barre, my daughter. Her gentleman friend is Alex Hardy. They are with the English police, but we have nothing to fear."

"You idiot," said Rosa. "What will they think of us? Welcome, Lydia. It stunned me when Chidozie came home from the Museum to tell me the news—stunned but happy for him. I hope you will continue to visit us. You are both welcome in our home, any time."

"I didn't think this weekend could get any better," said Lydia, leaning over the bar to hug Rosa. "Thank you. It means the world to me."

"What will you do tomorrow?" asked Rosa.

"We planned to continue sightseeing before lunch," said Alex.

"Then we're coming here to eat," said Lydia. "If it's okay with you, we'll spend our last few hours in Rotterdam with you both until it's time to drive to the Hook to catch the car ferry."

"That's settled then," said Chidozie. "Only one thing to do before you finally take your leave. You must tell us when you'll be back."

"We'll exchange contact details tomorrow," said Lydia. "We've used up several days holiday trying to find you, but we'll be able to take time off before Christmas."

"When we've closed this place for a fortnight, why not fly to Dubai, and I'll collect you from the airport," said Chidozie. "You can stay with us. We'll visit that restaurant Rosa was keen to tell you about."

"It sounds exciting," said Lydia. "Of course, we'd love to come if possible."

"You will make it happen," said Chidozie, "I know I can rely on you."

"Where do you stay when you're out there?" asked Alex.

"Chidozie bought an apartment by the Marina when he was there in 2007," said Rosa. "It was a wonderful investment."

"I recuperated in a small place nearby after the ship-wreck and decided I'd had enough danger at sea for two lifetimes. So, I contacted the shipping company and collected my outstanding wages, holiday pay, and long-service gratuity. Finally, I could buy an apartment in a new build that would set me back half a million euros today."

"Wow," said Lydia, "that's amazing."

An hour later, Alex and Lydia unsteadily returned to the hotel. Chidozie was right. It had been a long day. They both slept well.

They just about made the check-out time of eleven

o'clock from the floating hotel. It cut short the sightseeing tour, and Alex elected for water taxi trips to avoid adding to the ache he felt in his leg from the exercise yesterday.

Sunday afternoon was a pleasant, relaxed affair, just like Sunday afternoons with friends should be. But, after the lunch Lucas prepared for them, Lydia hoped that her father could somehow hang on to the talented chef for a bit longer.

It was difficult saying goodbyes to Chidozie and Rosa and leaving the 'Lady Eleanor' to return to the port to catch the ferry. However, it had to be done if they wished to return to Harwich in time to arrive at the Crime Review Team office at nine. Alex planned to catch up on sleep on Monday night if Lydia kept him awake on the ferry because she was too excited to sleep. So when they arrived back in Chippenham early this morning, there was only one matter to get sorted.

Lydia knew that she had to tell Eleanor that they had met Chidozie.

Should they mention the name of the bar? What if Eleanor searched online and found it for herself? How would she react?

Alex had noticed Chidozie's slight frown when they had exchanged contact details. Had he hoped Lydia would give him those for Eleanor Scott too? Rosa and Chidozie were an item, that's for sure. Alex had to watch that Lydia's romantic notions didn't drive a wedge between the couple. Eleanor and Chidozie had moved on with their lives over the past quarter of a century. There was no turning back the clock.

# All Things Bright: Chapter Three

Gus glanced at the clock on the office wall. It was almost ten-thirty.

"Do we have everything ready to take to London Road," he asked.

"Five minutes, guv," said Lydia. "Sorry, I'm still buzzing after the weekend."

"I look forward to hearing about it later in the week," said Gus. "If time allows. Until I've met with the ACC, I have no clue which case is in his in-tray for us this time."

Five minutes later, the relevant files were ready. Gus walked to the lift and headed to the car park. As soon as he was safely off the premises, Lydia gave the gang a minute-by-minute account of their adventure. It was too good to keep quiet any longer.

Meanwhile, Gus eased the Focus into the mid-morning traffic and headed for Devizes.

The sun always shines on the righteous, he thought, as he pulled off the London Road and into the visitor's car park. The upstairs window at the far left of the building caught the full blast of the morning sun. In his customary position, Kenneth Truelove stood, jacketless, staring at the worker ants.

Gus always found it difficult to gauge whether the ACC was in a good mood from his vantage point on the car park asphalt. Discretion persuaded Gus to trot up the steps and get upstairs as soon as possible. He would keep the delay at Seend because of roadworks to himself.

It was so regular an excuse that he didn't think the ACC believed a word even though genuine. As he reached the admin area on the first floor, the clock had ticked to seven minutes past eleven. Gus gave a brief wave to Vera and Kassie, pointed to his watch, and tapped on the ACC's door.

"Come," said Kenneth Truelove.

"Geoff Mercer not here this morning, sir?" asked Gus realising he was the ACC's only visitor.

"Mercer has been and gone, Freeman," said the ACC. "He appreciates how busy my role is these days."

Ouch, thought Gus. No need to guess which mood he's in.

"My team struggled to get the details together in time," said Gus. "Neil Davis and Luke Sherman worked on the case in South Wales on Saturday. We should congratulate them for going the extra mile to tie up loose ends on the case, plus they reunited Mrs Kendall and her daughter. An excellent result, I'm sure you'll agree."

"Well, if you put it like that, I suppose," said the ACC. He was out of his seat and back by the window.

"Do you believe Cardiff Central can pin the murder on these Corbett characters?"

"They have more than enough, sir," said Gus. "West-bury is also in receipt of fresh evidence showing that the

Corbett brothers knocked Sid Dyer off his motorcycle with their van too. Everyone's a winner."

"Not me," said Kenneth Truelove, "It's me who has to explain the unauthorised overtime you sanctioned on Saturday. The bean counters don't credit us for solving a murder on the books for four years. They're more interested in the financial implications. As for Dyer, that got ruled an accident. Now you've uncovered evidence that proves it was deliberate, is that right?"

Gus nodded.

"There you are," groaned the ACC. "That will rebound on me too. Unravelling the packaged paperwork on that caper will cost a pretty penny. Also, it doesn't show the original verdict from the coroner in a good light. I wish you looked before you leap, Freeman. We spent years fostering good relations with various branches of the justice department, and in a matter of months, you ride roughshod through the lot of them, highlighting their inefficiencies."

"We do our best, sir," said Gus. "Might I ask a question?"

"Does it involve an expense that will bankrupt the force?"

"I hope not, sir. I was thinking about the dogs when I was telling DI Williams the good news this morning."

Kenneth Truelove had returned to his desk and was leafing through the files in the folder on his desk.

"Bubble and Squeak?"

"The very same, sir," said Gus. "Dai Williams is interviewing the brothers as we speak. He anticipates requiring several sessions to bring them to their senses. The chances are that the dogs didn't last long after Ivan Kendall's murder. There was no sign of any dogs when the brothers got picked up in Tredegar."

"Why the concern?" asked the ACC.

"After investigating the Malone case, I realised that dogs were important to people in more ways than I imagined. My parents never had pets in the home when I was a kid. I didn't think to ask whether it was because we couldn't afford them or they had an aversion to animals. Then I uncovered that dreadful drug smuggling business where innocent pups had quantities of heroin sewn inside their bodies. When we dug into this latest case, another opportunity for the dogs' illegal use proved to be the motive for Kendall's death. I had no idea dogfighting was still an issue, especially since the Dangerous Dogs Act passed in 1991."

"What do you think you can do, Freeman," said Kenneth Truelove. "It's not the Crime Review Team's role to chase organisers of illegal dog fights. Geoff Mercer has people he can assign to that dirty business when it raises its head on our patch."

"Where is Geoff Mercer, anyway?" asked Gus. "It is ages since I had a conversation with him. We keep missing one another here at London Road."

The ACC was wandering again. He stood by the window and rested on the sill.

"There was a genuine reason for his absence at first," said the ACC. "Geoff attended a course on a new initiative that the Police and Crime Commissioner championed. The usual rubbish. Typical of Mercer, he shone in the sessions he attended and attracted someone's attention. West Mercia is headhunting him for a vacant Assistant Chief Constable position."

"That's good news, isn't it?" said Gus. "Although I'll be sorry to see him go."

"It was selfish of me, I admit," sighed Kenneth Truelove, "but, as you know, I'd set my heart on retirement at the end of next year. After Sandra Plunkett's demise, the PCC twisted my arm to become Acting Chief Constable until the dust settled and the right candidate turned up."

"You were hoping to keep Geoff Mercer at London Road by putting his name forward to the PCC, am I right?"

"Yes, my wife reluctantly agreed to put up with a Chief Constable working after he'd agreed to retire and start cruising the high seas. I informed the PCC that I would continue if he needed me, provided he made the promotion permanent. I was biding my time to engineer Mercer's upgrade when the PCC suddenly dropped the diversity initiative on me. When I looked around at my senior team, the only name that made sense was Mercer. So, I told the PCC Geoff would be the right chap to attend. Of course, the glowing comments that have filtered back from the course mean that the PCC now says my choice was inspired and keeps telling me it proves what a good Chief Constable I will make. I've shot myself in the foot, Freeman."

"How does Geoff Mercer feel about leaving London Road?" asked Gus. "I reckon Christine would have reservations."

"I've never told Mercer that I planned to ensure he stayed close to me if I accepted the late boost up the ladder," said Kenneth Truelove. "If I had, he might have dismissed the approach from West Mercia out of hand. If I mention it now, he'll think it's just an eleventh-hour attempt to hold on to him."

"Is Geoff determined to leave?" asked Gus.

"I don't know," said the ACC. "He spends as little time in my office as possible. He confines our conversation to the matter at hand. Mercer dashed off earlier to avoid seeing you."

"I was a few minutes late," said Gus. "I apologised."

"It wouldn't have mattered," said the ACC. "Geoff was itching to leave. He knows that when the two of you get together, he relaxes and he's scared that if you get a sniff of what's going on, you won't let him leave until you worm it out of him."

"He's a friend," said Gus, "not that I ever thought I'd say that. Now I know there's a danger that he'll disappear to another part of the country. I'll say my piece when I catch up with him. He'd be a fool to leave London Road. With you at the helm and Geoff as one of your ACCs, it would have the makings of a dream team."

"I never know when to take you seriously, Freeman. Is this another of your wind-ups?"

"Don't be daft, sir. You've always been a great copper, the archetypal administrator. The role you've tried to avoid is tailor-made for a man of your calibre. The other officers on the same ACC rung of the ladder are dedicated professionals, but they don't have the gravitas you possess. Mercer is the perfect piece of the jigsaw to complete the Wiltshire picture. We need to work together to make sure it happens."

"We agree on something at last," smiled Kenneth Truelove. "It might need work, but I can see a way forward now. Thank you, Freeman. Now, back to business."

**Grab your copy...**
**vinci-books.com/allthingsbright**